AFTERMATH

LEVAR BURTON

AFTERMATH

ASPECT®

WARNER BOOKS

A Time Warner Company

Aspect name and logo are registered trademarks of Warner Books, Inc.

Warner Books, Inc., 1271 Avenue of the Americas, New York, NY 10020

 A Time Warner Company

Printed in the United States of America
First Printing: January 1997
10 9 8 7 6 5 4 3 2 1

Library of Congress Cataloging-in-Publication Data

Burton, LeVar.
     Aftermath / LeVar Burton.
        p.   cm.
     ISBN 0-446-51993-6
     I. Title.
PS3552.U774A69   1997
813´.54—dc20   96-23329
                                                            CIP

Book design by H. Roberts

For my wife, Stephanie, who is my beloved and my best friend,
and has always got my back.
For my children, Eian and Michaela,
may they never be afraid to be exactly who they are.
Most of all for my mother, Erma,
who gave to me her love for the written word and
taught me how to dream.

I'm a big fan of the science fiction genre and have been for most of my life. As a young child growing up in Sacramento, California, I would spend countless hours on my bed in my room or under a tree in the backyard or even down at the public library on Amherst Road, losing myself in the fantastic worlds that had been crafted by the masters in the field. Asimov, Clarke, Heinlein, Bova and others held me firmly in their spells, all the while inviting me to expand my concept of the universe. They dared me to contemplate two of the most powerful words in the English language—"What If?" What if—like the heroes in their books—I could actually create for myself a future of my own choosing, on my own terms, in **my** own image?

Sadly though, what I always found lacking in those stories were heroes who looked like me. Rarely did I encounter characters of African descent or other people of color populating those worlds. I grew up in an America where depictions of African-Americans in the popular culture were few and far between. I suppose that's a large part of the reason I found myself so attracted to the world of *Star Trek*. Gene Roddenberry's vision for the future was definitely about diversity and inclusion. The presence of Nichelle Nichols as Lt. Uhura assured me that not only would people who looked like me be a part of the world of the future, we would play a vital role in the continuing evolution of the human experience. That validation was not only enormously reassuring to me, it was critical to the development of my self-esteem. This goes to the heart of why I am so grateful to have the opportunity to create an experience like *Aftermath*.

For me, part of the power of science fiction literature is that it encourages us to use our imaginations; it invites us to dream. There is an undeniable link between what we imagine to be so and that which we create in reality. I am convinced that the reason we have the flip phone today is due, at least in part, to *Star Trek* and those indelible images of Captain Kirk reaching back to that secret place on his hip, pulling out his communicator and flipping it open. Likewise, I am awed by the fact that right now scientists are developing a device for the blind that is modeled on the VISOR worn by Geordi LaForge on *Star Trek: The Next Generation*. Which brings me to a word about the Neuro-Enhancer, a device in this book that heals the body of all disease by maximizing whole brain functioning. Even though there are no prototypes in existence (that I am currently aware of), I invite you to ask yourself the big question—What if? What if there were such a machine? What if we could achieve the same results without the use of a Neuro-Enhancer?

It is an essential part of our process as human beings that we continually strive toward our own highest level of expression. Science fiction literature has and will continue to provide necessary inspiration for us as we navigate the never-ending journey of self-discovery. I am extremely proud to add my voice to what is an already proud and noble tradition.

Chronology of Events Leading to the War of 2015–2018

2009

America launches *Space Station Alpha*. Built and supplied by numerous shuttle launches, the space station houses a crew of sixty scientists and engineers. It is a proud day for the United States, but there is considerable grumbling among members of Congress about the cost of the project. Many think the money could have been better used to provide services for the country's growing number of homeless.

Elsewhere in the world, skirmishes, minor wars, droughts, famines and overpopulation have brought global economy to the brink of disaster. Struggling with its own financial problems, the United States can no longer provide financial assistance to other regions.

2010

Senator Lawrence Everette, a black Democrat from Ohio, announces his bid for the presidency. An outspoken advocate of racial equality, he vows to increase spending for the homeless and needy, rebuild America's inner-city areas, and end the stranglehold big business has on government. Although his plans don't sit well with those already empowered in Washington, he proves to be a popular choice with the people and soon leads the race.

2011

NASA atmospheric scientist Leon Cane publishes a report in *Scientific American* linking the space program to violent weather patterns throughout the world. His article creates a national scandal, causing Congress to stop all NASA funding, and ground shuttle launches, until a solution to the problem can be found.

2012

Lawrence Everette is elected President of the United States. Four days later he is assassinated by a white extremist in a chemical bomb attack. Riots break out in Los Angeles, Miami, New York and Atlanta. The U.S. government responds by sending in the National Guard.

2013

May—The New Madrid Fault in southern Missouri shifts, causing an earthquake of 9.1 magnitude. St. Louis and numerous other Midwestern cities are destroyed. Thousands are killed, millions left homeless.

The United States government is slow in responding to the situation in the Midwest, which leads to rioting and looting. The cry of "Remember Everette" becomes the official anthem of the poor, the homeless and the oppressed. In an attempt to stamp out the flames of revolution, the government sends federal troops into the area.

November—Tensions reach an all-time high as winter sets in. Millions of people are still homeless, many more lack food, fresh water and the other basic necessities of life. St. Louis, Chicago, Kansas City, Nashville and other cities erupt in fighting. Additional troops are called into these areas, but many minority soldiers refuse to fire on their own people. A rift develops in the military ranks.

2014

The nation teeters on the brink of civil war. More troops are called for, but the government no longer has the funds to supply them.

Emergency food and relief efforts grind to a halt as funding runs out.

Numerous insurance companies file for bankruptcy.

July 8—The stock market crashes.

Thousands of banks fail. Many more are forced to close their doors, declaring a bank holiday to prevent customers from making massive withdrawals.

The U.S. economy fails and the country enters another major depression.

Stranded since shuttle launches were halted, with little hope of coming home, the crew of *Space Station Alpha* begins to fight. A fire is started, which escalates in the oxygen-rich atmosphere. Millions watch at home, horrified, as all those aboard the space station die. NASA collapses, and with it dies the dream of space exploration.

2015

In a last-ditch effort to prevent a possible race war, General Wyatt Dixon, one of America's most distinguished black officers, attempts to seize control of the army. His efforts fail and the United States military splits in half, with minority soldiers lining up behind Dixon. Fighting breaks out on military bases around the country. For the first time since the Civil War, American soldiers are fighting one another.

The public school system fails.

Social Security and Welfare fail.

2015–2018

Race war. Millions die, millions more are left homeless. Food shortages. Nationwide famine. Widespread disease.

Neighborhoods become walled communities as everyone tries to hold on to what little they have. Many towns and cities no longer have electricity or running water.

The governments of numerous Third World nations collapse as the United States is no longer able to support them. Mass panic and riots sweep through Europe, Asia, Africa and Latin America.

2019

The race war finally grinds to a halt with leaders from both sides signing a peace agreement. People of color have seized control of a great deal of power and land.

The United States begins the slow and difficult process of climbing out of the ashes. Millions have lost homes and loved ones during the conflict.

Broke and virtually powerless, the federal government delegates much of its authority to individual state governments. These governments set taxes as they see fit and provide what benefits they can for their citizens. States that are still productive, and suffered little in the war, are swamped by an influx of refugees from neighboring states, forcing some to close their borders to outsiders. Even then, they do not have the money, or the manpower, to stop the flow of refugees.

Along the nation's highways, shantytowns and tent cities have been erected. Many are home to impoverished refugees and victims of the war, a place to start over for those who have lost almost everything. Others are the domain of prostitutes, bandits and those who prey on weak and weary travelers.

PART I

"We have to keep in mind at all times that we are not fighting for integration, nor are we fighting for separation. We are fighting for recognition as free humans in this society."

—*Malcolm X*

"Those who make peaceful revolution impossible will make violent revolution inevitable."

—*John F. Kennedy, Jr.*

C H A P T E R

1

Leon Cane lifted the lid of the metal Dumpster and peered inside. He wasn't looking for food; he still had a few cans of tuna stashed away in the wooden crate he called home. Instead he was searching for reading material—books, magazines, newspapers—something to relieve the boredom that came with being homeless. On a good day he might come across a discarded newspaper or a dog-eared novel. Once he had found a copy of *Scientific American*, but he had thrown it away, the bitter memories too much to endure. Luck wasn't with him today, however, for the Dumpster was empty.

Disappointed, he lowered the lid and continued down the deserted alleyway, the soles of his oversized shoes clopping loudly on the pavement. Like the books he read, the shoes had also been found in a Dumpster. They were two sizes too big, and rubbed his feet when he didn't remember to line them with newspaper, but he couldn't complain. A lot of people he knew didn't even have shoes. They went barefoot, risking cuts and infections, or wrapped their feet in plastic bags and strips of cloth.

Aware of the noise he was making, Leon slowed his pace. The back streets of war-ravaged Atlanta were dangerous enough without letting everybody know you were coming. Silence was the rule if you wanted to survive. Stealth. The thieves and murderers knew it. They waited like spiders in the shadowy darkness of doorways and burned-out vehicles, setting traps for their victims. Mercy and compassion were never offered, only pain and sometimes death.

But for every thief and cutthroat that skittered about in the blackness, there were a dozen people who had survived the riots and race war and wanted nothing more than to put the hurt behind them and begin the healing. For the poor and homeless, race was no longer an issue, no longer a reason to hate. When a person was cold and starving it mattered not if the helping hand offered was white, black, yellow or red.

In the months following the war, thousands of shantytowns and tiny tent communities sprang up across the country in fields and city parks, and along deserted highways and country roads. Noisy, crowded affairs, often lacking fresh water and sanitation facilities, these new communities were a mixture of refugee camp, flea market and carnival. They were a place to go when companionship was desired or supplies needed, a place to share a joke, have a drink or find a shoulder to cry on.

At these makeshift communities, everything one needed could be had for a price: food, clothing, drugs, even sex. Some of the ones run by gangs offered guarded sleeping quarters where a person could enjoy a good night's rest without fear of being robbed. Others featured gaming tents and casinos, where robbery was a way of life. Either way, the same rule still applied: no one was ever turned away because of the color of their skin.

Leon wiped the sweat from his forehead and looked up. The afternoon sky was a hazy gray. To the south vertical towers of cumulonimbus thunderclouds rose like snowcapped mountains high above the horizon, threatening rain. He stood and watched the clouds for a moment, lost in his thoughts, feeling a twinge of the same joy and wonder he had once felt as a much younger man.

Leon had grown up in the town of Millvat, Pennsylvania, just across the Ohio River from the city of Pittsburgh. His father worked in a steel mill. His mother was a seamstress, babysitting on the weekends to supplement the family income. With three growing boys to feed there never seemed to be enough money. But his parents scrimped and saved, sacrificing so that Leon and his two older brothers never had to do without.

His mother, Jewel, instilled in Leon a strong sense of self and her passion for learning. She impressed upon him at an early age that in order to compete successfully with white men he would need to be similarly educated. By scrimping and saving, Leon's parents set aside enough money to send both him and his brother James to college, while Leon's older brother Richard followed in the footsteps of their father and went to work in a steel mill.

Leon graduated from Colorado State University with a degree in atmospheric science. After graduation, he had gone to work at the Center for Clouds, Chemistry and Climate, nicknamed C^4, in La Jolla, California. He and a team of university, government and industrial researchers worked side by side to study the radiative effects of clouds upon the earth's surface, gathering their information from satellites, sensors and spy planes.

He had been working at the Center for a little over two years when he met Vanessa Campbell, a registered nurse at the La Jolla Medical Center. She was tall and slender, extremely beautiful, with a smile that could melt glaciers and cause a lion and a lamb to lie down together. They dated, sharing a passion for the theater, old movies and moonlight walks along the beach.

They also shared a love for creating amateur works of art. Vanessa's speciality was watercolor paintings of wildflowers.

She was very talented, several of her paintings winning awards and honorable mentions at local art shows. On picnics together in the park Leon would carry the food and drink, while she brought along a fresh canvas and her sketch pad. After eating, he would lie on the grass and watch her paint, or close his eyes and listen to her hum different songs. She always hummed when she worked, usually something lively and flowing like the images she captured on canvas.

Leon wasn't a painter. His artistic talents birthed in the bowls and pots he created on a pedal-powered potter's wheel. He loved doing pottery; there was something satisfying and almost magical about it: the smell and feel of the fresh clay when he kneaded out the air bubbles, the thunk-thunk of the wheel as his hands carefully gave life to a spinning bowl or pot, the heat from the kiln, which was always two degrees hotter than hell. Vanessa used to tease him that his pottery satisfied a primitive male urge somewhat akin to sexual desire. Maybe so, but she had no qualms about adding her feminine touch to his primitive urges with a well-placed buttercup or two.

They had been dating for only six months when Leon and Vanessa decided to get married, both equally certain that they had found the person they wanted to share their life with. A few weeks later they were married at one of the many twenty-four-hour wedding chapels in Las Vegas, Nevada. Leon's mother had been upset that they didn't have a formal church wedding, but she quickly forgave them when he flew her and his father out to California for a visit. One year and three months after the wedding, give or take a few days, Vanessa gave birth to Anita Luanne Cane, the most beautiful little girl in the entire world— at least in Leon's opinion.

Although Leon's work at C^4 figuratively put his head in the clouds, his dreams went way beyond that, out past the stratosphere and monosophere, to the great vastness of space. He knew humanity's future lay in space exploration and wanted very much to be a part of that future. His dream came true when an old friend introduced him to the head of the meteorology department at NASA. Four months later, Leon was offered a job with the Space Administration. It was an offer he did not turn down.

From a rented condo in La Jolla, Leon and his family moved into a modest three-bedroom home, just five blocks from the Atlantic Ocean, in Cocoa Beach, Florida. His job at NASA was to study meteorological and infrared information beamed back to earth from weather satellites to determine if space shuttles, their payloads crammed with parts and supplies for *Space Station Alpha*, could lift off according to schedule. With launches coming every three weeks, he had been kept quite busy. But he didn't mind: the job was rewarding and the pay terrific.

During his first six months working for NASA, Leon had noticed peculiar disturbances in the earth's weather patterns shortly after the launch or reentry of a space vehicle. It seemed every time a shuttle or rocket went up, or came back down, someplace caught hell with violent storms, tornados, even floods. At first he thought it was nothing more than a coincidence. After all, how could a rocket or shuttle launched in Florida possibly affect weather conditions halfway around the world? But the more he researched the matter, the more he became convinced there was indeed some sort of connection. The atmospheric disturbances could be traced all the way back to the earliest launches of the 1950s.

Leon theorized that the different layers of atmosphere surrounding the planet—a soupy mixture of nitrogen, oxygen, argon, carbon dioxide, hydrogen, ozone, methane and a dozen other elements—behaved less as a gas and more as a semi-solidified gelatinous substance when compressed by the earth's gravitational field. Ripples were created in the upper atmosphere during the exit or reentry of a space vehicle, much like the ripples on the surface of a pond when a stone is tossed into the water. These ripples traveled outward as invisible gravitational waves, disrupting weather patterns in places where the layers of atmosphere were thinner.

He took his findings to his immediate supervisor, but was dismissed with a laugh and a wave of a hand. Disheartened, Leon brought his report home and tossed it on his desk, where it stayed until he decided to go public with his findings. Afraid he was placing his career in jeopardy, Vanessa tried to talk him out of his decision. But Leon refused to listen, convinced he was doing the right thing.

Ultimately, it was Leon's conscience that led him to share his findings with the press. His report appeared as "Do Space Launches Affect Our Weather?" in the March 2011 issue of *Scientific American*. It was a good article, well written, backed up by dates, figures and facts. The results were disastrous.

Radical political organizations, opposed to the space program and looking for a reason to shut it down, jumped on Leon's article as a means to pressure Congress into giving NASA the axe. His article was beamed around the world by way of the Internet, with dozens of news reporters and talk show hosts twisting the report into a prophecy of doom. Once the fire was lit it could not be stopped.

Leon was subpoenaed to testify about his findings before a congressional committee task force, as were several of his co-workers, his supervisor and the head of the Space Administration. Once they got started, the hearings lasted for four weeks and were carried live on national television, with highlights and commentary presented each night on the six and eleven o'clock news. Congress and the President of the United States, already struggling with a failing economy, inflation and racial tensions, saw the situation as a chance to direct public attention and concern elsewhere. The shuttle program was suspended, as were any future plans for the space station. Almost overnight, Leon had gone from being a simple scientist who loved his job to the Antichrist of the space program.

With the suspension of the shuttle program, thousands of NASA employees were laid off. Thousands more were laid off by multinational corporations whose business centered around shuttle launches, satellite deployment and space technologies. The economic impact on the Florida communities of Cocoa Beach and Titusville was devastating. Within only a few weeks, they became little more than ghost towns. Leon was also laid off, but he lost much more than just his job. Three weeks after Congress gave the space program the axe, someone threw two firebombs through his living room window. His wife and their three-year-old daughter died in the flames that engulfed his home.

Leon's mother had tried to teach him how to share her love for God, but even as a child, Leon found it impossible to respect a God who could allow the world to be so full of pain. Science had become his religion. Now, he had nothing.

Homeless, alone, his heart sick with grief, Leon had left Florida with the intention of returning to Pennsylvania to see his mother. His father had died the previous year from a heart attack, and his brothers were living in other towns, but his mother still lived in the same house Leon had grown up in. Both the house and his mother represented happier times, times of comfort and simplicity.

But Leon never made it to Millvat; he got only as far as Atlanta, Georgia. On November 13, 2012, he arrived in the city of Atlanta with only the clothes on his back and twenty dollars in his pocket, arriving just in time to witness the riots following the death of President-elect Lawrence Everette.

He had watched as thousands of angry people ran through the streets, smashing windows, overturning cars and setting buildings on fire. Downtown Atlanta became a war zone as police officers squared off against armed protesters. Hundreds of people were killed in the fighting; many more were wounded and maimed. The gutters ran red with their blood, and the night was filled with screams.

He hadn't gotten caught up in the madness that swept the city during the riots, hadn't looted, robbed or even raised his fist in anger. The truth was he didn't care. Life no longer had much meaning for him. His world had become an empty wooden crate, one meal a day—if he was lucky—and a tattered, faded picture of the wife and daughter he had lost.

Leon Cane lowered his gaze, pushing back the memories that always brought tears to his eyes. He stuffed his hands into his pants pockets and continued slowly down the alley, searching for something to read to kill the pain.

CHAPTER

2

*D*anger.

Dr. Rene Reynolds looked up, studying the faces of those who watched her. Twelve men and seven women, experts in the fields of science and medicine—most of them representing major medical corporations—sat on folding chairs and observed her movements with keen interest. She found no warmth in their faces, but she found nothing to indicate a threat of any kind.

Dismissing her feelings as nothing more than a case of pre-presentation jitters, she turned her attention back to the computers, EKG and biofeedback machines, checking gauges and adjusting knobs where necessary. Her hands trembled slightly as she connected several electrodes to the elderly woman lying on the examination table in the center of the room. The woman's name was Irene McDaniels, and up until a few short weeks ago she had been suffering from both Parkinson's disease and cancer of the colon.

Rene heard a chair squeak as one of the visiting doctors stood up. She watched out of the corner of her eye as he walked across the room to the folding table set against the wall. On the table were a coffeepot, cups, paper plates and a tray loaded with cookies and snack cakes. Most of those in attendance had already helped themselves to the goodies. Rene smiled inwardly. Part of being a good scientist was never missing out on a free meal.

Beyond the table, the blinds covering the windows had been drawn tight to keep out the harshness of the summer sun. Even then the antique air conditioner, which was powered by a row of solar panels on the building's roof, had to struggle to do its job. The room was stuffy, and Rene felt a trickle of sweat leak down her back.

She couldn't complain about the heat, however, for the Institute was the only building on the block to even have air-conditioning, and one of the few places to have electricity for more than a few hours a day. Electrical power was rationed, like a lot of other things. Fortunately, the city of Atlanta considered the Hawkins Neural Institute important enough to give them extra kilowatt hours. What they received from the city went to operate scientific apparatuses and medical equipment. Nonessential items, such as the air conditioner, had to share the trickle of power provided by the solar panels.

Turning back around, Rene noticed her reflection in the large mirrors that covered most of the opposite wall. The woman who stared back at her was a twenty-nine-year-old African-American who, up until a few years ago, had spent most of her life in the pleasant suburbs north of Atlanta. She stood a trim five foot seven, with long straight hair that was probably the hereditary result of her great-grandmother being full-blooded Cree Indian. During her transition into puberty, Rene's hair had developed a somewhat shocking white streak.

Most women would have colored the streak, but Rene considered it a badge of honor, a symbol that she was different from most people. It was that feeling that drove her in life, causing her to strive for goals most never dreamed of reaching. Even as a teenager, when other girls were going on dates or hanging out, she had been busy setting in motion her plans for the future, determined to achieve greatness in her life and do something that would benefit all of mankind. Graduating high school with a 4.0 grade point average, she attended Duke University, earning a Ph.D. in neurophysiology. After college she came to work for the Institute, quickly becoming one of the company's top researchers.

On a small cart beside the examination table, in a gray padded case, was the culmination of years of Rene's hard work. Rene opened the case and removed a handheld microcomputer called the Neuro-Enhancer. Two thin cables connected the Enhancer to a copper headband lined with electrodes. Stretching the cables out, she carefully slipped the metal band on Irene McDaniels's head.

Rene had spent years mapping the neural networks of the human brain, using everything from nuclear magnetic resonance scanners to high-speed computers to record the firing order of each individual neuron. Working closely with computer designers and electronic engineers, she had developed the Neuro-Enhancer. The device repeated neuron firing orders, but at an increased rate, sending tiny electrical impulses shooting through the hundreds of electrodes lining the inside of the copper headband.

She had been looking for a cure for Parkinson's disease, which slowly destroys a tiny section of the human brain called the substantia nigra. It is the substantia nigra that supplies the neurotransmitter dopamine to a larger area in the center of the brain, called the striatum, which controls movement and motor skills of the human body. As dopamine supplies to the striatum dry up, movements slow and become erratic, eventually grinding to a complete halt. Although Parkinson's disease is not usually fatal, many of those afflicted die from injuries suffered in falls. Others end up wheelchair-bound, unable to move or even speak.

After only a few weeks of testing with the Neuro-Enhancer, Rene noticed a remarkable transformation begin to take place in her patients. In almost every case the uncontrollable tremors of hands and legs, characteristics of the disease, were completely eliminated. Motor skills and muscle strength also returned. In less than three months, ninety percent of her patients were again walking and talking normally.

Excited over the prospect that she might have actually found a cure for Parkinson's, Rene was absolutely stunned when she discovered that treatment with the Neuro-Enhancer also resulted in the elimination of chronic pain, an increase in memory and, probably the most important of all, the complete regression of cancer cells within the body. The regression did not stop when treatments were halted, but continued until the cancer was completely eliminated.

With sixty-five percent of Caucasians suffering from skin cancer due to a depleted ozone layer, and with the steady increase in the reported number of cases of carcinoma, leukemia, lymphoma and sarcoma in the general population, the country was on the brink of a major health collapse. Since the Neuro-Enhancer had proven effective in the battle against all types of cancer, it could just be the invention of the century.

Adjusting the metal band on Mrs. McDaniels's head, Rene inserted a coded micro CD, containing neuron firing patterns, into the Neuro-Enhancer's microcomputer. If the visiting scientists had come to see a show they were going to be disappointed. There really wasn't anything to see. No flashing lights or fireworks, no lightning bolts coming out of the sky like in the old Frankenstein movies, nothing but a mild hum and the readout of the instrument gauges to show that the device was even working. Nor was the healing visible to the eye. Cuts did not vanish with the wave of a wand. Tumors and infections did not run screaming from the body. The healing that occurred took days and weeks, not minutes and hours.

Rene flipped a switch on the computer console. On the wall behind her a projection scene lit up, displaying the read-outs of Irene McDaniels's pulse, blood pressure, EKG and bio-rhythm. She flipped another switch and a video movie appeared next to the readouts. The video showed Mrs. McDaniels as she was eight weeks ago: suffering from the advanced stages of Parkinson's disease, barely able to walk or get out of a wheelchair, unable to feed herself or even speak clearly. Rene allowed the video to play uninterrupted for a minute, then turned to face her audience.

"Welcome, Doctors. I'm glad that you could be here today. Thank you for coming." She picked up a small laser pointer and switched it on, aiming the tiny red dot of light at the screen. "The lady in the video is Mrs. Irene McDaniels; she is a patient of mine. These pictures were taken a little over two months ago. As you can see, Mrs. McDaniels suffered from Parkinson's disease. Like many who are afflicted, she was no longer able to move about without the aid of a wheelchair. Nor could she feed herself or engage in normal conversation. Prior to coming to the Institute, she had been treated by several other doctors in the Atlanta area with a variety of different medicines, including lev-odopa. Unfortunately, what little relief the drugs provided proved to be only temporary."

"What about fetal tissue implants?" someone interrupted. Rene turned and offered a slight smile. Even after thirty years, the implanting of brain cells culled from aborted fetuses into the striatum of a patient was still a controversial operation. Not only were moral issues raised, but surgeons often disagreed as to which of the two sections of the striatum should receive the implanted tissue. There were also debates about how much tissue was needed, how to prepare it for transplant, and whether to place large quantities in a few locations or small quantities in numerous locations.

Rene paused the video. "Fetal transplants were a possibility," she said, nodding. "But if you look at the patient's medical charts, in the folders handed out earlier, you'll see that Mrs. McDaniels also suffered from colon cancer and was in poor physical health."

She paused to allow time for the visiting doctors to check the charts before continuing. "Performing craniotomies on the surgical controls, as in fetal tissue transplants, can result in the formation of blood clots. Patients have also suffered strokes and heart attacks while undergoing such operations. Even if the surgery is a success there's still the danger of side effects, such as respiration problems, pneumonia and urinary tract infections. With Mrs. McDaniels's poor physical condition, I felt that such an operation would not be safe."

She unpaused the video and fast-forwarded the film. The image of Irene McDaniels jerked and shook like a high priestess in a strange voodoo ritual. Rene slowed the action. "This footage was taken a little over two weeks ago."

The video showed Irene McDaniels sitting at a table, writing a letter. Gone were the herky-jerky movements of her hands and head. Gone too was the unsmiling, unblinking facial expression typical of those who suffered from the disease. The last section of video, taken a few days ago, showed Mrs. McDaniels working in a backyard garden, pulling weeds, planting flowers and performing a host of tasks that should have been impossible for someone suffering from Parkinson's. Rene looked away from the video screen to study the reactions of those in the room, amused at the stunned expressions on the faces of the visiting scientists.

"Bullshit. It's a hoax," someone in the back row whispered, loud enough to be heard. "The woman in the video is an actress."

Rene stopped the video and shook her head. "I promise you that Irene McDaniels is no actress. If you look in the folders you will find complete medical reports from four of Atlanta's top doctors. If Mrs. McDaniels is an actress, then she's good enough to fool all four of them. She's also talented enough to fake blood tests, X-rays and lab work. And as you can see by the reports, not only has she been cured of Parkinson's disease, she has also been cured of colon cancer. Even the melanoma on her arms and the back of her neck have disappeared."

She paused to allow the information to sink in. Several doctors flipped through the folders given to them, reading the day-by-day progress of five of Rene's patients. The others stared intently at the charts displayed on the projection screen.

In the back row sat a large Caucasian man, powerfully built, his face and arms covered with a patchwork of dark brown skin grafts. Rene recognized the man, having seen his picture in numerous scientific journals. He was Dr. Randall Sinclair, one of the nation's foremost authorities on the treatment of skin cancer. Dr. Sinclair made worldwide headlines three years ago when he invented "skin fusion," a process of grafting skin from African-Americans, and other dark-skinned ethnic groups, onto Caucasians in order to increase skin pigmentation to stop the spread of skin cancer. The process was often effective, but it was very expensive and only the very wealthy could afford it.

The Neuro-Enhancer, on the other hand, was affordable and would be available to everyone. It was a cheap cure-all for the masses. With so many poor and dispossessed people dying from lack of even minimal health care, the Enhancer would go a long way toward bringing the country back together. If Rene never did another thing in her life, the Neuro-Enhancer would have made her existence meaningful.

It was Dr. Sinclair who finally broke the silence. "So you're claiming that this device of yours"—he glanced at the papers in his hand and cleared his throat—"a Neuro-Enhancer, also attacks cancer cells?"

Rene shook her head. "Unlike chemotherapy and other common treatments, the Neuro-Enhancer does not directly attack cancer cells. Instead it stimulates the neurons of the human brain, activating regions not normally used. Those regions have a direct effect on a person's health by not only increasing the body's natural ability to fight off infection and disease, but promoting a process of regeneration as well. In other words, the Neuro-Enhancer allows the body to heal itself."

She turned and aimed the laser pointer at the monitor displays on the projection screen. "This is the EKG and biorhythm of a normal mind at rest. Note the level of alpha, beta, theta and delta waves being produced. The alpha waves indicate the readiness of the cerebrum to respond to stimuli."

Turning back around to the examination table, she switched on the Neuro-Enhancer. A soft hum could be heard, like the humming of a lazy bee. On the projection screen, the EKG showed a noticeable rise in the level of alpha and beta waves being produced inside Irene McDaniels's head.

"The increase in alpha waves means that Mrs. McDaniels is now entering a deep state of mental relaxation, similar to the state one reaches right before going to sleep or while in deep meditation. At the same time, the rise in her Beta II waves indicates she is experiencing an intense period of mental activity."

Rene faced the audience. "Obviously, one cannot be both relaxed and mentally active at the same time, not under normal circumstances. What is happening is that the electrical impulses passing between the neurons are now operating at three times their normal speed. The brain compensates for this overload by bringing more neurons and neural regions into play. In effect, Mrs. McDaniels is now using more of her brain, and technically has more brain power, than she did only moments before. Since she is not taking a test, reading or doing anything where mental power is required, the energy is directed to the areas where it is needed most: healing the body."

"Are there any side effects?" asked a tall man with scarecrow-thin arms.

"None that we know of," Rene lied. A few people had in fact experienced some rather peculiar side effects from using the Neuro-Enhancer. But since none of the effects were dangerous, she had chosen not to mention them in any of her reports.

She continued, "Doctors, I understand your feelings of doubt. In the past few years there have been a lot of so-called miracle cures, everything from herbal enemas to megadoses of vitamin C. Those cures were ineffective because they relied on an outside substance being introduced into the body. With the Neuro-Enhancer there is no outside element. It is not a vitamin, chemical, gas or radioactive isotope." She glanced at Dr. Sinclair. "Nor does it require donor skin grafts. It uses one thing and one thing only: the power of the human mind.

"Mind over body is not a theory. It's a fact. The Chinese have been incorporating it into their medicine for years; so have the American Indians and many South American and African tribes. Only Western cultures have ignored this important truth. We have lived in a world of prescription medicines and needless operations, closing and locking the door on the one true cure." She pointed at the Neuro-Enhancer for effect. "But now we have the key to unlock our minds, and rid society forever of sickness and disease."

"So what's the catch?" someone asked.

"Catch? There is no catch." Rene set the pointer down. "But there is a problem. The Hawkins Neural Institute operates on a very limited budget. We need financial backing to finish development on the Neuro-Enhancer, which includes patent applications, seeking government approval and the production of additional models. For a modest investment sum your company will receive copies of all records concerning the project, including patient test data. You will also receive one fully functional, ready-to-use Neuro-Enhancer."

"What exactly do you call modest?" asked an auburn-haired woman sitting in the front row. Rene wasn't sure, but she thought the woman was the director of a cancer care clinic.

"I'll be happy to provide price information to those who are interested," Rene replied, setting the hook in a potential customer. "But I must add, this exclusive offer is for a limited time only. In six months we plan to go public with our findings."

"How many Enhancers do you have now?" the woman asked.

Rene pointed at the prototype lying on the table. "Just the one."

C H A P T E R

3

Amy Ladue could not remember her parents. Nor did she know her exact age. She thought she was ten years old, but maybe she was only nine. She did remember, however, the earthquake that destroyed the city of St. Louis; she had been about three years old at the time. It was her earliest childhood memory.

On the morning of May 16, 2013, the New Madrid Fault in southern Missouri had shifted, sending shock waves racing in all directions. The first of those waves hit St. Louis at 4:32 in the morning, a time when most people were still in bed. Those that were up and about recalled a strange stillness, which settled over the city just prior to the earthquake. In the downtown area cleaning crews and police officers watched in awe as thousands of pigeons suddenly took flight, leaving behind statue and ledge. They circled the city once and then flew to the east, crossing the Mississippi River, seeking safety in the Illinois countryside. In the suburbs surrounding the city, crickets and tree frogs fell silent, their nocturnal serenades replaced by the eerie howling of hundreds of dogs. A few minutes later a deep rumbling could be heard, like the sound of distant thunder, as the first of the shock waves reached the area.

In the early morning darkness, the ground rippled and shook like a giant serpent flexing its muscles. Houses were torn from their foundations and smashed flat, while towering apartment buildings and gleaming high-rises collapsed upon themselves like giant stacks of cards. In the first thirty seconds of the earthquake over twenty thousand people died as their homes and apartments crumbled on top of them. Those not trapped beneath tons of concrete, wood and steel fled onto the streets.

There was no safety to be found in the streets, however, as hundreds of underground gas lines exploded like artillery blasts, sending billowy clouds of orange flame high into the sky. Driven by the wind, the fire spread quickly through the residential areas. With water mains broken and the streets blocked with rubble, the fire departments could do nothing to stop the raging inferno. They could only stand by and watch as entire neighborhoods burned to the ground. Thousands of people trapped inside their homes perished in the flames.

The earthquake was no less devastating in the downtown area. Built upon a network of underground caverns, the city of St. Louis was unable to withstand such violent tremblings. As the ground shook and rolled, the roofs of several of the caverns collapsed, causing giant fissures to suddenly appear. People, automobiles, even entire buildings were swallowed up, never to be seen again.

While the land rose and fell, the mighty Mississippi—father of all American rivers—abruptly reversed its course and flowed north instead of south. The river overflowed its banks, the raging water roaring into the city and sweeping away everything in its path.

Only once before had the river reversed its course. On December 16, 1811, an equally powerful earthquake had rocked the area, causing the Mississippi to change direction and flow north for over one hundred miles. The epicenter of that quake was also the New Madrid Fault, located about 150 miles south of the city of St. Louis.

Seismographic records show that the earthquake of 2013 lasted only for a few minutes, but the damage and destruction it left behind would last forever. Gone were the museums, fine restaurants and historic buildings the city was known for. Even the Anheuser-Busch Brewery was no more. Gone too were the public utility buildings, police stations and fire houses. There was no electricity or fresh water, and the few hospitals still standing quickly filled to capacity with the injured and dying.

In the St. Louis area alone, fifty thousand people died and more than a million were left homeless. Broken and charred bodies were stacked in the streets like cordwood. Others were left to rot where they lay. The stench was incredible. Flies, rats and starving dogs fed on the bloated bodies, spreading sickness and disease throughout the city. Makeshift shelters were set up in some neighborhoods, but with shortages of food, water and medicine, and a complete lack of sanitary facilities, they became little more than places of pain and suffering, places to die.

Two days after the quake, a rescue team found Amy wandering alone through the streets, a naked little white girl with a fractured right arm. She was taken to a Red Cross field hospital, where she was given food and clothing and treated for her injuries. Not knowing her real identity, one of the officials at the hospital gave her the name Amy, for the nurse who found her, and Ladue, for the subdivision where she had been wandering. Amy didn't remember what her real name had once been.

St. Louis, St. Charles, Little Rock, Memphis and several other cities were declared federal disaster areas; the government, however, was unable to cope with devastation of such magnitude—especially coming only six months after the riots that followed the assassination of President-elect Lawrence Everette. Too little, too late, that was the story. Frustrated and angry, many of those left homeless by the earthquake turned to looting in order to survive. Riots broke out, with the call of "Remember Everette" becoming the battle cry of the destitute.

While she didn't recall her real name, Amy remembered the riots and the war. Sometimes, when she closed her eyes to sleep, she could still see the tanks and the bloody bodies of dead soldiers, could still hear the explosions of artillery rounds and the screams of women and children caught in the crossfire. She didn't know why the black people and white people were fighting, couldn't understand why they hated each other so much. All she knew was that mommies and daddies, even little babies, were being killed and that was a bad thing.

Now, standing on the bank of the Mississippi River, Amy felt her stomach rumble and tried to remember when she had eaten last. She thought it was yesterday, but it might actually have been the day before. If she went to one of the shelters for homeless children she might get something to eat—a sandwich maybe, or a bowl of soup. But she hated the shelters and even the thought of food could not get her to go there. The people who ran the shelters didn't want to let the children leave once they fed them, locking the windows and doors at night so they couldn't get out. They said that it was for their protection, to keep the little kids safe, but that wasn't true. It was a whole lot safer sleeping on the streets than at the shelters.

Nighttime at the shelters was bad, real bad. The big kids, especially those in gangs, always picked on her and punched her when she didn't do as they said. Some of them hit her for no reason at all, just to watch her cry. Amy didn't belong to a gang, didn't have anyone to protect her, so she had to do what she was told or get beat up. The big kids also made fun of her because she'd sometimes wet the bed when thunder shook the room. Amy couldn't help it; she always thought the thunder was another earthquake, or a bomb going off.

Amy did learn how to swim at one of the shelters, which was a good thing. And she learned how to read. She wondered what Tom Sawyer—a character from a book she had read—

would think about the Gateway Arch sticking up out of the middle of the river like a giant, twisted pretzel. The Arch had once stood on dry land, but that was before the earthquake made the Mississippi change its course. It now stuck up out of the water and boats had to be careful not to hit it.

In the book, Tom Sawyer and his friend Huckleberry Finn had built a raft out of logs and sailed it down the Mississippi. One day she too would build such a raft and let it carry her far, far away. Maybe she would ride it all the way to Hawaii. She heard it was nice in Hawaii: sandy beaches, palm trees, lots of things to eat. They even had schools.

Amy had never been to school, but she had seen a picture of one. The school in the picture was a big gray building, with trees, green grass and a flagpole. She dreamed of one day going to school, riding on a big yellow bus, carrying her book bag and lunch box. She wondered what school kids had for lunch. Peanut butter and jelly sandwiches were her favorite. They probably had real milk too, not the nasty-tasting powdered stuff they gave you at the shelters.

It would be so wonderful to go to school. She'd sit in the front of the classroom in her new, clean clothes and raise her hand whenever the teacher asked a question. Maybe the teacher would walk her home after school, or let Amy live in her house.

The little girl's dreams of happiness faded as a dead cat floated past her, its swollen body bobbing along in the muddy river like a furry fishing cork.

With a heavy heart, Amy knew that she would never get to go to school. There were no schools. No classrooms. No teachers with bright smiles and happy eyes. All there was were dead cats, garbage, broken buildings and homeless people. God had raised his fist and punched the city flat, smashing forever her dreams. She would live on the streets and beg for food until she grew very, very old—if she didn't get murdered or die of cancer first.

She watched the cat float away and felt tears form in her eyes. In another time, another place, the cat might have been loved, maybe owned by someone like her. Now it was just a dead thing, floating away to the sea. She wished she too could float away . . . far, far away.

Amy heard a cough and turned. A short, bald-headed man walked down the hill toward her. He was a white man, but on top of his bald head were several patches of black skin. The man was a zebra, which was what you called a white person who had a black person's skin glued on. Not that they really looked like zebras, which were horses with stripes, that's just what everybody called them. Only rich people could afford to be zebras. Poor people had to get by with open sores and funny-looking moles covering their bodies.

"Lovely day for a picnic, isn't it?" said the bald man as he approached her. Amy took a step back. On the streets it paid not to trust people.

The man, who was dressed in very clean clothes—black pants and a blue shirt—sat down on an old car tire near the water's edge. He carried a brown paper bag, which he placed on the ground beside him. Curious, she watched as he opened the bag and removed two sandwiches wrapped in plastic. One he set on top of the bag, the other he unwrapped and began to eat. Amy felt her stomach rumble again.

After a minute, the man looked back and saw her standing there. "Would you like to join me?" He patted a patch of bare ground beside him. "I have plenty of food and I don't mind sharing." When Amy didn't respond, he smiled. "Please, picnics are no fun when there's just one." He picked up the uneaten sandwich and held it out to her. "It's peanut butter and jelly."

Amy looked at the man, who was obviously rich and seemed very nice, and then looked at the peanut butter and jelly sandwich. Her favorite.

Deciding that the man could be trusted, she accepted his offer, sitting down on the ground next to him. "Thank you," Amy said, unwrapping the sandwich he gave her.

"Not at all. Not at all," the bald man replied around gooey mouthfuls of peanut butter and jelly. "Only too happy to share." He reached into his bag and pulled out two cans of cola, giving one to Amy.

They ate their sandwiches, washing down each bite with warm cola, and talked about the weather and other things. Amy tried to chew slowly, but she was hungry and the sandwich was gone before she knew it. Only the plastic wrapping was left, which she licked until there was no more to lick. She had just finished her drink when the bald man snapped his fingers.

"Dessert! I've forgotten the dessert!" He jumped up. "What kind of picnic would it be without dessert? Why, it wouldn't be a picnic at all." He started to walk away, then stopped and looked back at Amy. "Don't you want dessert? It's chocolate cake. I left it in the car. Hurry now. Come along."

Amy jumped up. She didn't know which surprised her more: that there was chocolate cake for dessert, or that the man had a car. No one she knew owned a car. Few people did. Cars were expensive; so was the gas they ran on.

After hurrying to catch up, Amy walked with the bald-headed man along the waterfront past crumbled buildings and vacant lots. Suddenly, the man grabbed Amy by the arm and pulled her into an empty building. The building was tiny and dark, and smelled of garbage and rats. She tried to scream, but he clamped his hand over her mouth and pushed her to the ground.

"We're going to have dessert, all right," the man said, holding her tight. "But it's not going to be chocolate cake."

The man climbed on top of her; his weight crushed her chest and made it hard to breathe. Leaning closer, he kissed her face and neck, slipping his hand beneath her T-shirt. His breath came harder as he removed his belt and fumbled to unzip his pants.

Amy was terrified. She knew what was about to happen. She had seen the same thing happen to Sissy Roberts at the shelter late one night. Two of the older boys had done it to her, even though Sissy had begged them to stop. Sissy's bottom had bled for days and she eventually died. Amy didn't want to bleed, didn't want to die.

Desperate, she kicked and fought back, squirmed and managed to get loose. She tried to crawl away, but the man grabbed her from behind and pulled her pants down.

"Don't that feel good?" he asked, thrusting his hand between her legs. "You nasty little girl. You dirty little girl."

Amy screamed. His fingers were like sandpaper: rough, hot. They grabbed her and poked her, sending rivers of shameful pain burning through her body. He grabbed her by the back of the neck and pushed her face into the ground. The dirt smelled sour, like the sweat of the bald-headed man.

Amy tried to fight back, but the man was too strong. He held her tight, her face to the ground, her bottom high in the air. He held her with one hand, and fumbled to remove his pants with the other.

"You're going to get it now. Yes you are, you nasty little thing."

Terrified beyond words, she frantically felt along the ground, searching for something to defend herself with. Her fingers glided over cigarette butts and bottle tops, finally coming in contact with the jagged remains of a broken beer bottle.

Amy grabbed the bottle and pulled it to her. Twisting suddenly, she rolled over on her back. As she did, she stabbed upward, driving the broken bottle into her attacker's face.

The bald-headed man screamed like a woman as the beer bottle ripped across his face, cutting his left cheek to the bone. Blood squirted bright red from the wound, splattering Amy's arms, chest and face.

He let go of her and grabbed his face, trying to keep his blood from gushing. Amy dropped the beer bottle and rolled away from him. Pulling her pants up, she ran for the doorway.

"Put that on your stupid chocolate cake!" Amy yelled as she fled back into the harsh brightness of day. In the darkness behind her, the bald-headed man continued to scream.

CHAPTER 4

The stars dotted the night sky like a thousand tiny campfires. Beneath those stars, on a lonely South Dakota hilltop, sat Jacob Fire Cloud. For three days and three nights the elderly Lakota medicine man had sat there, without food or water, with only a thin blanket to protect his naked body from the cold. Praying to the Great Spirit for guidance, he listened for a voice that did not come.

His throat parched, his body weakened from the ordeal, Jacob could no longer stand and barely had the strength to raise his pipe in offering or wipe the tears of sadness from his eyes. Yet he refused to give up, dared not give up.

Time was running out for Jacob Fire Cloud, running out for his people. The Great Shaking was drawing near. The third and final one. Man had not listened to the Creator's voice, had not taken his wisdom and teachings to heart. The world was corrupt, evil, lost. Nothing had been learned from the mistakes of the past. Those who had died had done so in vain.

Jacob was only a boy, living on the Pine Ridge Indian Reservation, when the elders told him how, long ago, the Great Spirit had gathered together the four races of man, giving each a responsibility known as the Guardianship. To the red people He gave the Guardianship of the Earth, bestowing upon them the sacred knowledge of plants, minerals and animals. To the yellow race He gave the Guardianship of the Wind, teaching them about the sky and how to draw air within their bodies for spiritual advancement. Chinese monks, their lives spent in ancient monasteries, still relied on those teachings in their daily meditations.

The black race was given the Guardianship of Water, the chief of all the elements. It was the most humble element, yet the most powerful. Because of this sacred knowledge given long ago, it was a black man who discovered blood plasma, for blood is the most precious of all waters.

The white race received the Guardianship of Fire. Even today, one had only to look to the center of the things the white race invented to find that fire. It was in their lightbulbs, their cars and their weapons of destruction. It was also in their hearts. Like fire, the white man had moved across the face of the earth, never still, consuming all that lay in his path.

Fighting off the weakness that blurred his vision and made his bones ache, Jacob let the blanket slip from his shoulders. The cold night air chilled him, caused him to shiver, but it also refreshed and cleared his mind. Leaning forward, he fumbled with the knotted cords, which held tight the edges of his medicine bundle.

The bundle was made of buckskin, stained and brittle with age, its edges carefully decorated with bead- and quillwork. Some of the rows of beads were missing, but Jacob didn't mind. The value of the medicine bundle did not lie in its colorful decorations. It was what was on the inside that mattered.

Removing the cords, he unwrapped the bundle to reveal an assortment of dried herbs, which he used for healing both the body and spirit, a half dozen hawk feathers, two tail feathers from a golden eagle, a twist of sweetgrass, sage, a leather pouch filled with tobacco, a pocket lighter and his medicine pipe.

Jacob picked up the pipe and slowly filled its blackened bowl with tobacco. The pipe's bowl was made from a piece of red pipestone, carved in the shape of a rattlesnake's head. The stem was hickory, wrapped in leather and trimmed with gray rabbit fur. A tattered eagle feather hung beneath the bowl, held in place by a piece of imitation sinew. The feather was one of a matched set. Jacob had placed the other feather upon his wife's chest the day he buried her on a lonely hilltop behind his house.

After filling the pipe's bowl, he dug a tiny hole in the earth and placed a small pinch of tobacco in it for Grandmother. A second pinch was tossed into the air as an offering to the Great Spirit. Placing the pipe to his lips, he lit the tobacco with his lighter and inhaled the fragrant smoke deep inside his body. He let out his breath and raised the pipe above his head.

"O Grandfather, hear my prayer, for I am but a child lost in the wilderness. Look down upon me with pity and compassion, for many years I have walked the medicine path. I am old now, Grandfather, and I know that my time upon this earth grows short. Soon I will join my ancestors around the great council fire."

Again he puffed on the pipe and offered it to the Creator. "Please hear me, Grandfather, for I do not pray for myself, but for the people of this land. The Great Shaking is coming. I know this to be true, for it is written in the sacred tablets guarded by the Hopi people at Third Mesa . . ."

Before sending the four races to different parts of the world, the Great Spirit gave each of them a pair of stone tablets upon which were written prophecies of the future. The prophecies warned that if the four races did not live together as brothers, the Great Spirit would grab the earth and give it a shake.

According to the tablets, the first shaking would take place around the time the people saw giant beetles moving across the land. These beetles would be shaken so hard they would be knocked off the earth and into the sky, flying through the air like grasshoppers. In 1908, when the Model T Ford was mass-produced, the elders knew that these were the bugs the tablets told about. A few years later, Europe erupted in the flames of World War I. The flying grasshoppers turned out to be the air-planes that soared over the battlefields.

A sign of light will appear, but it will tilt and bring death. And the sun will rise, not in the east as we know it but in the west. Those were the words that foretold the coming of the second shaking. As the elders at Third Mesa pondered over the meaning of the tablet's words, an insane corporal rose to become a dictator in Germany. His heart black with evil, he took an ancient religious symbol used by Native Americans and their brothers far to the east—reversed and tilted it—and called it the swastika.

And the sun did rise in the west instead of the east: the rising sun of the empire of Japan. Once again the sacred tablets had predicted the future. Once again the earth was shaken by the devastation of war.

"Please, Grandfather, speak to me. Let your words of wisdom fill my mind. Let me feel your sacred breath upon my flesh. Too long I have cried in the wilderness, searching, listening for your voice. If I am worthy, and if it be your will, please send me your guidance so I may help my people . . . before it is too late."

Jacob Fire Cloud knew that the third shaking would happen soon, for it was written that it would occur in the days when men became women and women became men, and when species of animals long extinct were brought back to life to again walk the earth. Finally, the third shaking would occur in the days when men put "the house in the sky." Even though it was now just a ghost house, *Space Station Alpha* rose in the east like a brilliant star as it made its nightly climb into the heavens. Jacob watched the space station, his heart heavy.

Time was running out.

CHAPTER
5

Dr. Reynolds's presentation had gone better than she had hoped. Several of the medical company representatives had expressed serious interest in the Neuro-Enhancer. With any luck, the Institute would soon have the financial backing it needed to get the Enhancer into production. With the realization that her dreams of helping others on a large scale might soon become a reality, she had felt a great weight lift from her shoulders.

Rene had actually been in a good mood when she took the Institute shuttle to the walled neighborhood where she lived, in what had once been an affluent suburb just north of Atlanta. The neighborhood was now somewhat run-down, but for the most part it had been spared any real damage during the war. A tall concrete block wall topped with razor wire and broken glass, and armed security guards, kept the residents safe from those who would prey upon them.

The trip home had been uneventful; the driver had stayed on the main thoroughfares to avoid the most dangerous sections of the city. Even then, they had to pass through the downtown area, which still bore the scars of the riots and war. Beautiful high-rises were now mere skeletons, their glassless windows staring blindly like the eyeless sockets of skulls. Many of the buildings had been taken over by gangs and squatters; others sat empty and desolate. Once the glistening jewel of the South, Atlanta was little more than a burned-out memory of its former glory.

To pass the time on the trip home, she had struck up a conversation with one of the security guards riding shotgun on the shuttle. His name was Harold, a white man, about thirty-four years old, with a pleasant smile and a wonderful sense of humor. He told Rene that before the war he had worked as an accountant for a large advertising agency. He even pointed out the remains of the building, just a few blocks west of where the Coca-Cola Bottling Company once stood.

But that had been hours ago. Rene now stood across the street from the Hawkins Neural Institute. The building sat in darkness, empty; all of the scientists and lab assistants had gone home for the evening. There were no security guards either, no one to question her motives for returning at such a late hour.

But what were her motives? What had compelled her to leave the safety of her home, paying one of the neighborhood rent-a-cops to bring her back downtown? She knew the deserted streets of Atlanta were home to thieves, murderers and thousands of desperate people. They were dangerous enough to walk in the daytime, far worse at night. A woman like her, someone who still had a job and a home, still had money, would not be welcome in the inner city, not at night. It was dangerous, she knew that. Still, she had returned. Why?

Was it because she had a bad dream? No, not a dream; it was something more than that. She had been awakened with a premonition, a warning of things to come. Unable to shake off the feeling that something bad was about to happen, she had returned to the Institute seeking the source of her uneasiness.

Crossing the street, Rene hurried to the front door of the Institute. She looked around, made sure she was alone, and then punched the four-digit code into the automated door lock. A green light shone and the door opened with a click.

She entered the downstairs lobby, closing the door behind her. The building was eerily quiet, spooky, the darkness held at bay by a row of dim security lights set in the ceiling.

She crossed the lobby and followed a long corridor to a flight of stairs. Halfway down the corridor, she passed the examination room where she had given her presentation to the visiting scientists. The rows of folding chairs had been removed, but the room still smelled of coffee and cookies.

Rene had lied when she said the Neuro-Enhancer caused no side effects. Use of the device had in fact caused some very curious side effects in a couple of her patients. But instead of drowsiness, dry mouth, itchy rashes or other by-products normally associated with experimental treatments, they reported suffering from such peculiar oddities as premonitions of the future and mental warnings of impending danger. Unwilling to believe such things were possible, Rene began testing the Neuro-Enhancer on herself, with equally startling results.

She took the stairs to the second floor and turned left. Her office was two doors down on the right. Opening the door, she was relieved to find everything exactly as she had left it: her desk, her computer, the framed photo of her father. Rene paused to look at the photo, as she did each and every time she entered the room. The hurt still tugged at her heart, but not as strongly as before. The pain had faded with the passage of time.

Leyland Reynolds had been a history professor at the University of Georgia. He was a humble man, soft-spoken, respected by both students and fellow faculty members. A man of profound culture, he had used his wealth and talent to promote an understanding of classical art and music in the city of Atlanta. Twice he was elected chairman of the Atlanta Endowment of the Arts, in charge of arranging symphony concerts and arts exhibitions and funding scholarships for worthy fine art students. He was also the editor of *Atlanta 2000*, a critically acclaimed cultural review magazine.

When his wife, Rene's mother, died from a rare blood disease, Leyland took over the role of raising Rene. Setting aside his commitment to the arts and the community, he dedicated his every free minute to his daughter's education and happiness. It wasn't until many years later that he again focused his attention on matters outside the home.

It was as a result of her father's fierce devotion to her that Rene developed her enormous self-confidence. She was only five when her mother died, and no matter how hard she tried to retain them, the few memories she had of her seemed to fade with each passing year. Throughout her life it had always been "Daddy" who had been there, for everything from a scraped knee to her first date, with Lonnie Preston when she was fifteen. It was Leyland who had set the standard that Rene had been striving to live up to for as long as she could remember.

Some of her most indelible memories as a child were of the two of them sitting on the porch swing of the house on Lakeland Street, on languid summer evenings, spinning her future out before them like some intricate web. These dreamfests always had one central theme at their core: Leyland's repeated insistence that there was nothing that was beyond Rene's grasp in this life if she put her mind to it. He was forever emphasizing to Rene how special and unique she was, and how she would grow up to accomplish great things in her life. He had drummed into her the importance of following her own voice and the value of keeping her own counsel. Being the only child of a great man like Leyland Reynolds had certainly provided Rene with considerable benefits and privileges, but it was also a situation not without its drawbacks.

In 2010, Leyland had vigorously supported Senator Lawrence Everette in his bid for the presidency, helping the senator organize campaigns and fund-raisers throughout the

Southeast. He believed in Everett's dream of building a better America, a place of equality and freedom, no matter what color a person's skin.

Senator Everette's campaign for racial equality, environmental protection and economic reforms did not sit well with big business and those already in power within the government. Nor was the senator's political platform very popular with many of Leyland Reynolds's colleagues at the university. His show of support for the black candidate quickly alienated them, but Leyland didn't care. His dream of a better tomorrow was much more important than being invited to a few faculty social events.

Professor Reynolds continued to work tirelessly throughout the campaign, even though he had his doubts that an African-American would ever become President. But despite the odds, Lawrence Everette did win. America had elected its first black President.

Rene remembered going to the polls with her father on election day to cast their votes, the first and last time she had ever voted in a national election. She had been nervous and excited, but not nearly as nervous as she was later that night when they sat in front of the television set, watching as the election results slowly trickled in. When it was finally over, when it was clearly decided who the winner was, her father had gotten up and gone out onto the balcony to smoke his pipe. A few minutes later the phone rang. It was Lawrence Everette, calling to personally thank Leyland for all his hard work and dedication, and to invite him to a little victory celebration that weekend in Richmond. She had been thrilled, but her father had accepted the invitation with the mantle of quiet dignity he always wore.

Four days later, President-elect Lawrence Everette was killed in a chemical bomb attack while having dinner in an exclusive Richmond restaurant. Twenty-seven other people also died in the attack, including Professor Leyland Reynolds. The attacker who set the bomb was a twenty-two-year-old ex-marine from Davenport, Iowa; a card-carrying member of a militant extremist group that wanted to keep America "pure," meaning white.

No sooner had reports of Everette's assassination been aired on television and radio than riots broke out in Los Angeles, Miami, New York and Atlanta. African-Americans, Mexicans, Puerto Ricans and other minorities, enraged that their hopes of racial equality had been destroyed, took to the streets, smashing cars and windows, setting fires and pelting the police with rocks and bottles. For the first time since Sherman's march to the sea, the skyline of Atlanta glowed red as fires burned in the downtown area. By midnight the situation was completely out of hand and the police could do little more than pull back, turning control of the city over to the angry mobs. Government troops were called for, but they didn't arrive until two days later. In the meantime, Atlanta burned.

Rene looked at the photo of her father. At least his death had spared him from seeing his beloved city become a battlefield, from seeing the university campus baptized in the blood of young men and women. She, on the other hand, had witnessed all the atrocities of war in glorious Technicolor.

Circling her desk, she opened the safe sitting in the corner of the room and removed a gray padded case. Inside the case were file folders, two micro computer disks and the Neuro-Enhancer. Rene double-checked to make sure everything was still there, and then breathed a sigh of relief. Her worries had been for nothing.

Danger!

The word cut through her like a burning knife, a whispered word of warning that only her mind could hear. She spun around. Something was wrong, terribly wrong. Something bad was about to happen.

Rene placed the Neuro-Enhancer back in the safe and locked the door. She started to leave the office, but noticed she had accidentally left the microdisks lying on the desk. They were her original and a backup, each containing a set of binary codes that duplicated the firing order of the brain's neurons. Without the disks, the Neuro-Enhancer was useless; safeguarding them was critical.

Grabbing the disks, Rene turned to unlock the safe again but was interrupted by the sound of glass breaking.

Startled, she hurried to the door and opened it, leaning her head out into the hallway. She listened for a minute but didn't hear anything. All was quiet. Still, Rene knew she wasn't just imagining things. The sound of glass breaking had come from somewhere in the building. Maybe someone had tossed a rock at one of the office windows. If so, then the building would be unsecured. Rene owed it to the company she worked for to investigate the sound. She'd call the police, but no one would come. Not at night.

Her heart thumped with fear as she left the office and crept along the hallway, her soft-soled shoes gliding silently over the carpeting. She paused at the top of the stairs to listen, wondering if the noise she heard had come from outside. Sounds had a way of traveling through old buildings, echoing along hallways and vibrating through walls. The noise might have been nothing more than the shattering of a wine bottle dropped by some old drunk in a back alley.

She descended the stairs to the first floor and started down the corridor, checking doors as she went. Most of the offices were locked, so she could do little more than pause to listen at the door. Those that were open proved to be undisturbed.

Rene was just starting to relax when she entered the lobby and felt a gust of fresh air. Turning, she saw that someone had knocked all the glass out of the front door, allowing the night to enter. She stared at the gaping opening for a moment, and then realized that the alarm should be ringing but wasn't. It could only mean that someone had disconnected it prior to smashing the door.

Panic raced through her. This was no random act of van-
dalism; someone hadn't just thrown a rock through the door for
the hell of it. This was thought out and deliberately planned.
Someone had broken into the Hawkins Neural Institute and was
probably still inside the building somewhere. She was not alone.

The sound of a door slamming echoed from the second
floor, causing her to jump.

Burglars! They must have used the stairway at the opposite
end of the building. While she was coming down, they had
been going up. A thought flashed through her mind: she had
left her office door open, left the lights on, her purse sitting on
the desk. They would know that someone else was in the building. She had to get out.

Rene turned and ran for the front door. She was halfway
across the lobby when a white man, dressed in jeans and a
black T-shirt, stepped through the open doorway.

She froze; so did the man. They stood at opposite ends of
the lobby, eyeing each other. A tense moment passed, then the
man smiled and spoke. Rene saw that he was wearing some
kind of throat mike and earpiece, probably a two-way radio.
"I've got her," he said. "She's in the lobby."

From the second floor came the sound of footsteps running
down the hall. The man with the mike reached beneath his shirt
and unclipped something from his belt. Rene didn't wait to discover what that something was. She turned and fled, racing
toward the back of the building.

The hallway turned left; Rene followed it. She knew better
than to try any of the doors; they would be locked. So would
the fire exit at the rear of the building, but only to the outside.
If she could reach the fire exit, she might be able to get away.

She turned right at the next hallway, pausing long enough
to tip over a trash can in an attempt to slow down her pursuer.
The trick worked. The man with the mike came around the corner and hit the trash can at full speed, tripped over it and
crashed into the wall.

The emergency exit was in sight, the bright red door illuminated by a lighted sign above it. Rene was almost to the exit when she was tackled from behind.

She went down hard and slid, elbows and chin rubbed raw on the carpeting. But as she went down, she kicked out and felt the hold on her legs loosen. Slipping free, she rolled across the floor, collided against the wall, and stood up. Her attacker also got to his feet.

He was a white man, but not the same one she had seen in the doorway—the one who had tripped over the trash can. Tall and muscular, he too was dressed in a black T-shirt and jeans. He stood between her and the doorway, blocking the exit. Rene thought about running back down the hallway, but the man who had tripped showed up.

She was surrounded, trapped, two against one. But she wasn't about to give up without a fight. Her father wouldn't have; neither would she. Pushing herself off the wall, Rene charged straight at the man blocking the emergency exit. He braced himself for the attack, spread his arms to grab her.

Rene pulled her right arm back and made a fist. The move was a fake. When the man blocking the door raised his hands to protect his face, she dove past him.

She hit the floor, crawled, jumped up and threw herself against the safety bar. The door opened and she ran out into the night.

Rene sprinted down the alleyway, her attackers right behind her. She was halfway down the alley when she spotted a third man in front of her. At first she thought it was another burglar, then realized it was just a homeless black man rummaging through the trash bins. The man looked up as she ran toward him.

"Help me!" she yelled. The homeless man looked at Rene, then looked past her and saw the two men chasing her. His eyes widened in fear and he turned to run.

"Please, help me!"

She was almost to him when a blinding pain ripped through her hips and back. Rene's legs went numb. She staggered a few feet and fell into the arms of the homeless man. Looking down, she saw two tiny electronic darts sticking out of her right hip.

No. Oh, God, no. She could no longer feel her legs, the numbness spreading quickly throughout her entire body. As unconsciousness raced to overcome her, Rene pushed the code disks into the hands of the homeless man.

"Run. Run. For God's sake, run."

He hesitated, saw the men racing toward him, and then let go of her. The last thing Rene saw before a blanket of darkness descended over her was the man fleeing for his life down the alleyway.

CHAPTER
6

Leon Cane faded around the corner and took off, running for his life. His oversized shoes echoed loudly off the pavement, threatened to slip off his feet and go flying through the air. Still, he didn't dare slow down. He had just witnessed a crime. Robbery, rape, murder; he wasn't sure which. It didn't matter. He had seen the men involved, two white men, had seen their faces. Criminals showed their faces only when they knew there would be no witness left alive to describe them. If the men caught him they would surely kill him.

What about the woman? Was she dead? Had she been beaten and raped, her naked body left like garbage in the alley? A wave of guilt tore through him, causing him to slow his pace. He stopped and looked behind him. No one followed.

Did they kill her? The guilt he felt grew stronger, tightened his throat and squeezed his heart.

"I couldn't do anything," he said aloud, shaking his head. "They had guns. They would have killed me." He spoke the truth, but his words were hollow and did nothing to change his mood. The woman had cried out to him, cried out for help. Like his wife had . . .

Leon shook his head again, pushing back the images that threatened to form in his mind. Painful images from long ago. No matter how many times he tried to push them down, bury them in the cobwebs of time, they bobbed back to the surface to rip out his heart.

She needed my help.

"I could do nothing!"

He looked down and opened his right hand. The woman had given him a pair of computer microdisks. He had no idea what was on them, obviously something important—something her attackers wanted. Maybe he should take the disks to the police. They would know what to do with them.

Leon thought about it and then decided against the idea. The police would be of no help. At best, they would ask him a lot of questions he couldn't answer. At worst, they would lock him up.

If Leon had a computer, he could find out what was on the disks. He smiled. There were no computers among the homeless, no televisions or electricity. The country was broke, as were most of the people in it. But there was one place where he might find what he was looking for.

Slipping the disks into his shirt pocket, he walked along Marietta Street until it crossed International Boulevard. Leon followed International until he reached Centennial Park, which was no longer a park but a community of simple wooden shelters, cardboard boxes, tents and lean-tos. A tall cyclone fence had been erected around the park, leaving only one entrance open on the north side. Above the entrance someone had jokingly painted a sign, christening the new community "Second Chance."

Two men stood guard at the entranceway: one black, the other white. Both of them were members of the Eternal Brotherhood, an organization made up of several local gangs.

The Brotherhood had come into existence shortly after the war ended in an attempt to bring peace back to the streets of Atlanta. Based upon an uneasy alliance, the members offered their service in positions once provided by the government. They functioned as the police officers, fire fighters and sanitary engineers of the homeless and displaced. They were also judge and jury, dealing out swift punishment to those who broke the laws of the street communities.

Leon didn't see any weapons, but knew both men would be armed. He also knew neither one of them would hesitate to shoot an unwelcome intruder. Fortunately, he had been to Second Chance enough times to be recognized, even known. As he approached, the guards relaxed their stance and smiled.

"Hey, Leon. What brings you out so late at night?" one of them called. "I thought you'd be home, snug in your bed by now."

"I *was* on my way home," Leon replied, "but I wanted to stop by to see the Junkman." He stepped up to the gate and raised his arms out to his sides, allowing himself to be frisked. The black guard, who went by the name of T.J., patted him down and found no concealed weapons.

"Give me lovin'," he said, grabbing Leon in a bear hug.

Leon hugged T.J. back, and then hugged his partner. He wasn't sure, but he thought the other man's name was Slide.

"You'd better watch out for the Junkman," T.J. warned. "He's a smooth operator."

"Yeah." Slide grinned. "He'll talk you out of your pants and then sell them back to you. Make money doing it too."

"I'll be careful." Leon nodded, entering the village.

Unlike many of the tent cities, Second Chance had been laid out with some thought to order. The tents and other shelters had been set up in neat rows, with space behind each row for growing vegetables or hanging laundry. In the center of the park, an area was left open for leisurely activities, monthly

Brotherhood meetings and Sunday worship service. Tonight the members of the community were being treated to the vocals of a young woman, accompanied by two men on acoustic guitars. Her voice was clear and pleasant; she might have been a professional singer in a previous era. The woman stood upon a plywood platform and sang to an audience of fifty or so spellbound listeners.

Leon wanted to listen to the performance, but business came first. Weaving around the people listening to the concert, he made his way to the opposite end of the park, to a section known as trader's row. Here rows of booths and tables had been set up, displaying a variety of items for sale or trade. Just about everything could be had for a price.

There were booths featuring homemade lye soaps, shampoos and perfumes. Others offered slightly used shoes and articles of clothing. Loaves of bread covered one table, baked fresh in the small brick oven behind it. Next to the bread table, pieces of meat simmered over a small barbecue pit. Leon suspected the meat was either alley cat or rat.

Behind the booths lived the traders, their tents and shacks often as cluttered with merchandise as their stands. It was still early, so quite a few of them were up and about. They sat around tiny campfires, keeping an eye on their wares, hoping a potential customer would come along. Leon nodded to a few of them as he walked past.

At the end of trader's row stood a large gray tent, its canvas walls mildewed with age. There were no tables or booth, but everyone knew that the man who owned the tent was indeed a trader. In fact, he was the most profitable trader in the entire village. If Shaky Larkins, alias the Junkman, did not have what you were looking for then he could probably get it.

Stepping up to the tent, Leon knocked on the piece of board hanging from a length of frayed rope. He had to knock only twice before being answered.

"Go away! I'm closed!"

Leon smiled. Shaky was never closed; it was just his standard reply. Ignoring the remark, he opened the flap and entered the tent.

"Can't you hear? I said I was—" Shaky looked up, saw who it was, and smiled. "Leon. Leon Cane. How the hell are you? Don't just stand there. Come in. Come in." He stood up and gestured for Leon to enter. Shaky's real name was James, but no one ever called him that. Bony, wrinkled and gray-headed, the Junkman looked much older than his actual age of sixty-five.

Squeezing his way between piles of mechanical parts, clothing, used appliances and other miscellaneous junk, Leon took a seat on a chair made from scrap pieces of wood and automobile tires.

"You're just in time for coffee," Shaky said, removing a dented metal pot from a small fire. Leon watched as he slowly poured a stream of thin brown liquid into two tin cups, spilling some in the process.

Since the economic collapse, coffee, like a lot of other things, was in rare supply. With prices starting at thirty-five dollars a pound, few could afford the real stuff anymore. Instead, they substituted with a variety of other ingredients. In the South roasted acorns or pecan shells were used. Up North the drink of choice was made from hickory and walnut shells.

Shaky handed Leon a cup of what proved to be pecan coffee. "So what brings you to this neighborhood at night?" he asked. "Get tired of living by yourself?"

Leon shook his head. "I was hoping you might have something I need."

"Shopping, are we? For what?" Shaky snapped his fingers. "Wait. Don't tell me. I know. It's books, isn't it? It's always books with you. Never met someone who read so much in all my life. But you're in luck. I've got a few new titles you might be interested in. Hardbacks. Real difficult to come by nowadays." He set his cup down on a small wooden crate and started searching through his piles of odds and ends.

"Shaky, stop," Leon said. The old man ignored him and continued to toss hubcaps and old toasters out of the way.

"Most folks don't read books nowadays; they just use them for starting fires or wiping their butts. A damn shame if you ask me. Such a waste. But they won't be wiping their butts on these. No sir. At least not till you're done with them."

"Shaky, I don't want any books!" Leon said, raising his voice to be heard. Shaky stopped digging and turned to face him.

"You don't?" He straightened. "Then why didn't you say so instead of having me bust my back looking for you." He shook his head. "That's the trouble with you young uns: no respect for your elders." He sat down in a chair opposite Leon and snatched up his coffee cup. "Like I ain't got anything better to do than to look for books for someone who don't want any."

Leon waited for the old man to stop fussing and then said, "I don't need books. What I need is something that will play these." He pulled the code disks out of his shirt pocket and placed them on the wooden crate that served as a table. Shaky picked up the disks and looked at them.

"Where'd you get these? Pull them out of a Dumpster?"

Leon explained what had happened, describing in detail the woman in the alley and the men chasing her.

"Did you go to the police?" Shaky asked, turning the disks over in his hands.

Leon shook his head. "I didn't think the police would believe me. You know how it is; they'd probably blame me for the whole thing."

Shaky thought it over, then nodded. The police departments operated on a shoestring budget, those that still operated at all. They didn't have the funds or the manpower to go chasing down criminals, not unless you could afford to pay them. Since Leon was homeless, they probably wouldn't even bother to file a report.

"Can you help me?" Leon asked.

Shaky looked at him a moment, then handed the disks back. "Sorry. I haven't seen a working computer in years, especially one new enough to play these." He made a sweeping gesture of the room. "Now if it's junk, old clothes or appliance parts you need, you're in luck."

"Thanks anyway," Leon said, disappointed. He finished his coffee and stood up. As he started to leave, Shaky stopped him.

"Wait a minute," the old man called. "I do have something for you. Just got them in yesterday." He rummaged through a pile of clothes and pulled out a pair of black running shoes. "These should fit you," he said, tossing Leon the shoes.

The shoes were almost brand-new, with only one small scuff to show they had ever been worn. Turning them over, Leon saw that they were size ten. His size.

"I don't have any money," Leon said. He started to toss the shoes back, but Shaky put his hands on his hips and shook his head.

"Damnit, Leon. Who said anything about money?" He pointed at Leon's feet. "I'm tired of hearing you clop around in those oversized gunboats you're wearing. Make enough noise to wake the dead. I figure the only way I can get you out of them is to give you something else to wear. Besides, I still owe you for that radio you gave me. All it needed was a transistor. Take the shoes; maybe now I can get a little peace and quiet around here."

Leon accepted the shoes with a nod, waiting until he stepped outside before slipping them on. They fit perfectly; he didn't even have to stuff the toes with newspaper. Knowing Shaky could sell just about anything, Leon left his old shoes sitting in front of the tent.

The young woman with the pretty voice had quit singing by the time he left Shaky's tent, but Leon didn't mind. He felt good in his new shoes, his feet springing off the grass and bouncing off the pavement. He felt so good, in fact, that he started to jog. By the time he left Second Chance, his feet had adjusted to the shoes and he was running as fast as he could.

He ran the remaining five blocks to the alley where he lived. The alley was narrow and almost unnoticeable, a mere crack between two deserted brownstones. Two hundred yards from the street, the alley dead-ended against the side of a third building. Where it terminated, a high fence and a sturdy gate guarded an area once used to store trash cans and building supplies. Leon had sold all but one of the trash cans for scrap years ago, and the building supplies had been used to reinforce the wall of a large wooden crate that sat in the back corner of the fenced area. A wooden crate he now called home.

Leon preferred a solitary lifestyle to living in one of the street communities. For one thing, he felt safer. The crate he lived in sat in continuous shadows, hidden from view. And since he had the only key to the gate, his home was far more secure than most. But as he entered the alley, his pace going from a jog to a walk, he saw that the gate stood open. Something was wrong.

Someone had broken into his sanctuary, invading his private world. The broken pieces of the padlock lay on the ground, evidence of the invasion. He tensed. Perhaps that someone was still around.

Stopping just inside the gate, Leon picked up a board and slowly approached his home. He circled around to the doorway and squatted down, prepared to defend himself if necessary. The piece of plywood that served as a door stood open, further evidence that someone had been there.

He listened for a moment, heard nothing, then leaned the board against the side of the wooden crate, close enough that he could still grab it if needed. Reaching in his pocket, he removed a pack of matches and lit one. The tiny flame of the match pushed back the darkness enough for him to see that his home was empty. But someone had been there; his simple belongings lay scattered about on the floor.

"Damn."

Leon lit a second match and located one of his candles. The candle's pale amber glow revealed his worst fears to be true. He had been robbed. Gone were his blankets, his clothing and his meager supply of food: three cans of tuna, a couple packets of dried soup and a half-eaten loaf of bread. Also missing were his books, the homemade shelves they had sat upon empty and bare.

His heart nearly broke when he saw that the thieves had not been content with just robbing him. Out of meanness, they had destroyed the only thing in life that held any meaning for him. Lying at Leon's feet were the tattered remains of a photograph of his wife and daughter. The faded picture was the one thing he considered sacred, his most prized possession. But now that too was gone, destroyed, torn into tiny pieces by a nameless, faceless villain.

There was no one to vent his outrage on. No one he could punch and kick to rid the anger that flooded his heart. He sobbed, his soul tearing, as the sorrow of the situation rushed in on him.

"Why me, God? Why is it always me?" Leon sat down heavily, his body weak, waiting for his breath to return to normal. When it finally did, he leaned forward and carefully gathered up the pieces of the mutilated photograph. And then, his eyes still blurred with tears, he slowly started to put the picture back together. One tiny piece at a time.

PART II

"There is something in every one of you that waits and listens for the sound of the genuine in yourself. It is the only true guide you will ever have. And if you cannot hear it, you will all of your life spend your days on the ends of strings that somebody else pulls."

—*Howard Thurman*

C H A P T E R
7

The sun shone bright and warm, golden in a sky of blue. The air was filled with the delicate scent of peach blossoms and the melodies of a mockingbird. Rene felt the sun upon her face, like the breath of a warm puppy, as she ran through a field of tall flowers. She held a piece of string clasped firmly in her right hand. At the other end of the string a red kite danced with the clouds, carried upon invisible currents of wind. She laughed as the kite bobbed and weaved, happy as only a child of twelve could be, calling for her father to hurry up and not fall behind.

Leyland Reynolds chased after his daughter and the dancing kite. Smiling, laughing, he ran across the field where the peach trees grew and the mockingbirds sang. Rene turned to watch her father. He was tall and strong, his hair just starting to turn gray at the temples; his smells a mixture of cologne and black cherry pipe tobacco. Behind her father, the city of Atlanta rose like a magical kingdom, stretching mirrored towers and castle walls high into the sky.

Suddenly, the sky went dark and breathless; the dancing kite fell from the clouds. The string slack in her hands, Rene watched as the kite fell to earth and lay like broken dreams upon the ground. She looked to her father for help, but he was no longer there. The gas had taken him. Thick, yellow, it rolled across the ground, turning the trees into withered skeletons and stealing forever the mockingbird's song.

She tried to run from the gas, but the numbness in her legs slowed her. Each step was agony, bringing tears to her eyes.

The field was no longer empty. Others ran, screaming, from the soldiers with their guns and tanks. They fled from the bullets, the bombs and a thousand other horrors the war brought. Women ran with children in their arms only to be cut down in a hail of bullets, their blood mixing with that of the husbands and fathers who already lay dead on the ground. The blood blended together and ran in rivers across the field, turning the ground into mud. Bloody red mud. The mud sucked at Rene's feet, slowed her down even more. She called to her father for help, but he did not come. He had gone to Richmond to die in the yellow gas.

Jet fighters screamed overhead. The ground shook with the explosions of their rockets and bombs. Rene watched as buildings disappeared with a flash and a bang, entire neighborhoods baptized in flames. Schools, where children once played, became charred skeletons, the laughter and happiness gone forever.

Rene ran from the bombs the jet fighters brought, ran from the gas, but she could not get away. The bloody ground grabbed at her feet and pulled her down, sucking her into a muddy red grave. She tried to struggle, but couldn't move her arms. She tried to call out, but dirt filled her mouth and choked her. She couldn't breathe . . . could not breathe.

Rene awoke with a start, gasping, struggling to draw breath into starved lungs. Her heart and head pounded as she slowly became fully conscious, realizing with relief that she wasn't buried beneath the ground. It had been a dream. A nightmare. But as she tried to move, she discovered that her wrists were handcuffed and knew the nightmare was far from over

I've been kidnapped.

Everything came rushing back to her: the break-in at the Institute, the men who attacked her, her apparent abduction. She started to panic, but forced herself to remain calm. It would do no good to become upset. Her only hope lay in rationally thinking the situation through.

Okay, first things first. Where am I?

She lay on her back in complete darkness, staring up at a ceiling she could not see. Her arms were numb, which meant she had been lying on them for some time, probably for hours. Rolling on her side, she bit her lower lip to keep from crying out as the circulation slowly returned to her arms and hands.

As she lay with her face to the floor, Rene became aware of two things: first, the floor was made of metal and not wood. Second, the vibrations felt through the metal floor told her she was moving. If that was the case, then she must be in the back of a truck or a van. Listening carefully, she could hear the sound of the vehicle's tires humming on the road.

Another thought sprang to mind, sickening her. When the feeling finally returned to her fingers, Rene checked to make sure that she still wore clothes. She did—and she felt okay—so she had probably not been raped while unconscious.

Thank God.

So why had she been abducted? If robbery was the motive behind the break-in at the Institute, why hadn't the thieves just killed her? It would have been simpler. No doubt they knew she was in the building. Rene remembered the man with the mike telling his companion: "She's in the lobby." They had probably followed her, or watched her enter the building and knew she was alone. Apparently, they also knew there were no guards.

What did they want from her? Ransom? What a joke. She had no family, no one to pay the money. The company she worked for couldn't afford to pay for her return. The Hawkins Neural Institute operated in the red as it was. Surely her kidnappers would know that.

She thought of the men who grabbed her, trying to picture their faces in her mind. A wave of fear washed over her as she realized that both of them were white.

Was her kidnapping racially motivated? During the war the groundswell of pent-up anger went on to manifest itself in a purging of all the hate-mongering institutions that the minority population had been subjected to for so many years. Klansmen, neo-Nazis and skinheads had been hunted down and systematically executed. Many were publicly hanged by angry mobs, just as blacks had once been hanged by white-robed assassins.

But despite all efforts to stamp them out of existence, many hate group members had managed to escape execution or imprisonment. In certain states militant groups were re-forming, wanting nothing more than to stir up the flames of racial tension once again. Still, Rene could not imagine what such organizations would want with her. It had to be something else.

Whatever the reason for her abduction, she knew her life was in danger. When the circulation finally returned to her arms, Rene struggled and squirmed to work the handcuffs down the back of her legs and over her feet, bringing her hands to the front of her body. Now she would be better able to defend herself. If only she could find a weapon.

Crawling on her hands and knees, she searched the floor for a wrench, a tool, anything she could use in a fight. Finding nothing on the floor, she stood up and slid along the walls, hoping to find something useful hanging from a hook. Again she found nothing.

Her frustration mounting, Rene paused when she reached the back doors. There was no handle on the inside of the doors, no latch of any kind. They were locked from the outside and would not budge, not even a little bit. Freedom was only inches away, yet she could do nothing to attain it. Thwarted, she turned away from the doors and walked forward until she reached the front wall. On the other side would be the driver's cab and the men who abducted her.

Rene had intended to kick the wall to vent her frustration and let her kidnappers know how angry she was about being a prisoner. But she stopped herself, the mood slowly fading. It would be foolish to advertise the fact that she was awake and moving about. If they thought she was asleep they would be less cautious, maybe even a little careless. Perhaps they would stop soon to check on her. When they opened the doors, she would have a chance to escape—not a great one, but a chance nonetheless.

In the meantime, she needed to quit wasting energy by moving about. She would wait, mentally and physically prepared, for her chance at freedom.

With that thought in mind, she sat down with her back against the front wall. Rene placed her ear against the wall to see if she could hear anything. She couldn't. The thickness of the wall, or a space between the cab and the truck, prevented her from hearing conversation or anything else that could be useful. Disappointed, she closed her eyes and tried to gather her thoughts.

But as Rene started to relax a face suddenly flashed to mind: the face of the homeless man she had given the Neuro-Enhancer's code disks to. A faint glimmer of hope entered her heart. The man had witnessed her abduction and would notify the police. She smiled. It was only a matter of time till she was rescued.

Doubt entered her thoughts. The glimmer of hope faded and died. The police wouldn't get involved in a simple kidnapping, not when robbery and murder was a way of life on the streets of Atlanta. Even if they did get involved, they had no way of knowing where she had been taken. If only there was a way to tell someone where she was.

Maybe there was.

In addition to premonitions, another curious side effect of using the Neuro-Enhancer was the ability to project thoughts from one person to another. So far this mental telepathy had shown up in only two people: Rene and one of her elderly patients. Since she had been experimenting with the Enhancer on a daily basis, Rene's new-found mental ability was much more advanced than that of her patient. Even so, the phenomenon had only occurred a few times in the carefully controlled atmosphere of the laboratory. Could such a thing be possible now, without the Enhancer? Could she awaken the dormant portion of her brain to reach the same state of awareness needed to project thoughts? One thing for sure, she had nothing to lose by trying.

Closing her eyes, she willed her mind to grow calm and forced her body to relax. She inhaled deeply to slow her breathing. In through the nostrils; out through the mouth. In and out. Relax. Breathe. Relax.

Rene thought of how it was when she used the Enhancer: the icy numbness that slowly seeped into her body, starting in the toes and gradually coursing up through her legs; her muscles tingling with energy as the neural regions in her brain went into overdrive. And as she thought about it, she once again felt the numbness in her feet—felt the tingling flow from her shoulders to her fingertips.

It's working! She fought her sudden excitement, forcing herself to remain calm. *Breathe. In and out. That's it.*

The numbness turned her legs to lead as it seeped into her calves and crept up her thighs. It moved into her hips and stifled the nervous quivering in her stomach. The numbness and tingling merged; she felt relaxed and yet charged with energy at the same time.

As her body reached a state of deep relaxation, Rene's thoughts became focused and crystal clear. Programmed and conditioned by the Neuro-Enhancer, her mind now called upon neural regions normally not used. Thousands of electrical impulses raced through her brain from one neuron to the next.

Rene did not concentrate on what her brain and body were doing. Instead she focused her attention on the man she had given the code disks to, fixing his image firmly in her mind. Straining with such mental exertion that her body shook, she projected her thought toward him. One thought. Only one.

Help me!

C H A P T E R
8

The night is always coldest just before the dawn. Jacob Fire Cloud knew that to be true. He sat shivering on a lonely South Dakota hilltop, with nothing but a thin blanket to keep him warm. And though his naked body was weak from lack of food and water, and numbed by the chill night air, his mind was unaffected, his thoughts clear.

People who didn't know any better often thought that the visions experienced on a vision quest were nothing more than hallucinations brought on by starvation, lack of water, intense climate or drugs. They had never experienced the clarity of mind that occurs when the body is deprived of food and cleansed in the sweat lodge. Had they known the truth, or been willing to believe, there might have been more people seeking guidance in the wilderness. Just about every hill would have had someone on it, crying for a vision. But most people didn't believe in Indian medicine, or visions, so they didn't come. Jacob was quite alone.

He sat on the hilltop, his pipe cradled in his lap, facing east, watching the coming rays of dawn. In the valley below the creatures of the night were making their way back to their homes, replaced by the day's early risers. He saw a rabbit emerge from its burrow, nose twitching, ears upright and alert. The rabbit moved slowly, munching the tender shoots of new grass, mindful of the presence of a redtail hawk circling high overhead.

Jacob watched as the sun appeared over the hills to the east, painting the gray sky with streaks of pink and orange. It was going to be a beautiful day, but the old medicine man found no happiness in his heart. Three days had already passed and still his vision had not come. He knew he could not hold out much longer; he wasn't a young man anymore. The emptiness in his stomach filled his mind with thoughts of food and warm drink. Soon the temptations would become too strong to resist and he would give in. Failure was inevitable.

Jacob shook his head in an attempt to free himself from thoughts of food. He would not give up, dared not give up. His people depended on him. He had to put aside all thoughts of bodily comfort and concentrate instead on his reason for being there. "Think only of the shaking," he told himself. "Think of how little time is left."

To focus his attention, he watched the hawk circle in the eastern sky. With wings bronzed by the sunlight, the majestic bird soared lazily over the valley, gliding on invisible updrafts of air. The wind carried the hawk's piercing cry to Jacob. A hunting cry. The bird was searching for his breakfast.

He shook his head and smiled. "Breakfast. You're thinking of food again."

Jacob turned his attention back to the valley below, but he could no longer see the rabbit. The warmth of the sun had embraced the remaining chill of the night, covering the narrow valley in a thick layer of mist. He watched as the mist slowly curled along the valley's floor, moving like a herd of—

He blinked and looked again, not believing his eyes. The mist was changing shape, growing darker, turning into something else. Horns and heads appeared. Creatures with fur and hooves. Spellbound, he watched as the mist slowly transformed into a herd of buffalo.

Jacob sucked in his breath. What he saw was impossible. All the buffalo were gone. The white man had killed them long ago. Even those protected in the national parks had been slain by poachers for their meat when food became scarce. The buffalo were gone, extinct, yet below him in the mist he saw a herd of the great beasts. A spirit herd. His vision had come.

No sooner had Jacob realized that he was receiving his vision than all the buffalo in the valley below began to change back into mist and disappear. All except one.

One solitary brown buffalo cow remained, slowly walking up the hill toward him. As the buffalo approached, it dropped to the ground and rolled over, the color of its fur magically changing from brown to red. Halfway up the hill, it rolled over again, changing from red to yellow. The spirit buffalo was only twenty feet away when it rolled over once more and changed from yellow to white.

Jacob's hands shook uncontrollably; it was all he could do to hold on to his pipe. Tears of joy streaked his cheeks. His prayers had been answered. The Great Spirit had sent him a vision, the greatest of all visions. He had sent His personal messenger, the white buffalo, guardian of the north and bringer of wisdom.

The ground shook with each step as the white buffalo cow approached. Her breath was like an arctic blast; where she stepped the ground froze. Trembling with both fear and excitement, Jacob raised his pipe before him and offered it to the sacred spirit. The white buffalo rolled a final time. This time, however, the buffalo didn't just change color. It changed form.

Jacob Fire Cloud's heart burst with joy as his eyes beheld the vision standing before him. She had returned to save her people, the woman who had taught the Lakota how to pray. She had returned, her voice carried upon the wind. The White Buffalo Woman had come home.

She had returned once before, coming back in her animal form. In 1994, a white buffalo had been born in Janesville, Wisconsin, bringing great prosperity upon the Native American people. Many tribes had grown wealthy from their casinos, buying back some of the land stolen from them by the white man.

Now she was back to unite the four races, bringing all of mankind together as brothers and sisters. She alone could stop the third shaking. She alone could save mankind.

Jacob wept openly as he gazed upon the White Buffalo Woman. She stood no more than ten feet away, dressed in white buckskin, her face as radiant as the sun. She looked at him and smiled, her voice and thoughts filling his head. And then she snatched Jacob's spirit from his body, carrying him high into the sky.

They danced among the clouds, their spirits touching as they sailed over the earth on the wings of eagles. As they soared over the distant mountains, Jacob heard a voice like thunder and knew it was the Great Spirit who spoke.

The Creator told him what had to be done if his people were to be saved. Jacob listened carefully, setting each word to memory. When the voice ended, so too did the vision. He was again on the hilltop. Alone. The White Buffalo Woman had gone.

A great happiness filled the heart of Jacob Fire Cloud as he slowly placed his pipe back in his medicine bag. His body still weak, he somehow found the strength to stand and walk. It was a long way back to his home, a very long way, but he would make it. He was sure of it.

His prayers had been answered. The vision he had prayed so long and hard for had finally come, answering questions and offering guidance for him and his people. She had returned; he could still hear her voice deep inside his head, calling him.

Jacob smiled. The White Buffalo Woman had returned, only this time she was black.

CHAPTER
9

A voice woke him. Thinking that the thieves who robbed him had returned, Leon put his hands out to protect his face. Always protect the face, protect the head, that was the rule of the streets. It was a lesson learned in the school of hard knocks. Those who didn't follow it sometimes ended up as mindless, drooling zombies, or dead. He had been beaten twice before: once by cops, and once by two men who wanted what little money he had. Neither was a pleasant experience. This time, however, there was no one around. He was alone.

Leon sat tensed, listening, making sure someone wasn't sneaking around the humble wooden crate he called home. But he heard nothing to alert him that danger was near. No footsteps. No voices. The only sound was the plop-plop of raindrops hitting the roof. He must have been dreaming.

Lowering his hands, he breathed a sigh of relief. For once the danger was only imagined. He rubbed his eyes and sat up, pushing open the makeshift plywood door. A new day had dawned, but it was overcast and raining, draping a blanket of gray over an already gloomy city. The rain gave a sickly, slimy look to the surrounding buildings and caused the sour odors of garbage and urine, long since soaked in and forgotten, to be released again from the pavement. Oily rainbows formed where the rain gathered in puddles.

Leon watched the rain, his soul as gloomy as the day. He had been right last night; he knew it was going to rain. But the rain wouldn't last. Patches of blue sky were already poking their way through the gray. By mid-morning the rain would stop, and by afternoon the sun would be out in full force to suck up the puddles and turn the day into a humid steam bath.

The pleasure he took in knowing he could still accurately predict the weather was overshadowed by what had happened the night before. He had been robbed, his blankets and provisions stolen. There would be no breakfast, no lunch or dinner either, unless he managed to find work somewhere. That sometimes happened. If he was lucky, Leon got hired to do odd jobs for food. A sandwich or two. A bowl of rice. Nobody had much money nowadays.

If he wanted to work, he needed to get moving. It was a long walk to where the jobs were, and there were a lot of other hungry people out there.

Putting on his new shoes, Leon slipped on the same shirt he had worn the night before. He had just finished buttoning it when he spotted the photo of his wife and daughter on the floor beside him, looking like a badly assembled jigsaw puzzle. He had managed to piece the picture back together, but he had no tape or glue to hold it in place. He must have bumped the picture during his sleep, for several of the fragments were out of place.

Afraid the thieves might return and steal the picture out of meanness, he scooped up the pieces and placed them in his pocket. As he did, his fingertips brushed two micro computer disks.

His mind occupied with his own troubles, he had completely forgotten about the incident in the alley. He wondered what had happened to the woman, feeling a twinge of guilt for not going to the police. She had been in trouble. No doubt the men who chased her had been intent on robbery, or something far worse. Still, he knew the police wouldn't have done anything. Nothing at all.

Leon had just crawled from his wooden crate when he again heard a voice. A woman's voice.

Help me.

Startled, he stood up and turned around quickly. No one was there. Odd, he thought. It sounded as if a woman had been standing right behind him. He circled the crate, thinking she might be hiding. Still no one. The alley leading to the street was also empty.

Leon relaxed a little. Voices had a way of traveling in the concrete canyons of the city. The voice he heard could have been coming from a roof, from inside one of the warehouses, or from several blocks away. He stood and listened for a moment, but didn't hear it again.

He shook his head. "You're hearing things. That's all. Keep it up and you'll be talking to yourself like the old winos down at the park." He closed the front door of the crate and fastened it with a piece of rope. Again he heard a woman's voice.

Help me!

The voice came loud and clear, sounding like she was standing right next to him. Someone had to be playing a trick on him.

Leon looked around, searching for a hidden speaker or tape player. He checked around the wooden crate, under the pieces of wood and trash inside the fenced enclosure, even behind the garbage can, but found nothing.

"You're not fooling anyone," he shouted. "I know you're here. Somewhere."

There had to be a speaker, maybe one of those tiny ones. No other answer could explain it . . . unless he was going crazy. Leon touched his head, as though he could tell by the shape of his skull whether or not he was losing his mind. Nothing seemed out of place; his head felt the way it always did. No abnormal, tumorous growth. No bump. He didn't drink or take drugs, so he wasn't hallucinating. What else could it be? Unless . . .

Help me.

His mouth dropped open in surprise. He wasn't hearing the voice with his ears. On the contrary, it came from somewhere deep inside his head, drifting up from the darkness of his subconscious like tiny air bubbles from the ocean's depths. They were words never spoken but heard all the same. Words meant only for him. A woman's voice. He knew that voice.

"Oh, dear God," he whispered.

Chills danced up and down his spine as he recognized the voice that came from deep inside his head. It had been so long, so very long, but there was no mistaking it. The voice he heard could belong only to Vanessa, his wife, speaking to him from the grave, calling him as she had done the night someone firebombed their house.

It had been September 21, 2012, one year after *Scientific American* published his article about shuttle launches affecting global weather patterns, six months after he had been fired from NASA. He had been in his study, typing up a résumé, when a firebomb crashed through his living room window. The flames spread quickly, racing across the carpeting and up the walls. A second bomb followed the first. More flames. The smell of gasoline heavy upon the air.

Leon hadn't heard the window break, but he heard Vanessa calling him from the bedroom, and the horrified screams of Anita, their three-year-old daughter. He rushed out of his study, only to find a raging inferno in his living room. He was cut off from his family, separated by a solid wall of flames.

He tried to reach them, but the flames licked his skin, burned him, drove him back. The fire in the living room spread down the hallway toward the bedrooms, sent crackling tongues of flame in search of his wife and daughter.

Terrified, Leon retraced his steps and ran out the front door. He raced around to the side of the house and used a brick to break out the glass in the bedroom windows. Even then he could not get to his wife and daughter. The security bars, installed only a few months earlier for protection against burglars, trapped them inside their bedrooms. The bars were bolted to the outside of the house, impossible to remove without tools.

Though he was not a particularly strong man, Leon tried his best to spread the steel bars to free his family. But no matter how hard he strained, the bars would not bend. He watched, helpless, as the hungry flames entered their rooms. He heard their screams of agony. His daughter, overcome by smoke, had fallen to the floor and could no longer be seen. His wife, her hair and clothing on fire, stretched her arm through the bars and gently touched his hand. And then she too was gone.

The bars grew hot, glowed red. Leon refused to let go. Only when the flames sprang from the window, singeing his hair and eyebrows, did he release the bars and step back. He did not feel the pain in his blistered palms, nor did he hear or see the fire engines racing toward his house. He felt nothing, and saw only the image of his wife—etched forever in his memory—reaching out for him, calling him.

"Help me!" Those had been her last words. He had failed her, failed his daughter, but he would not do so now. Somehow Vanessa called to him from beyond the grave, called to him for help. He had to go to her.

Leon Cane pushed himself away from his wooden crate and began to run.

CHAPTER
10

They stopped moving.

Rene Reynolds had been dozing, but came fully awake when she realized the truck had stopped. The gentle swaying that had been with her for so long was gone, as was the sound of the vehicle's tires humming on the road.

She tensed. Why had they stopped? Was it only for gas, or was this the end of the line? Either way, it might be a chance to escape, maybe her one and only opportunity for freedom.

Her heart pounded as she stood up and slowly inched toward the back doors. She took several deep breaths, but could not shake the fear that dug icy claws deep into her guts and threatened to turn her body numb. The muscles in her legs quivered as she stood crouched and listening.

She heard the driver's door open, and felt it slam. The passenger door also opened and closed. Footsteps. Muffled voices. Scraping at the back of the van. A lock was turned.

The back doors swung open and light entered, the artificial glow of fluorescent bulbs. Rene started to lunge, but two white men blocked her path. They were not the same men who had broken into the Institute, but it didn't matter. Each was armed: one with a pistol, the other with an electric stun gun. She froze. Even if she made it past them, she could not outrun the weapons they carried. The men must have seen the position she was in, noticing that her hands were now in front of her, and guessed her intentions. They both took a step back. The man holding the stun gun, who was muscular and covered with tattoos, raised his weapon and smiled.

"Don't even think about it," he said.

His partner, a tall man with dirty-blond hair and a goatee, gestured with the pistol he held for her to get out of the truck. "Climb on down out of there."

Rene stayed where she was. "I demand to know why I've been kidnapped." She tried to keep the fear from her voice but failed. "I'm a scientist, damnit. What do you want with me?"

"You'll find out soon enough, sweetheart," answered the tattooed man. "Now get out of the truck."

She shook her head. "Not until I know what's going on."

The tattooed man's smile melted. Rene was pushing her luck, but she hoped she was more valuable to her kidnappers alive than dead. "Lady, we were paid to bring you here alive. That's all I know. But no one said we had to bring you here undamaged."

Acting on cue, the man with the goatee cocked the hammer on his revolver.

"Now, are you going to get out of the truck? Or do you want my friend here to put a round through your kneecap?"

Rene looked from one man to the other. She found no compassion in either of their faces. No warmth. Their eyes were cold, deadly, like those of a snake. They would not hesitate to shoot her if necessary.

"Okay, you win," Rene said, giving in. The tattooed man's smile returned. He stepped forward and helped her down out of the truck. Once she was down, he grabbed her by the left arm and shoved the stun gun against her ribs.

"This thing fires two hundred thousand volts," he said. "Try anything funny and I'll light you up like a lamp." He led her away from the truck, his partner falling in several paces behind them. Rene held back, giving herself a little extra time to look around. They were in a parking garage, probably in the basement of a large building. Unfortunately, there were no signs on the walls, nothing to tell her where the building was located. They could have been anywhere.

An idea suddenly struck her. She turned and looked at the vehicles behind her. There were two cars and three trucks in the garage, including the one she had arrived in, each with a vehicle license tag registered to Cook County, Illinois.

I'm in Chicago!

Rene was stunned. What was she doing in Chicago? Why had they brought her here? She could think of no reason for being taken so far from Atlanta. She had no enemies in Chicago; she had never even been to the city before. If her abduction was for the purpose of ransom, wouldn't it have been simpler for the kidnappers to keep her hidden somewhere in the South?

At one end of the parking garage were two elevators. The man with the goatee stepped past them and pushed the button on the wall, summoning one of the cars. Entering the elevator, Rene saw there were buttons for only four floors. If the building wasn't tall, then it had to be long, because the garage had enough room for over a hundred vehicles. The goateed man pushed the button for level four and the elevator door slid shut.

When they arrived on the fourth floor, Rene was led down a long, narrow corridor. On first impression, she thought she was in a hospital. The walls were painted a creamy white, absent of any kind of decorations, and there was a lingering smell of chemicals and disinfectants. But if they were in a hospital, then they were on a floor that was no longer used. Cobwebs hung from the ceiling like delicate chandeliers, while dust covered the moldings and the doorknobs of the rooms they passed. The beige carpet they walked on was also soiled, and there were brown stains on the ceiling where water had leaked through. Overlapping the smell of disinfectants came the sour, musty odors of mold and rat droppings.

Twenty doors lined the hallway, ten on each side. They stopped in front of the last door on the right, obviously arriving at their destination. As the man with the goatee unlocked the door, his tattooed partner stepped in front of Rene and removed her handcuffs. She thought about running, but he still held the stun gun in his left hand. She didn't know if 200,000 volts was enough to kill a person, but she didn't want to find out.

A blast of stifling hot air billowed out into the hallway as the door was opened, carrying with it the stench of urine and vomit. Rene tried to retreat from the foul odors, but the tattooed man gripped her arm tighter and held her in place. Her eyes watering, she gazed through the doorway at a tiny, windowless room—a room which contained only a metal-framed cot, a sink and a toilet. Nothing more. Rene had never been in a jail before, but she knew a cell when she saw one.

Before she could complain about her accommodations, Rene was shoved into the room and the door closed behind her. She turned and beat on the door with her fist, only to discover that it was covered with gray padding. Even her strongest blow made only a muffled thump. The walls were also padded.

After giving the door a final kick, Rene turned to study her surroundings. She was grateful for the dim lightbulb, which burned in a recessed fixture in the ceiling. At least she hadn't been cast into complete darkness. Then again, in the dark she wouldn't have to contend with the dreadful sights that lay before her.

The metal-framed cot lined the wall to the left of the doorway. The bed had been made, but not recently. A tattered green army blanket and dirty white sheet covered a thin mattress that sagged badly in the middle. On top of the mattress rested a caseless pillow, stained from sweat and what might have been blood. Fastened to the cot's steel frame were four heavy leather straps, two at the head of the cot and two at the foot. Rene shuddered when she thought about what the straps might have been used for.

Across the room from the cot stood a sink and toilet, both stained the color of rotten teeth. The padded wall behind the toilet was also stained. Brown. Rene quickly looked away, her stomach turning, when she realized what had been smeared across the wall.

She crossed the room and tried the sink's faucet, but it didn't work. The toilet probably wouldn't work either. Even if it did, she had no desire to ever use it. The mere thought of her bare skin touching the diseased porcelain bowl was enough to turn her stomach. Instead she turned away from the sink and slowly approached the bed.

Brought up in a household where personal hygiene and cleanliness had been preached, and with her training as scientist, she knew that a million deadly germs existed in the world. Half of those germs probably resided in the cot's mattress and filthy coverings. The other half million undoubtedly crawled around on the concrete floor beneath it.

Rene grabbed the edge of the stained pillow and flung it across the room. The army blanket and sheet followed. She didn't see anything crawling on the mattress but flipped it over anyway, only to discover that one side was just as soiled as the other.

With no other place to sit, she overcame her revulsion and sat down on the edge of the cot. At least her captors had removed the handcuffs, but not before they'd rubbed a groove in her wrists. Rene knew the groove would fade in time. Other than that, she was physically unharmed. Her mental condition, however, was another matter.

Just thinking about her situation filled her with deep, black despair. She had been kidnapped and was now being held prisoner in a modern-day dungeon. No doubt her captors had some evil intentions in mind for her. Sex slave perhaps? A thousand possibilities popped into her mind, none of them pleasant.

"Stop it!" she said, shaking her head. It would do no good to let her imagination run away with her. She had to hold on to the positive. She was alive. She was unharmed. That meant something.

"Yeah, a healthy whore brings more money than a damaged one."

If her captors wanted slaves, why didn't they look closer to home? Why go to all the trouble of bringing her from Atlanta to Chicago? It didn't make any sense. Not unless her abduction was for political reasons.

Rene considered that possibility. She herself had no pull in any political circles, but her father had pull when still alive. He had publicly backed the man who would be President, meeting with and mingling with those in high places. Maybe Rene's captors had kidnapped her to get back at her father for something, not knowing that he was dead.

Then again, maybe this had something to do with someone she had met at one of the many political functions Leyland Reynolds had dragged her to. That had been so long ago. Never interested in politics, she had not bothered to remember the names or faces of those she met; therefore, she had no connections in the government, any government. Rene almost smiled. If her abduction was for political purposes, they had snatched the wrong person.

But she did have connections. Correction, she had one connection. She thought again of the homeless man she had given the code disks to. The break-in at the lab, and her disappearance, would be reported. Maybe the police would question him. If only she could mentally contact him.

Doubt tugged at her mind. The man was in Atlanta; she was in Chicago. How could she even think of mentally contacting someone so far away? Such a thing had never been done before. Even with the Neuro-Enhancer attached and running, the farthest she had ever projected a thought was a few blocks. To try to project a thought a thousand miles, without the Enhancer, was impossible. Absurd.

Rene felt her spirit lift a little. It was the impossible that drove her to become a scientist, saying yes when others said no. Besides, what did she have to lose? She wasn't going anywhere, nor did she have anything better to do. Knowing it was probably her only hope for being rescued, she again closed her eyes and thought of the homeless man, projecting her thoughts toward him.

Help me. Please, help me. I'm in Chicago.

CHAPTER
11

Jacob Fire Cloud tied an orange knapsack, a blanket and his leather medicine bundle to the handlebars of his old bicycle. Crossing the room, he took down a sacred wooden staff from where it hung on the bedroom wall. Carved from the branch of a willow tree that had been struck by lightning, the staff was about twenty-four inches long and two inches around. The blackened piece of wood was wrapped in buckskin and decorated with beadwork. Seven feathers were fastened to the staff: three eagle feathers and four wing feathers from a red-tail hawk. Like the staff itself, which had been kissed by the Great Spirit's fire, the feathers were considered strong medicine.

He removed a piece of red flannel cloth from the dresser that sat against the wall and slowly wrapped the staff, taking care not to damage any of the feathers. Once it was wrapped, he tied it to his medicine bundle with a length of cord.

"You're crazy, you know that?" said Michael Fire Cloud, watching him from the corner of the room. It was the first time his son had spoken in over an hour. Ignoring the remark, Jacob opened the top drawer of the dresser and pulled out a .357 revolver, slipping it through his belt.

"That thing hasn't been fired in thirty years."

"Forty," Jacob corrected.

"At least shake the spiders out of it."

Jacob smiled and removed a box of tarnished bullets. Putting the bullets in the knapsack, he turned and studied his son.

Michael Fire Cloud was thirty-two years old, tall and thin like his father, with long, raven-black hair—the color Jacob's hair had once been before time turned it white. But that's where the similarities between the two men ended. Jacob, rooted in tradition, walked the medicine path, keeping alive the teachings and wisdom of his ancestors. Michael, on the other hand, was a prodigy of the modern age. Raised on the reservation, he had moved to Los Angeles shortly after graduating high school. There he had enrolled in college, learning the white man's ways. He became a computer engineer, designing programs for a device that Jacob could never figure out how to use.

Unfortunately, like many Indians who leave the reservations and move to the big cities, Michael was never able to fit in. He felt alienated, alone, a person by himself in a world of many. He cut his hair and dressed like those around him, even got an earring and a few tattoos, but that didn't help. No matter what he looked like, deep inside he was still an Indian.

Michael's frustration at not being able to fit in turned to anger. He became politically motivated, joining one cause after another. He fought for racial equality, the homeless, gay rights, the environment, even to save the whales. When the riots broke out after the assassination of President-elect Everette, he too took to the streets to voice his anger, smashing windows and helping overturn cars. He was on the front lines when government troops arrived in Los Angeles to break up the riots. Arm in arm with his fellow demonstrators, he marched boldly toward the soldiers, never dreaming the Guardsmen would open fire on fellow Americans.

The soldiers' rifles sounded like firecrackers on a Chinese New Year. The bullets sliced through the crowd of unarmed protesters like a giant sickle, ripping flesh and splintering bone, leaving hundreds dead and dying in the streets.

Michael watched in horror as the rows of marchers in front of him were shot down in cold blood. He tried to turn around and flee, but the people behind him kept pushing forward, unaware of the slaughter that was taking place. A bullet buzzed past his head like an angry hornet. A second bullet struck the woman beside him. She grabbed her stomach and crumpled to her knees, blood spurting from between her fingers. The woman's name was Elizabeth; she was nineteen years old and three months pregnant with Michael's child when she died.

Stumbling over the bodies in the street, Michael fought his way to the sidewalk in an attempt to flee down an alleyway. He had just reached the sidewalk when a bullet tore through his left thigh. The pain ripped a scream from his lips and sent him sprawling to the pavement. Knowing he would be crushed to death by the panicked crowd if he did not get back up, he struggled to his feet and limped into the alley. Halfway down the alley, he collapsed and passed out.

He would have bled to death if one of his fellow demonstrators, a black man whose name he did not know, hadn't come along and tied a tourniquet around his leg to stop the bleeding. The man then carried Michael to a hospital, where the bullet was removed and his wound treated. He remained in the hospital for nearly a week. When he got out, he no longer had any desire to march or protest. The bullet that pierced his leg, and the horrors he had witnessed, had taken all the fight out of him. Heartsick, disillusioned, he had withdrawn into his shell—and into a bottle.

One year later, Jacob Fire Cloud found his son passed out drunk in a tiny, roach-infested apartment. With the help of a neighbor from across the hall, he carried Michael down the stairs and placed him in the back of his pickup truck. He brought

Michael back to the reservation where he belonged, brought him home, saving him from the bottle, the city and the war.

The days following his return were not easy ones for Michael as he struggled to fight off the demons that infected his soul. Jacob had been there for him every step of the way, taking him through sweats to cleanse and strengthen his body, teaching him wisdom to clear his mind, and performing sacred ceremonies to heal his spirit. He was there when Michael awoke late at night, the demons of his city life torturing his dreams. On those lonely nights, when the wind howled and Michael cried, he would hug his son until the shaking stopped and the tears dried. It hadn't been easy, but in the end Jacob had won. The evil that claimed Michael's soul had finally given up the fight. He had his son back.

"You're crazy," Michael said again. "How can you be sure the White Buffalo Woman has returned? You can't just go running off, not at your age!"

"We will talk," Jacob said. He took his son by the arm and led him outside. They walked around to the back of the house and up a tiny hill upon which grew purple wildflowers and sage. At the top of the hill a simple wooden headstone marked the resting spot of Emma Fire Cloud, Jacob's wife. They had been married for over thirty years, and he was as much in love with her the day she died as the day they married. Earlier, Jacob had climbed the hill alone to sit by his wife's side and speak of the things he must do.

Reaching the top of the hill, Jacob pulled his small personal pipe from the pocket of his denim shirt and loaded the bowl with tobacco. Michael remained silent, patiently waiting, for he knew his father always smoked first before talking of important matters. Tossing a pinch of tobacco into the air, as a gift to the Great Spirit, Jacob lit the pipe with his lighter. He smoked for several minutes before speaking.

"What do you see?" Jacob asked, pointing toward the refugee camps in the distance.

"Tents, shacks . . ." Michael said.

"What else?"

"People."

Jacob nodded. It was the answer he was looking for. "Hundreds and hundreds of people. They have all come here for a reason. Most come here seeking cures for their illness: medicines for their oozing sores, magic for their blindness and withered limbs. They have heard that I am a man of medicine, so they come."

He turned and looked at Michael. "I have no cures to give them. Gone are the plants which used to grow wild on this land. The white man has destroyed them with his pollutions and poisons. Grandmother's womb is bare; she can no longer produce the little plants which heal."

He again pointed at the refugee camps. "Those who are not physically ill come here seeking cures of the spirit." He shook his head. "Again I have nothing to offer them."

He smoked his pipe in silence for a minute. "It is written in the Hopi prophecies that there will be three shakings—"

"Haven't there already been three?" Michael interrupted.

Jacob shook his head. "There have only been two."

"What about the war, and the earthquake in the Midwest?"

"Those were only warnings," Jacob answered. "The third shaking is still to come. When it does, our people will be no more." He looked at the sky, searching for something that could not be seen in the daytime. "It is written that the shaking will occur soon after a house is put in the sky. That time is now."

Jacob looked his son in the eyes. "But it is also written that before it happens, the Great Spirit will send down a messenger to try one final time to bring the four races of man together. That messenger has been sent. It is her voice I hear calling me, asking for help. I must go to her."

"But what of the people who need you here?" Michael said, alarmed that his father was serious about leaving. "Who will they go to for guidance or medicine?"

Jacob laid his hand on his son's shoulder. "You. They will come to you."

"Me? But I'm not a medicine man. I don't know anything."

"You know more than you think." Jacob smiled. "You have learned a lot since you returned from the city. The people will come to you and you will help them. You'll see."

Michael shook his head. "I don't know all the words to the ceremonies. I'll mess up."

"If you do the ceremony with a good heart, and for a good reason, it does not matter if some of the words are forgotten. The medicine will still be honored by the Great Spirit. That is a promise He made to our people long ago. He has never broken that promise and will not do so now. You will do fine."

Jacob patted his son's shoulder and walked back down the hill. He went inside and got his bicycle, leaning it against the side of the house. He waited until Michael came down the hill, and then gave him a hug goodbye.

"You're not coming back, are you?" Michael asked.

Jacob shrugged. "I don't know. Grandfather has not allowed me to look into the future to see how my journey will end." He smiled. "But I am like an old dog that nobody wants. I think I will be back."

Jacob Fire Cloud climbed on his bicycle and started to slowly pedal away. He was still a little weak from his vision quest, even though he had eaten twice since returning from the ordeal. Michael watched his father for a moment, and then called after him.

"The voice you hear. How do you know it's her? How do you know it's the White Buffalo Woman?"

The old medicine man looked back over his shoulder. "The elders said she would return one day. They said she would reappear in the east . . . and that is the direction from which the voice comes."

"From the east?"

Jacob nodded. "From Chicago."

12

Amy felt as dirty as the waters of the Mississippi looked in the early light of day. The rich bald-headed man had tried to do something terrible to her: he had tried to rape her. She could still feel his touch upon her skin, his rough hands as unclean as a dead rat. The thought of him pulling her pants down, touching her, made Amy's stomach churn and her throat tighten. She bent over and threw up, emptying her stomach of what little food she had eaten the day before. What was left of the peanut butter and jelly sandwich, given to her by the rich man, was sprayed over the weeds poking through the cracks in the pavement.

She had cleansed her stomach, but she still couldn't rid her body of the lingering touch. Nor could she free herself from the fear, loathing and guilt that she felt. The man had tried to rape her, true, but she had cut him with the jagged edge of a broken beer bottle and that was also wrong. Maybe she had even killed him.

Amy thought about it. Had she killed the bald-headed man? If so, that would make her a murderer. The police would be looking for her. They put murderers in jail, locking them away until they died of old age and rat bites. Sometimes they strapped them into an electric chair and fried them until their eyes popped out and their skin sizzled like bacon. She had never seen anyone electrocuted, but the older kids in the shelter told her that's what happened to people who committed murder. Amy didn't want to go to jail, or have her eyes pop out of her head. She had to hide.

She looked around, trying to decide on a hiding place. There were plenty of places to hide along the waterfront: empty buildings, abandoned warehouses, burned-out cars, maybe even a few of the caves beneath the city. She had once hidden in the wrecked remains of a big silver boat called the *Admiral*, but a couple of old drunks had chased her out. Still, she couldn't hide forever. Sooner or later she would have to come out to look for food. Even rats had to eat. When she did, the police would grab her and drag her off to jail.

If she couldn't hide, then she had to get away. That was it, she had to leave the city. A frown tugged at the corners of her mouth. If she left St. Louis, she would be giving up any hope of ever finding her mother. The people at the shelter had told Amy that her mother was dead, but she didn't believe them. Her mother was still alive, somewhere. She just didn't know where.

Maybe she could go away for a little while, until the police quit looking for her. Sooner or later they would get tired of searching and give up. Then she could come back and everything would be like it was before. But how would she get out of the city?

Good question. She didn't have a car, didn't know anybody who did. She didn't even own a bicycle. She looked at the river. If she had a boat she could get away. Or a raft . . .

A smile unfolded on her face as she spotted a tugboat pushing a string of coal barges up the river. "A raft!" she said, excited. "A really big raft!"

Amy studied the barges for a moment and then turned and looked upstream, focusing her attention on the twisted remains

of the Eads Bridge. Part of the bridge had been destroyed during the earthquake. What was left of it stuck out over the water
like a giant diving board. If she could reach the bridge before
the barges passed beneath it, she might be able to jump onto
one of them. It was quite a fall, but the piles of coal should
cushion her landing and keep her from getting hurt. At least she
hoped they would.

Amy had just formed the plan in her mind when someone
shouted, "Hey, you there!"

She turned and saw a policeman coming down the hill
toward her. Her blood went cold.

Oh no, she thought. He must have died, the rich bald-
headed man who tried to rape her. All his blood must have
leaked out and he had died. She had killed him. She was a murderer. But how did they know she was the one who did it? How
did they find out?

He must have told someone before he died. Or maybe he
had written her name on the wall, carefully spelling each letter
with a finger dipped in his own blood. That must be it. Her
name was written in dried crimson. AMY LADUE KILLED ME. Now
the policeman was going to arrest her and take her away to jail,
where there would be rats and big kids who would punch her
if she didn't do what they said. They were going to put her into
the electric chair and fry her until her skin turned black and
crispy and her eyes popped out.

"Hold it right there," the policeman yelled. Amy looked at the
policeman, looked at the string of barges, and took off running.

"Stop!"

Amy didn't stop. She ran like a frightened rabbit for the
Eads Bridge, pumping her arms as hard as she could. The
policeman chased after her.

Would he shoot her? Did policemen shoot little kids in the
back? Amy wasn't sure, but she thought they did. Why else did
they carry guns? She had never been shot and could only imagine what it would feel like: the bullet going in, all hot and

smoking, tearing through muscle and bone. It had to hurt, just had to hurt really bad.

Last summer, she had seen the body of a man who had been shot. He was lying in the weeds, next to the crumbled wall of an abandoned building. His body was swollen from the heat and smelled really bad, and there were flies crawling all over it. He lay on his back, his eyes open and glassy, like the eyes of a dead fish, staring up at the sky as though he could still see. A small round hole was in the center of his forehead. A bullet hole. Blood had oozed from the hole to dry on the man's face and neck. Just a little hole, smaller than a dime, but it had killed him dead.

She turned and looked behind her. The policeman was still chasing after her, but he hadn't drawn his gun. Maybe he only wanted to catch her, saving her for the electric chair. Either way, dead was dead. She didn't want to be dead and swollen, with glassy fish eyes that couldn't see. She ran faster.

Amy reached the bridge and started across. She was well ahead of the policeman, but now she had to slow down and choose her steps carefully. Though part of the bridge still stood, it was in bad shape. Chunks of concrete had broken loose and fallen into the river, leaving behind steel girders and reinforcement rods that stretched across the empty spaces like twisted, frozen snakes.

"Don't look down. Don't look down," she told herself, but did anyway. The river wasn't deep yet, no more than ten or fifteen feet. Jagged chunks of concrete and metal that had fallen from the bridge stuck out of the water like the teeth of a hungry fish. Amy knew she would splatter like an egg if she fell on those pieces.

She had just taken another step when she heard a groaning, cracking noise, like nails being pulled from a board, and felt the bridge shift beneath her feet. Amy screamed as a crack opened before her and a section of the concrete gave way. She barely had time to grab the bridge's railing as a four-foot piece of cement fell into the river below.

Heart pounding, the taste of fear bitter in her mouth, she stood on the base of the railing, clinging to one of the upright steel girders. Her eyes were closed, and she was much too afraid to open them again. Only when she could again breathe normally did she sneak a peak.

The section of bridge where she had stepped was gone. It had fallen into the river. She too would have fallen had she not jumped when she did. The mere thought of what almost happened made her legs tremble.

"Don't move."

The voice startled her. Turning, she saw that the policeman had caught up with her. He was only about twenty feet away, carefully working his way across the bridge.

"Stay where you are," he ordered. "I'm coming to get you." He must have seen the fear in her eyes, because he held out his hand and said, "I'm not going to hurt you. I only want to talk."

Her muscles tightened. She started to flee from the approaching officer, but something in his voice held her in place. He said he only wanted to talk. Was he telling the truth? She wanted to believe him, but could she? Before Amy could make up her mind, she heard someone else shout: "That's her, officer! She's the one! Arrest her!"

Amy turned to see who was doing all the shouting and spotted the bald-headed rich man standing at the water's edge, waving his arms and jumping up and down. He still wore the same clothes he had the day before, but a large white bandage now covered the left side of his face.

Relief flooded through her. She was not a murderer after all, and probably wouldn't burn in hell for all eternity. She might not even get fried up in the electric chair. Her relief was only temporary, however, for the rich man continued to yell.

"Arrest her, Officer. Arrest that little bitch. She's the one who did this to me. I demand that you arrest her and throw away the key."

She may not be a murderer, but she had cut the man's face

with a bottle and that had to be against the law. The policeman wouldn't believe that she had been protecting herself, probably wouldn't even listen to her side of the story. The bald-headed man was rich, powerful. He could buy judges and policemen. Amy, on the other hand, was nothing. A nobody. They would lock her in jail and throw away the key. That's where they kept all the rats.

"I only want to talk to you," the policeman said again.

"Liar!" she yelled, backing away from him. "I'm just a river rat. You're going to arrest me and put me in jail!"

Terrified of being locked up, Amy held on to the railing and hurried the rest of the way across the bridge. The policeman yelled for her to stop, but she didn't listen.

She made it to the end of the bridge, but the barges were still too far away. The policeman would catch her before she could jump. Knowing she could not wait, Amy climbed onto the bridge's railing.

The police officer stopped dead in his tracks. "You don't want to do that."

Amy looked at him and smiled. "Yes, I do."

She took a deep breath and then jumped. Her arms flapping wildly, she plummeted toward the river. The fall seemed to take forever, an eternity in slow motion. She saw the bridge flash past her, the policeman watching her in wide-eyed terror, and was captivated by the jeweled reflection of the river's surface. She struck the water feetfirst, the impact stinging the bottoms of her feet and stealing her breath away.

Down, down, down she went, deep within a world of swirling darkness, tumbled and tossed about like a kite in a thunderstorm. She struggled against the current, fighting to get back to the surface, but the river was too strong for her, dragging her deeper into its ebony womb.

Kick. Kick. Kick, she told herself, remembering the swimming lessons she had been given at the shelter. She was a good swimmer, but that had been in the calm waters of an enclosed pool, not in the raging torrents of the Mississippi.

Water entered her nostrils, bringing with it the smells of the river: the odors of fish, sewerage and slimy, dead things. Amy wanted to cough, but dared not. If she did, water would rush into her mouth and fill her lungs. She would drown and be like the cat she had seen the day before. Maybe that's what the river wanted. Maybe it wanted to make her part of its cold, watery world; drag her down to the blackness at the bottom and bury her in the soft mud, forever.

Fighting the sensation to cough, fighting the river's icy grasp, she swam as hard as she could for the surface. Her lungs ready to burst, her head finally popped above the raging water.

Amy coughed, gasped for breath, and choked as water entered her mouth. She swallowed, coughed some more and drew in shuddering lungfuls of air. She had made it to the surface, but she still wasn't out of danger. The river carried her downstream, spinning and tossing her about like a piece of driftwood. Turning, she saw the approaching barges and realized in horror that she was on a collision course with them.

The river's current was carrying her straight at the oncoming barges. She would be run over, killed, her body crushed and then chopped into little pieces by the tugboat's propellers. Fish food.

She swam harder, fighting the current to get out of the way. She spotted a chain hanging from the side of the lead barge. Amy reached out and grabbed the chain, clung to it for dear life. The little girl was so exhausted she didn't even feel her body bouncing against the barge's metal side.

Her strength slowly returning, she managed to pull herself up the chain and tumble inside the barge, landing on a soft pile of coal. Bruised and battered, she lay there as the barge passed beneath what was left of the Eads Bridge. Above her, the policeman leaned over the bridge's railing and stared at her in disbelief.

Amy smiled at the policeman, and then lifted her right hand, extending the middle finger in a gesture of defiance. She was now an official river rat, heading upriver on the world's largest raft.

CHAPTER
13

Leon Cane stood in the window, feeling the wind upon his face. Cool, caressing, like the kiss of angels. It whispered in his ears, sharing with him secrets of faraway places and times long past. He closed his eyes and imagined himself flying with the wind, soaring like a bird up to the sun. Soaring, soaring, soaring, never falling, sweeping over mountains and deserts, touching ancient temples and forgotten cities of stone. His spirit passed beyond the reach of day, into the cool darkness of the night. Following the path of dead kings, he drank from sacred pools of water, which glowed like jewels in the moonlight.

He sighed and opened his eyes. Leon was on the twentieth floor of the Atlanta Hilton and Towers, looking out over what had once been the heart of Atlanta. Most of the downtown area had been destroyed during the riots, the once-glittering high-rises looted and burned. The remaining buildings had been pock-marked and scarred by rocket and artillery attacks during the war.

But Leon hadn't climbed twenty flights of stairs in a burned-out hotel just to admire the view, not that it was worth admiring. He had come seeking peace for a troubled soul, to rid himself of guilt and anguish. He had come to join his family again, forever.

His throat tightened as memories of his wife floated through his mind: Vanessa curled up on the sofa, watching television, a bottle of mineral water on the end table beside her. The smell of her hair, the feel of her flesh when they made love, the whisper of her voice late at night when she lay beside him and spoke of her dreams for the two of them and for their daughter.

Tears slowly trickled down Leon's cheeks as he thought of Anita, feeling the emptiness that lay within his heart. There was no way to describe how badly he missed his daughter, for it was beyond description. Never again would he be able to hold his little girl on his lap, hug her, listen to her laughter when he playfully tickled her feet, or see her lower lip turn into a pout when she was mad. Words alone could not begin to tell of the loss he felt, or the guilt.

It was his fault that his wife and daughter had died. His and his alone. Vanessa had begged him not to publish his article about space launches affecting global weather patterns, but he had refused to listen. Leon thought he was doing something important, looking out for the welfare of mankind. Instead he should have been thinking about the safety of his family.

Because of that cursed article his home had been fire-bombed and his family murdered. The joys of being a husband and a father had been taken away from him. There would be no more quiet walks along the beach, no more casual conversations at the dinner table. He and Vanessa would not grow old together; Anita would not grow up, fall in love, and get married. She would never even have a boyfriend, or ride a bicycle. Gone, gone, gone, all of it gone; a world of hopes and dreams destroyed forever in a fiery blaze. A blaze he had brought upon them.

Leon wiped his eyes and looked down. The street below was deserted. There was no noise, only the sound of the wind as it blew through the concrete canyons of the city. The air was almost clean—almost, for it carried upon it the all-too-familiar fragrance of burning shit. Even this high up he could not escape the noxious odor.

With a shortage of electricity, natural gas and fuel oil, many residents of the city had resorted to using dried human excrement as a means of cooking meals and providing warmth on cold winter nights. It was an odor Leon could never get used to, no matter how often he smelled it.

Help me.

The voice was loud and came so unexpectedly that he nearly fell out the window. He hung on, barely, teetering high above the street. A stick figure, dressed in baggy clothes, dancing with the pigeons.

Vanessa called to him, needed him. He had failed her once before, but he would not fail her now. He would go to her, crossing over to the other side. There was nothing keeping him in this world, nothing at all. He was just a homeless refugee, living from day to day, sleeping in a box, trying to survive. There was no real reason to continue living.

The street looked like a tiny black river. Just one step was all it took. Just one. Would he feel the impact? How bad would it hurt? He shook his head. What difference did it make? What was one brief second of pain compared to the lonely agony that haunted his every waking minute? One brief second was all it took for everlasting peace.

Leon took a deep breath and looked up. He focused his attention on the sky as he tightened the muscles in his legs. Gripping the window's edge, he prepared to step off into space.

Please help me.

The voice came again to fill his mind, this time carrying with it an image of the person who called him. The face of a young black woman. Not his wife.

Leon suddenly realized that the voice he heard was not Vanessa's. It was the voice of a woman he did not know.

"Who are you?" he asked aloud. "How can I hear you?"

There was something vaguely familiar about the woman's face, as though he had seen her someplace before. He concentrated on the mental image, racking his brain to come up with a name to go along with the face. A few moments passed, and then everything clicked into place.

The woman in the alley! It was her face, her voice that he heard. But how? A chill danced up his spine. Had she been killed? Murdered? Was it her ghost who called him, haunting him?

Leon thought about it. He believed in the existence of ghostly spirits, a belief passed on to him from his mother and grandmother. At holidays, and other gatherings, the family members would talk about having "seen" or "heard from" his aunt Gertie—a relative who apparently drowned at the ripe old age of eleven. Once during such an occasion, the whole room had been silenced by the laughter of a child who could be heard but not seen.

Even though Leon believed in the existence of spirits, he was certain the voice he heard did not belong to a ghost. For some strange reason, he felt the woman was still very much alive. But if the woman was alive, how was she getting inside his head? There had to be a rational explanation for what he was experiencing. Maybe he was just tired. It could be fatigue. Perhaps it was guilt for not helping the woman. Or maybe after all the years of living alone, all the heartaches and sorrows, he had finally gone crazy.

Help me.

"Leave me alone!" he yelled, cupping his hands over his ears. The sudden movement caused him to lose his balance and tumble backward into the room. He landed on his butt, jumped up and yelled again. "Go away, I tell you. Get the hell out of here!"

Help me. Help me. Help me.

"Go away. I cannot help you. I can't even help myself." He was talking to thin air, talking to himself like a crazy man. "Go away and leave me alone."

Help me. Help me. Help me . . .

He looked around the room, hoping to find someone hiding, playing a trick on him. No one was there. Except for a few pieces of broken furniture, the room was empty.

"Why me?" he yelled, angry. "I don't even know you. I don't want to know you. Choose someone else."

He waited for the voice to speak again, but it had grown silent. The anger slowly leached from his body, replaced by a weary sadness. Why did she call him? He didn't know her, owed her nothing; he had his own problems.

A troubling thought crossed his mind. Maybe the woman called to him because she had no one else to call. Maybe she too was alone in life. Alone, lonely, such a terrible way to be. He had been alone for so very long. But now someone spoke to him, called him, needed his help. Vanessa had also needed his help, but he had failed her.

"Not this time," he whispered. "I won't fail this time." He took a deep breath and looked around the room. Inside of him an ember was stirred, glowing with the tiny flame of his spirit. For the first time in years, Leon felt that his life might have some meaning and a purpose after all. Someone actually needed him, needed his help.

But the flame almost died again as the shadow of uncertainty crept over him. "How can I help you?" he asked aloud. "I don't even know where you are."

He stood in the center of the room, quietly waiting for the voice to again enter his mind. When it did, it spoke only one word.

Chicago.

In a field of wildflowers and weeds, beneath the pale light of a crescent moon, shadowy figures hunched around a hundred tiny campfires. Waiting, listening, they spoke only in whispers, their voices like the gentle murmuring of a babbling stream. Leon Cane also sat by a small campfire, carefully feeding it twigs and dried pine needles. He too waited and listened.

Before coming to the field on the outskirts of the city, he had gone to see Shaky, the Junkman. Leon wanted to say good-bye, because he wasn't sure when he would make it back to Atlanta—if he ever came back at all. The old man had been visibly upset about him leaving.

"You're going where?" Shaky had asked, jumping up from his seat.

"Chicago," Leon answered, knowing how dumb his plans sounded.

"Chicago? Chicago? What's in Chicago? You got relatives up there or something?"

Leon shook his head.

"Then what are you going for? There isn't any work in Chicago, if that's what you're looking for. And the winters are cold as hell. You ever experience a Chicago winter?" He didn't wait for a reply. "Well I have, and I can tell you they aren't any fun. Nothing but snow and ice, and the damnedest wind. You can't go anywhere, can't even get out of the house. You'll freeze to death. So what the hell are you going to Chicago for?"

Leon explained about the voice he heard and his reason for going. Shaky looked at him for a moment in stunned silence, then commenced to yell.

"That's about the craziest damn thing I've ever heard! A voice. You hear a voice." He pointed a finger at Leon. "Well, let me tell you something, I hear a voice too. Right now that voice is telling me you've gone off the deep end, you don't have both oars in the water, the lights are on but nobody's home."

"I'm not crazy," Leon argued.

"No, of course not," Shaky said. "Everybody hears a voice that tells them to run off to Chicago."

"I do," Leon said calmly.

Maybe there was something in the way Leon said it—something in his voice—or maybe it was the look in his eyes. Either way, Shaky calmed down and stopped yelling.

"You're serious. Aren't you?"

Leon nodded.

The old man blew out his breath; his shoulders slumped. "You got any money for the trip? Any food?"

Leon told him about being robbed the night before.

"And they took everything?" Shaky shook his head. "I told you you shouldn't live by yourself. It's not safe. Not that things are much better in the camps, but at least you've got somebody watching your back." He turned away from Leon and started rooting through a pile of junk. A few seconds later Shaky tossed him a beat-up canvas knapsack. "Here, take this."

"I don't want any charity," Leon said, starting to toss the knapsack back. The old man turned on him like a bulldog.

"Charity! Who said anything about charity? I'm a businessman; consider this a trade."

"A trade?" Leon was confused.

He nodded. "That's right, a trade. You're leaving, probably won't be coming back, so I'm claiming ownership to that wooden crate you call home and everything left in it—before someone else does. I can use the materials for a few projects I've got in mind."

Along with the knapsack, Shaky added three cans of tunafish, a can opener, a rusty steak knife—just in case Leon ran into any trouble on the road—a thin army blanket and five crumpled one-dollar bills.

"Now get out of here before I change my mind," he said with a wave of his hand. "Lord knows I've done too much for you the way it is."

Leon put the cans of tuna and other items in the knapsack, and stuffed the dollar bills in his pants pocket. He then stood up and gave Shaky a hug goodbye. The old man started to push Leon away, then changed his mind and hugged him back.

"Take care of yourself," Shaky said, showing his true feelings for one brief moment. He broke the embrace. "Now get out of here. I'm busy enough without having you hanging around all day." With a nod and a smile, Leon shouldered the knapsack and left. It was a long way to Chicago.

Leon Cane smiled to himself in the darkness, thinking about what might have been his very last visit to the Junkman. He was just about to add another stick to his tiny fire when he heard a long and mournful call, like the howl of a dying wolf.

"Train!" someone yelled.

Instantly, all the campfires were extinguished and the field was again cloaked in darkness. In that inky blackness, men, women and children gathered together their belongings and moved up the hill to a strip of trees bordering the railroad tracks. Leon too gathered his stuff and started up the hill. Halfway to the top he turned and looked behind him. In the distance, the single headlight of an approaching freight train glowed like the eye of some prehistoric beast. A cyclops. But it was a beast that spelled freedom for many.

With the collapse of the American economy, few people had enough money to afford a car. Those that did often couldn't afford the gas to keep it running. Public transportation had also come to a standstill. Buses no longer traveled the highways, planes no longer filled the sky. Even the subway systems had ground to a screeching halt. The only things still operating, on a somewhat limited basis, were the trains, and they were used strictly for hauling goods and materials from one city to the next. With passenger trains no longer in existence, the freight train had become the taxi of the poor, providing free rides to those quick enough to climb on board.

The train drew closer, its light stabbing the night. Leon heard its engine strain as it started up the hill. The train would be moving its slowest as the engine topped the hill. That's when several hundred people would rush the cars in an attempt to climb aboard.

Leon's heart beat faster; he felt the excitement and fear of those around him. The engine sped by and the crowd surged toward the tracks. Jostled and elbowed, he was swept along with the mass of people. One slip and he would be trampled by those behind him.

The fastest runners reached the train and slid open the doors on the boxcars. Leon felt the wind of the passing train as he ran alongside it and knew that death missed him by only a few inches. He grabbed for an open door, but was shoved from behind by someone also trying to board the train. He stumbled, nearly fell, and tasted the metallic, bitter taste of fear.

The train slowed almost to a complete stop as the engine topped the hill. Only a few seconds before it would again pick up speed. Like a swarm of ants, the people shoved and pushed, fighting to get on. Leon saw a man slip and fall, heard him scream as the steel wheels ran over his legs.

The train sped up, sending the crowd into a blind panic. They clawed and punched, pushing people out of the way, not caring if those people lived or died. Leon grabbed hold of a door, but someone jumped on his back, using him as a human ladder to board the train. Angered, he drove his right elbow straight back, heard a groan, and felt the weight fall off him. He quickly pulled himself up and into the boxcar.

Hands grabbed him, helped him to his feet. The boxcar was already full, people packed in like cattle. He had expected it to be empty, but then realized that Atlanta wasn't the first city where people had boarded. All along the line, whenever a hill or curve slowed the train enough to make it reasonably possible, people would attempt to get on. He wondered how many mangled bodies lined the nation's railroad tracks.

He had just stood up when someone screamed. Startled, he turned around and saw a young woman in the doorway, reaching out to a little boy who clung by one hand to a metal latch on the outside of the boxcar. The latch was bent downward, and the child's grip was slowly slipping along its length to the end. Soon the boy would fall. Chances were he would be crushed beneath the train's wheels. Even so, those standing closest to the door made no effort to help. They just stood and watched as though it was all part of a show.

Elbowing his way to the doorway, Leon threw himself on his stomach and reached out to the child. "Give me your hand!" he yelled. The little boy looked at him in wide-eyed terror.

"Hurry, damnit, give me your hand." He stretched even farther. The little boy hesitated, and then grabbed Leon's hand.

As the boy let go of the latch, his feet dragged the ground. Leon felt himself slipping and knew he was going to be pulled from the boxcar. They would both be killed. The only chance he had of saving himself was to let go of the little boy, and he wasn't about to do that.

He was only inches away from falling when someone grabbed his ankles and pulled him and the child to safety.

Leon lay on his stomach, panting, weak from exertion. Several seconds passed before he was able to catch his breath. He sat up and turned to see who had pulled him inside, but there was no one there. His savior had vanished among the crowd. The little boy and his mother had also disappeared.

Getting to his feet, he squeezed his way through the crowd to the back of the boxcar. He found an empty spot along the wall and sat down. The excitement and fear of his near-death experience had left him, replaced by a black cloud of despair and humiliation. He had tried to save the boy's life and failed. Some hero. If it weren't for the efforts of some unknown helper he and the boy might have died.

He closed his eyes and leaned his head back against the wall, feeling the swaying motion of the train. He thought about his reasons for going to Chicago. What good could he be to the woman whose voice he now heard? How could he help her when he couldn't even help a little boy? Why was he doing it?

Someone touched his shoulder. Leon opened his eyes. Even in the darkness, he could see that it was the little boy he had tried to save. Small. Thin. Wide eyes set in a tiny brown face. The little boy held out his hand, offering something. Leon looked and saw it was an orange. Food. The most precious gift the child could give him. A thank-you.

He smiled and took the orange. The child smiled back and turned away, vanishing among the shadows and crowd. Why was he going to Chicago? Because it was the right thing to do.

PART III

"We used to wonder where war lived, what it was that made it so vile. And now we realize that we know where it lives, that it is inside ourselves."

—*Albert Camus*

CHAPTER
14

Rene Reynolds had no way of telling time in her windowless cell, no way, other than counting aloud, to mark the passing of the minutes and hours. She didn't wear a watch and her surroundings never changed. The temperature never got any hotter, or any cooler, and the dim lightbulb in the ceiling above never varied its shade of sickly yellow.

But even in her unchanging environment, she knew that time was, in fact, passing. Her body's internal clock told her this. Since her arrival, she had used the toilet four times. Overcoming her revulsion for the soiled cot, she had also slept twice. Rene had no idea how long she had slept. It might have been hours; it might have been days.

Trays of food had been brought to her, carried into her cell by a silent guard. It was always the same guard, and he had always greeted her questions with a glare and icy silence. She had thought about slapping him just to see if he was able to speak, but the gun he wore held her at bay. Since the guard refused to answer her questions, and he wore no wristwatch, the length of her captivity remained a mystery. The food offered no clue either, since it was always the same: a ham and cheese sandwich on wheat bread, an apple and a carton of warm fruit drink. Nothing on the menu indicated whether it was being served for breakfast, lunch or dinner. For all she knew, the trays might have been brought once a day, twice a day or once every other day.

As the hours trickled slowly by, Rene's frustration with the hopelessness of her situation grew. She paced the room, occasionally punching the padded walls to vent her anger. When she grew tired of that, she would sit on the edge of the cot and attempt to transmit her thoughts. She had all but given up on contacting the homeless man in Atlanta, knowing that he was probably too far away to be reached and much too far away to be of any help. Instead, she sent her thoughts out at random, hoping somebody, anybody, would hear her silent callings and come to her aid.

She had also tried to probe the mind of the guard who brought food, but was unsuccessful. The most she got for her efforts was a slight headache and a feeling of boredom, which could have come from the guard or been merely a reflection of her own state of mind. Still, she was determined to keep trying. After all, there wasn't much else to do.

Danger.

Rene opened her eyes and sat up straight. She had been leaning against the wall, attempting once again to mentally call for help. The warning had stopped her transmission as effectively as hanging up a telephone.

She looked around the room. Nothing had changed; the danger had not yet arrived. Almost on cue, she heard a lock click and the door to her cell swung open. Instead of the familiar guard with a tray of food, two armed men stood just beyond the threshold. "Come with us," one of them ordered.

Rene's heart began to beat wildly. She tried to calm herself, but could not stop her hands from trembling. She slowly got to her feet; her legs feeling like lead as she crossed the room. She dreaded what was about to happen, expecting the absolute worst.

The men positioned themselves on each side of her as she stepped into the hallway, preventing any chance of escape. Escape? What a joke. She was so scared she could barely walk, let alone run. Escape was out of the question. All she could do was cooperate and hope for the best.

Rene was led to the end of the corridor and down another hallway. At the end of the second hallway they stopped before an elevator, waiting while a car was summoned. They rode the elevator down to the third floor. Stepping from the elevator, she was taken down yet another corridor.

She was surprised at the cleanliness of the third floor compared to the level above it. While the carpeting may not have been new, it looked like it had at least been vacuumed once in a while. The walls were also clean, as was the ceiling, and the lights burned a bright white instead of a diseased yellow. Obviously, the third floor was used for something other than keeping prisoners.

Halfway down the hallway, they stopped before a door of polished oak. Her escorts didn't knock as they opened the door and ushered her inside, closing the door behind her. Rene heard a click and knew she was locked in.

The office she found herself in was spacious and plush, the office of a company president or CEO. Padded leather chairs and bookshelves filled one end of the room. At the opposite end sat a massive wooden desk, a water cooler and several straight-back chairs. Rene took all this in in a glance, focusing her attention on the man who sat behind the desk.

He was a large man, muscular, the type who might have once played professional football. He wore a short-sleeve white shirt, his arms and face a patchwork of skin grafts. He studied Rene as she entered the room, sizing her up with the eyes of a predator. But it was the wave of black hatred pouring off him that caused her to break out in a cold sweat.

She recognized the man behind the desk as Dr. Randall Sinclair, the same Dr. Sinclair who had been in the audience when she demonstrated the Neuro-Enhancer. He stared at her for a moment longer, and then smiled. The smile was false, a mask to hide behind. She could still feel his loathing for her.

"Good evening, Dr. Reynolds. I hope your being brought here wasn't too much of an inconvenience." His voice was sweet, patronizing.

"No. Not at all." She forced a smile. "I enjoy being physically abducted and held a prisoner against my will."

His smile faded. "Most unfortunate. I do apologize. But I'm afraid it was all very necessary. We saw no other way to get you here."

"Wherever here is." She crossed the room and looked out the windows. Across the street, several high-rise buildings and what looked like a warehouse sat in darkness, offering absolutely no clue as to her whereabouts. She turned back to look at Dr. Sinclair. "What is this place?"

"It used to be a home for the mentally disturbed, but that was many years ago. Now it is a medical research facility. Nothing more. You might find our labs a little bigger, our staff a little larger, but other than that it is very similar to where you work."

"We don't have armed guards and jail cells where I work," she countered.

"No need to be bitter, Dr. Reynolds. You're a scientist; you know the need for security. It would not do for some of our projects to fall into the wrong hands or become public knowledge before they were ready."

"Why have I been brought here?"

He ignored the question. Reaching into his desk drawer, he produced a small notebook and a stack of paperwork. Rene recognized the notebook as being hers, probably taken from her office by the same men who abducted her. A flush of anger warmed her face, but she held her tongue and didn't say anything. If Dr. Sinclair had her notebook, then he might also have the Neuro-Enhancer.

"I've been going through your reports about the Neuro-Enhancer," he said, setting the notebook and paperwork on the desk in front of him. "Fascinating reading. Between the reports and that little demonstration you gave, I'd almost believe it to be true."

"It is true!" she blurted before she could stop herself.

He raised his eyebrows. "Come now, I'm not a stupid man. Do you really expect me to believe that you have invented a device that can cure the body of so many ailments?"

He was goading her, trying to get her to blurt out something else. She remained silent.

Randall Sinclair stared at her a minute, then flipped through the stack of paperwork. "It's all so interesting. What a shame your device has to be destroyed."

She was horrified. "Destroyed! Why?"

"You're a research scientist, Dr. Reynolds. You get paid to search for the cures to human misery."

"I've found the cure!" she yelled, her emotions overcoming her.

Randall Sinclair slammed the top of his desk with one huge fist. "What you've found is the fucking unemployment line. The end of everything. Think, woman. Think. We are paid to look for cures; we are not paid to find them. That little device of yours, if it works as well as you and your patients claim, will mean the end of medical science as we know it. There will be no need for scientists and doctors if the human body is able to cure itself—no need for us. All funding will be cut off, without so much as a 'thank you' or a pat on the back. You will have saved mankind, but in doing so you will have cost us our jobs, our livelihoods and virtually destroy medical science."

"You're forgetting one thing," she said, finding her voice.

"What's that?"

"Too many people already know about the Neuro-Enhancer. You can't keep it a secret."

Dr. Sinclair smiled. "Only a handful of scientists and a dozen or so patients know about the device. With the disappearance of the Neuro-Enhancer, those scientists will be convinced that your little show was nothing more than an elaborate hoax—an attempt by the Hawkins Neural Institute to obtain money illegally. I imagine such a thing can be very damaging professionally.

"As for your patients: they will continue to praise your miracle machine, but few will listen. They will become like the lunatics who run around claiming to see UFOS or the image of Elvis in a bowl of corn flakes. To those that do listen, the Neuro-Enhancer will become the next Holy Grail—a thing of dreams and nothing more."

Convinced that Dr. Sinclair did in fact have the Neuro-Enhancer, and fearful of his intentions for it, Rene tried a new strategy. "But there's more than one Enhancer."

He shook his head. "Nice try. In your situation, I probably would have claimed the same thing. But no, there is only one Enhancer. You said so yourself at the presentation."

"I lied to create a bidding war and up the sale cost," Rene said. "We've got several Enhancers ready for market."

"Dr. Reynolds, that's not true. We've gone through your personal records and that of your company. There is only one Neuro-Enhancer and I have it."

He stood up and came around from behind his desk. "No. The Neuro-Enhancer can never be mass-produced, that would be much too dangerous. We would become expendable, tossed out on the streets to starve with the masses. I don't like starving, Miss Reynolds. Do you?"

Rene stood rigid as he stepped behind her, laying his massive hands upon her shoulders. "If the Neuro-Enhancer was kept a secret, used only by certain individuals for their own personal needs, I might be willing to go along with the project. In fact, I might be very willing." He slid his hands beneath her hair and slowly upward, caressing her neck and the base of her jaw. She shuddered at his touch.

"There are certain men in this country, very powerful, very rich, who would be willing to pay a lot of money to cure what ails them. You could become a very wealthy woman. Very wealthy indeed. Where are the codes, Dr. Reynolds?"

"Someplace where you'll never find them," Rene answered.

The hands that caressed her neck tightened like a vise. Dr. Sinclair grabbed her by the throat and bent her backward, stretching her spine dangerously close to snapping. She tried to scream, but he clamped his hand over her jaw.

"Who was the man in the alley, Dr. Reynolds?" He whispered, his face only inches from her ear. His hot breath was sour. "Who did you give the computer codes to?"

She tried to talk, but he held her jaw too tight. She could barely shake her head.

Randall released her jaw and stroked her face with the back of his hand, running his fingertips over her lips in an obscene manner. Rene thought about biting him, but he still held her by the back of her neck. With his strength, it would take only a small squeeze to pinch a nerve or sever her spine, paralyzing her. "Who?" he again asked.

"I don't know," she answered.

"You're lying."

Her eyes watered, tears of pain rolling down her cheeks. "It's the truth, I swear it. I gave the disks to a homeless man. I'd never seen him before."

He caught one of the tears on the tip of his index finger and rubbed it with his thumb. "Why would you give the codes to a complete stranger?"

"I was scared," Rene whispered.

Dr. Sinclair wiped the tear off on her shirt, then slowly ran his fingers across her breast and down her stomach. Slipping his hand beneath her shirt, he traced around her navel and along the belt line of her pants. Rene shuddered with revulsion at his touch, feeling violated, like she had just been raped. She felt bile burning its way up her throat and swallowed to keep from gagging.

"Scared enough to give away your life's work?" he asked.

She tried to nod, but couldn't. "Yes, rather than have it stolen."

His grip suddenly tightened. "I don't believe you. There must be a set of backup disks somewhere . . . your home, perhaps?"

"The backup was with the original," Rene cried, pain exploding down her back and through her legs. "I don't have any other copies."

"Liar!"

"It's the truth. The disks were kept in a safe; they never left the building. I hadn't made any duplicates yet."

Dr. Sinclair's grip loosened. "What about re-creating the disks?"

Rene coughed. "Even with all my notes it would take months. Maybe years."

Dr. Sinclair held her for a moment longer in that back-breaking position and then straightened her up. He let go of her and walked back behind his desk. "In that case, Dr. Reynolds, you'd better pray that we find the man you gave those disks to." He pressed a button on his desk. A few seconds later the door opened and the guards stepped in.

"Take Dr. Reynolds back to her room," he instructed them. "And make sure she gets a fresh change of clothes. She seems to have had an accident."

Rene looked down and saw the stain in her white pants, feeling the warm wetness for the first time. She had been so scared, in so much pain, that she had wet herself. A flush of embarrassment passed through her, replaced by white-hot anger. She glared at Dr. Randall Sinclair, swearing to herself, swearing to God, that she would one day remove the smug smile from his face—even if she had to rip it off.

15

A golden eagle circled high in the cloudless South Dakota sky. Wings outstretched like feathery brown sails, the eagle soared over rolling hills, stands of pine forests and a deserted blacktop highway. Well, almost deserted. Jacob Fire Cloud slowly pedaled down the center of the empty road, his rusty old bicycle creaking loudly and threatening to fall apart at any moment.

His back wet with sweat, the muscles in his legs knotted and cramping, he plodded on, one painful pedal push after another. Oblivious to his surroundings, he set his gaze on the shimmering eastern horizon, answering the summons of a voice only he could hear. But with each passing mile his determination began to wane a little and Jacob knew that his mission was doomed to fail. He was not a young man anymore. Even if he was, it would be foolish to try to ride a bicycle all the way to Chicago. The distance was just too far. His son, Michael, was right. He should have stayed home.

Jacob took a deep breath, coughed and shook his head to clear the doubt from his mind. The voice was there, strong as ever, the voice of the White Buffalo Woman, calling him, giving him strength to continue. He would not give up. No matter what, he would not quit. He whispered a silent prayer, asking the Great Spirit to aid him in his mission. Grandfather would provide; He always did. Somehow, He would help Jacob get to Chicago.

As if in answer to his prayer, Jacob heard the piercing cry of an eagle from high above. He looked up, his heart filling with happiness at the sight of a golden eagle gliding overhead.

"Aho, little brother. I see you."

Few eagles still existed in America. Most had been killed off during the Native American craze, which swept the country in the 1990s. With the release of movies such as *Dances with Wolves* and *Thunderheart*, it became popular among the white society to either claim to be Native American or to collect Indian artifacts. Eagles had been slaughtered by the hundreds, their feathers and claws sold to rich collectors and Indian wanna-bes. The birds had been almost completely wiped out before the fad finally faded. To see an eagle in the wild now was rare, so Jacob knew that this particular bird had been sent to him as a messenger from the Great Spirit. His prayer had been heard.

Unfortunately, the old medicine man's happiness was short-lived. Instead of watching the eagle, he should have been paying attention to where he was going. But Jacob wasn't watching the road, so it came as a complete surprise when the front wheel of his bicycle struck a large pothole. He wasn't going fast, but he hit the hole with enough force to be thrown over the handlebars. He landed on the side of the road and tumbled head over heels, ending up on his back at the bottom of the ditch.

Stunned, the breath knocked from him, he lay there looking up at the sky, wondering if he had broken any bones and where the eagle had gone. A few minutes passed. Jacob wiggled his toes and slowly straightened his legs. A flash of pain shot up his right side, but quickly faded. Nothing seemed to be broken. Except for a few new bruises and a scrape or two, he appeared to be none the worse for wear. He had gotten off lucky and he knew it.

"Stupid old fool." He slowly sat up and brushed himself off. "You could have broken your neck. Then where would you be?"

Jacob started to climb out of the ditch, but stopped when he heard the sound of voices. The voices were deep, masculine; the voices of men. They approached from the direction of the road, stopping where his bicycle probably now lay. He counted three voices, three men, but there might have been more.

Slowly, cautiously, staying low to keep from being seen, Jacob Fire Cloud crawled on his belly up the ditch until he could just see the road beyond. Three men stood around his bicycle: two Hispanics and a white man. All three were young, probably in their early to mid-twenties, with the rugged, hard-edged look that comes from life on the road. Each of them wore a collection of crude, bluish green tattoos adorning their arms and the back of their hands. Prison tattoos.

The men were probably convicted criminals: thieves, maybe even murderers. Because of the economic collapse of the country, many state and federal prisons had been forced to close. The prisoners they once housed had been turned loose to fend for themselves. With jobs unavailable, most had gone back to their former occupation of preying on the innocent as a means of survival.

The three men Jacob now watched had probably come out of the stand of pine trees bordering the opposite side of the road. Maybe they had a camp there. Since none of them appeared to be aware of his presence they had probably not witnessed his fall, coming upon the bicycle after he was already in the ditch.

Even so, he knew it would be only a matter of time before they started looking for the bicycle's owner. Few people would go off and leave a perfectly good bike, especially one with a backpack tied to the handlebars. They would find him, rob him, maybe even beat him and leave him for dead. Not knowing what else to do, and wanting to buy as much time as possible to think of a plan, Jacob decided to do the unexpected. He decided to be charming.

"Greetings, my brothers. You are just in time for lunch." Jacob smiled his friendliest smile as he climbed out of the ditch. His sudden appearance startled the three men. Two of them reached behind their backs to pull weapons, but hesitated when they saw it was just an old man. To keep from getting shot, Jacob kept his hands in front of him and made no sudden movements. "Please, join me. My food is in the orange backpack."

Suspicious, the men stared at him for a moment and then turned their attention to the backpack. They seemed to relax a little, obviously feeling he posed no threat. The two men who had reached behind their backs let their empty hands fall back to their sides. Jacob breathed a sigh of relief.

One of the Hispanic men opened the backpack and removed Jacob's supply of dried venison and his thermos of black coffee. They divided up the meat and began eating, pausing only to pass the thermos around. None of them offered Jacob any food, but he didn't mind. He was so nervous he could barely swallow spit, let alone meat.

Jacob studied the three men as they ate, trying to decide on a course of action. The two Hispanics looked like they might be brothers. Both were thin and muscular, with short curly brown hair and mustaches. They were dressed alike, wearing dirty blue jeans, collared shirts and white tennis shoes. Their companion, the white man, was a foot taller, with greasy blond hair and a scraggly beard. His face was a collection of pockmarks and broken veins, and when he opened his mouth to take a bite of venison Jacob could see that his front teeth were missing.

Halfway through his meal, the white man noticed Jacob watching him. His eyes narrowed. "What are you staring at, old man?"

Jacob felt his chest tighten. The young man was like a rattlesnake ready to strike. "Nothing," he answered.

The young man nodded. "That's what I thought." He ate the last of his meat, washing it down with some of the coffee. When he finished, he turned his attention back to Jacob. "Gee, where are our manners? We forgot to share. That's terribly rude of us, especially since it was your food." The others laughed, sharing the joke.

"What else have you got, old man?" he asked, the warmth gone from his voice.

"Nothing you would want," Jacob replied.

"Oh?" He nodded toward the leather medicine bundle tied to the handlebars of the bicycle. "What's in there? Money? Drugs?" He stepped toward the bike and squatted down to untie the bundle.

Anger surged through Jacob Fire Cloud. Outrage. The items in his medicine bundle were sacred, not to seen or touched by anyone but him. He could not stand by and allow the thieves to steal or damage his most precious possessions. If that happened, then his mission to help the White Buffalo Woman would certainly fail. All would be lost. He had to do something to stop them, had to do it now.

"Wait," Jacob said. "I do have this. Maybe you can sell it."

The young man stopped and looked at him. Jacob tried to keep his voice steady, not wanting to show how scared he really was.

"It's not worth much, I know," he said, continuing the dialogue. "Maybe only a couple of dollars. What do you think?"

Slipping his right hand beneath his shirt, Jacob drew and cocked his revolver. The young man's eyes went wide. He reached behind his back to draw his own gun, but he never got the chance.

The antique Magnum sounded like a cannon going off. Jacob fired twice. The bullets slammed into the young man's chest like a giant fist, knocking him straight back through the air.

The old medicine man turned and saw the other two men also drawing guns. He fired twice more. The first bullet hit the closer of the two Hispanic men in the shoulder and spun him like a top. The second round punched a hole in the back of his head, killing him instantly.

Jacob heard a sound like an angry bee and knew that a bullet had just missed his head. He pivoted and fired his revolver, emptying it. The bullets struck the last of the three men in the stomach. The impact of the slugs doubled the man over, knocking him to his knees. He tried to stand back up, tried to raise his gun to fire, but he toppled over on his side instead. A few seconds later, he breathed a heavy sigh and died.

The old medicine man stood in the center of the road, arms outstretched before him, the revolver gripped tightly in both hands. He aimed the pistol's smoking barrel from one young man to the next. No one moved. All three men were dead.

Jacob Fire Cloud slowly lowered the gun. He felt the blood pounding in his temples, felt the bile rising in his throat. He had never killed anyone before. He was a man of medicine, a man of peace; to kill a person went against everything he believed in. But he had had no choice. The thieves had already taken his food and would probably steal his medicine bundle and bicycle as well. He could not allow that. The voice of the White Buffalo Woman called for his help. He would not fail her.

If anything, Jacob could take comfort in the fact that he had acted the way a warrior should act. He had stood up to danger. He had not run. His ancestors would be proud.

He was so shaken over what had happened, so transfixed by the sight of the blood puddled around the bodies, bright red in the afternoon sunlight, that he didn't hear the approaching truck, never knew it was there until the blast of a horn caused him to jump.

Jacob turned quickly, bringing the empty revolver back into firing position. It was a black pickup, dusty from untold miles on the open road. The driver, a young Asian man, sat behind the wheel, staring in wide-eyed horror at the bodies lying in the road and the pistol in Jacob's hand. Before Jacob could even think to lower the gun, the driver jumped out of the truck.

"Don't shoot." He raised his hands in the air. "The truck's yours. Take it. Just don't shoot."

Somewhat embarrassed, Jacob lowered the gun. "I don't want your truck."

"I don't have any money," the man said, his hands still high in the air.

"I'm not a thief," Jacob said. He pointed at the three bodies. "They are. They tried to rob me."

He quickly explained what had happened, leaving out the part about his search for the White Buffalo Woman. The young man, who said his name was Danny Santos—a Filipino-American from Billings, Montana—listened in awe.

"Jesus, three against one. You're either one hell of a shot or a lucky son of a bitch."

Jacob smiled. "I think maybe a little of both."

Danny pointed at Jacob's bicycle. "You're not riding that thing, are you? In this heat?"

"It beats walking," Jacob replied.

"That depends on how far you're going."

"Chicago."

Danny looked at him, stunned. "What are you, nuts? Do you have any idea how far away Chicago is? It would take you a year to get there on that thing, provided you didn't get killed along the way."

"I don't own a car," Jacob said simply.

Danny looked at the bike for a minute, then turned back to Jacob. "I'm probably crazy for even thinking this, but you don't look like the criminal type. I'm going to Omaha. You can ride with me if you want. After that you're on your own. But I must warn you, I'm a talker. You've got to stay awake, laugh at my jokes, and give an occasional grunt to let me know you're still listening. You've also got to shoot anybody who tries to rob us along the way. Deal?"

"Deal." Jacob nodded.

Danny smiled. "Good. Now let's get your bike loaded and be on our way."

"What about them?" Jacob pointed at the bodies.

Danny shrugged. "I don't have a shovel, so we can't bury them. If you want, we can drag them down into the ditch."

They grabbed the three men by the legs and dragged them off the road. They also took the dead men's pistols—two revolvers and a .45 automatic—rather than just leave them lying around.

Then Danny helped Jacob load his bicycle into the back of the pickup, squeezing it among the boxes and wooden crates he was hauling. Climbing into the pickup's cab, Jacob was surprised to see an assault rifle lying on the floorboard. "You need my protection when you have that?"

Danny grinned. "It came with the job; this is my first run. I haven't even fired it, and probably couldn't hit anything if I did." He started the truck and shifted into gear.

As they headed down the road, Jacob happened to glance out the window and saw the golden eagle again fly overhead. He had completely forgotten about seeing the bird earlier. He smiled. The eagle was indeed a messenger. The Great Spirit had sent him a ride.

CHAPTER
16

Leon stared out the open doorway of the boxcar, watching the countryside slowly slip by. He was lulled to tranquillity by both the motion of the train and the beauty that he saw. Sometime during the night, while he slept curled against the wall, someone—some powerful unknown deity—had come along and stolen away the concrete sprawl of the city, replacing it with picturesque valleys of emerald green and misty rolling mountains. And even though it was already approaching midday, the air was still cool and crisp, scented with the fragrance of pine forests and wild flowers—a pleasant change from the stench of the city.

He wasn't sure where he was. He could only guess. Tennessee. Kentucky maybe. The northern part of Georgia also had mountains, but they had probably passed through those sometime during the night. Wherever they were, he was grateful that at least one part of the country remained apparently unscathed by the war. He was almost tempted to jump off the next time the train slowed, to lose himself in the quiet green of the forests. He could be happy here, he knew, seeking solitude away from the cities and the rest of humanity.

But how long could he be at peace before the guilt returned to him, bringing with it the same old nightmares? And what of the voice that now called him, a new torment, urging him to seek its source? Could he ignore such a summons? He doubted it. The voice would seek him out. Even deep in the forest it would find him, call to him. He would be powerless to resist that call, even if he wanted to.

No. The beauty outside the boxcar was not for him, not yet anyway. He had to at least try to locate the woman whose voice he now heard. His destiny lay not in quiet meadows and shadowy forests, but in the concrete corridors of a city much like the one he had just left. Somewhere in Chicago was the woman whose pleas for help now filled his mind. There awaited his future.

With a sigh, Leon tore his attention away from the scenic countryside. The boxcar he traveled in was less crowded than when he first boarded it the previous evening. Several times during the night the train had slowed to climb a mountain or round a curve. When it did a few more people had climbed on board, but twice as many had gotten off. There was room enough now to sit comfortably or move about.

At the front of the car, Leon spotted the little boy he had tried to save the night before. The boy sat with his mother, sharing a simple meal of bread and oranges. He watched as the woman handed her son an orange and pointed to a middle-aged man sitting by himself opposite the open doorway. Following his mother's instructions, the child walked over to the man and handed him the orange. He then returned to sit by her side.

Leon turned his attention from the boy to the man sitting by the doorway. He was Caucasian, probably in his late thirties, tall and thin, with shoulder-length red hair tied back in a ponytail. An equally red beard covered his face. The man wore an old purple T-shirt, blue jeans and a pair of open-toed sandals. A faded tattoo of the planet earth adorned his right forearm, the image blurred and misshapen from a patchwork of skin cancer scars.

The tattoo meant that the man was an Earthie, a member of the "screw the establishment, let's grow our hair long and live with Mother Nature" group that popped up shortly after the beginning of the new millennium. Earthies were a blending of the hippie movement of the 1960s and the New Age movement of the 1990s. Extreme pacifists, they lived on communal farms, growing their own vegetables—and in some cases their own marijuana—turning their back on government, world problems and society in general. They held no jobs, but existed entirely off the land and what money they could make selling fruits and vegetables. Needless to say, those who lived in states with moderate temperatures and longer growing seasons fared much better than their brothers and sisters in colder climates.

Unlike hippies, Earthies did not take to the streets to protest the war. They didn't burn flags, hold rallies or march on Washington. Instead they retreated deeper into the countryside, becoming an almost invisible element of society, tuning in on the harmonic energies of the solar system through yoga, meditation, Celtic ceremonies and a host of other spiritual nonsense. Only after the fighting stopped did members of their society start to reappear in public.

A thought crossed Leon's mind when he saw the little boy hand the man an orange. He grabbed his knapsack and slowly made his way over to where the Earthie sat. Sitting down next to him, Leon opened his knapsack and took out the orange the little boy had given him the night before.

"You deserve this more than I do," Leon said, holding out the orange.

The man turned and looked at Leon, then looked at the orange being offered. An amused expression crossed his face. "What for?"

"Wasn't it you that kept me from falling out of the boxcar last night?"

The man gave an indifferent shrug. "Someone had to do it, brother."

Leon cringed at being called brother. Whenever he heard the term, it was usually followed by a sermon of some kind. He forced a smile. "I didn't see too many volunteers offering to help."

The man smiled back. "Me neither. But keep the orange. I've already got one. Besides, it was a gift. You wouldn't want to hurt Edrick's feelings. Would you?"

"Who?"

"That's the boy's name."

"Oh." Leon looked past the man and noticed Edrick's mother watching him. Feeling like he had been caught doing something he wasn't supposed to do, he put the orange back in his knapsack.

The man's bearded face spread wide in a toothy grin. "You mean you saved somebody's life and you didn't even find out what his name was?"

Leon shook his head. "I didn't exactly save his life, I only tried. You saved his life. And no, I never asked his name. Didn't think it was important."

The grin faded. "Names are always important, especially nowadays. For some of us it's the only thing we've got left. Take away a person's name and they've got no reason for being." He stuck out his hand. "My name's Cinnamon Baker."

Leon almost burst out laughing. "Cinnamon?"

The grin returned. "What can I say? My old man had a warped sense of humor."

"Leon Cane," he said, shaking the man's hand. "With a name like Cinnamon, you must have caught hell growing up."

"Not really. I never told anyone what my real name was. Everyone just called me Red."

"Which do you prefer now?"

He shrugged. "I'm not picky."

"Less chance of me laughing if I call you Red." Leon smiled.

"Then Red it is.

"There, that takes care of the introductions. So tell me, Leon. What brings you on this trip? Are you a vagabond of the open road, like myself, seeking fame and fortune on the back roads of America? Or is it just the scenery that lures you from your home?" Red held up his hand. "Wait. Wait. Don't tell me. Let me guess."

He turned and scrutinized Leon closely. "Judging by your clothes, I'd say you are a man of the streets, but you are not a transient. I've met many a transient in my time and you, sir, are not one. You walk like a man who is painfully aware of his feet, which means that the shoes you are wearing are new—at least they're new to you. A seasoned veteran of the rail would never try to chase a train in new shoes. He'd break them in first."

Leon hadn't really thought about it, but the shoes Shaky had given him were rubbing his feet a little. He probably walked with a slight limp and didn't even know it.

"So I guess you are a man with a purpose," Red continued. "You are going to a specific place and not just traveling about. Am I right?"

Leon had to admit that he was, though he didn't elaborate on the reason for his trip. Instead, he took the offensive. "So what about you? What's your story?"

Red shook his head. "Sorry, but that's not the way the game is played. You have to guess first."

It was Leon's turn to do the scrutinizing. He looked Red up and down, cocking an eye for comical emphasis. "When you called me 'brother,' I thought you might be a Bible thumper. But we've been talking for few minutes and you haven't tried to save my soul, baptize me or get me to repent, so I'm not so sure now."

Red roared with laughter.

"Judging by that tattoo on your right forearm, I'd say you were an Earthie. But I'm not so sure about that either. Earthies are supposed to be farmers, toiling in the hot sun all day, but you're too fair-skinned. Then again, maybe you've been wearing long-sleeve shirts."

Red made a gesture of tipping an invisible hat to Leon. "Bravo, my friend. I'm obviously not dealing with your typical person. You have a sharp mind and a keen eye to go with it. Yes. Yes. You hit the nail right on the head. I was an Earthie for almost three years, still am in a way. I just don't live on a farm anymore. Blame it on the curse of the redheads; fair skin and sunshine don't mix. I spent all my time blistering and peeling. Either I had to give up the farm life, or die from skin cancer. I chose to give up the farm."

Leon noticed a small cross tattooed on the back of Red's left hand. "What does the cross stand for?"

A shadow crossed his face. "Ah yes, the cross. It was something I had done when I was a soldier, my own personal form of protest."

"You were a soldier?"

He cocked an eyebrow. "Does that surprise you?"

Leon admitted it did. "And now?"

"Now I travel the country, king of the rails, teaching people how to live in harmony with nature, how to stay in balance—that sort of thing."

"I see," Leon said, though he didn't really see at all.

"Do you?" Red smiled. "I think maybe you are just humoring me . . ."

Leon braced himself for a lecture on the joys of being an Earthie—at one with nature, Mother Earth, the great goddess what's-her-name, and a lot of other garbage, but Red was interrupted by sudden blasts of the train's whistle. Three shorts and two longs.

Red jumped up, a surprised look on his face.

"What is it?" Leon asked, concerned. "What's wrong?"

The Earthie frantically dug into his jeans pockets, pulling out a handful of change—pennies and dimes mostly. He turned to Leon. "Do you have any money?"

Leon hesitated. "A little, but—"

"A little's all we need. Fifty cents . . . a dollar if you've got it."

Leon stood up and reached into his pants pocket, pulling out one of the crumpled dollars Shaky had given him. He hated to part with the money, but Red had saved his life. He felt that he owed him something.

He handed over the crumpled bill. "At least tell me what you need it for?"

"Whistle-stop," Red replied, adding the dollar to his handful of change.

"Whistle-stop? What's that?"

"Watch and learn, my friend. Watch and learn." Red moved to the left of the open doorway and stepped closer to the edge. He grabbed hold of the side of the boxcar, so he wouldn't fall out, and leaned his head out. He looked toward the front of the train, the wind ruffling his beard and blowing his hair straight back. Pulling his head back inside, he turned to Leon.

"Get on the other side of the doorway and do what I do, but make sure you hold on or you'll fall out."

Still not knowing what was going on, Leon stationed himself on the opposite side of the doorway. Leaning out, he saw that the train was approaching a bend. Just before the curve, a small crowd of people were standing next to the tracks. Several of them held long, hooked wooden poles. Hanging from the hooks were small cloth sacks, bulging with some unknown contents.

"Get ready!" Red shouted.

"What'll I do?"

The Earthie grinned. "Lean out and grab one of the sacks."

The train's whistle sounded again as the engine reached the bend. Three shorts and two longs. The people standing along the tracks raised their poles and held them toward the passing train. Leon spotted other men hanging out of the open doorways of boxcars. As those men passed the people with the poles, they reached out and grabbed some of the cloth sacks.

In exchange for the sacks, they tossed coins and dollars from the train.

"Grab one!" Red yelled. Leon didn't need to be told. He was already leaning out of the boxcar, reaching out for one of the cloth sacks. He missed the first one he snatched for, but grabbed hold of the second one. He almost dropped it as it slid off the pole, but somehow managed to hang on to it, pulling it tight against his chest. Red also grabbed one of the sacks and then tossed his handful of money into the crowd.

Looking back down the tracks, Leon saw children scrambling between the adults to gather up the fallen currency. And then they were gone from sight, disappearing as the train rounded the curve.

Leon stepped away from the doorway and opened the cloth sack. Inside were a dozen or so deep-fried doughnuts, still warm from the oil. He inhaled deeply, savoring the aroma. He was still sniffing when Red joined him.

"A lot of people depend on the trains nowadays, and not just for getting places. For some it's their only chance to make any money." Red nodded toward the sack Leon held. "Those are for us. This sackful is for everybody else. You always buy two bags, that's the rule: one for yourself and one for those who don't have any money."

"Breakfast, everyone!" Red turned and handed his sack to a young couple standing near him. "Pass these around. See that everyone gets one." The young man and woman smiled, and did as instructed.

"Now, brother Leon, let's see if we can invite ourselves to breakfast." They walked to the other end of the boxcar, where Edrick and his mother were sitting.

"Do you mind if we join you for breakfast?" Red asked, pointing at the sack Leon held. "We have doughnuts."

"Yes, Cinnamon's doughnuts!" Leon added.

Red frowned.

"Sorry, I couldn't resist."

The woman looked at them, perhaps a little suspicious, and then smiled and pointed at the floor as if offering a chair to sit. Red flopped down in front of her. Leon joined him.

"I'm Cinnamon Baker, but please call me Red. This is my traveling partner, Leon Cane." Acting on cue, Leon set the bag of doughnuts in front of the woman. Her son made a grab for the bag, but she slapped the back of his hand.

"I'm María and this is my son, Edrick, who seems to have forgotten his manners."

The boy lowered his eyes sheepishly. "I'm sorry. May I?"

Leon nodded. "Yes, you may."

Edrick smiled and pulled a doughnut out of the bag. María also took a doughnut and offered a slight smile. "It's so hard to teach them manners. Times are difficult."

Leon noticed a slight accent in the woman's speech. She was obviously Hispanic, but he wasn't sure if she was Mexican or Puerto Rican. He wanted to ask her, but knew it would be rude. People were often touchy about their heritage since the war, refusing to offer any more information about themselves than was absolutely necessary.

As it turned out, María proved to be very warm and open and didn't mind at all answering personal questions. She and her son were originally from Puerto Rico, but had left to escape the poverty and escalating violence. Long dependent on American dollars, Puerto Rico's economy had collapsed shortly after that of the United States. There had been riots and widespread looting, with gangs taking over everything. Many people fled the country, only to find things just as difficult in the States.

María had left Puerto Rico five years ago, moving in with relatives in Orlando, Florida. She was now on her way to spend time with a cousin who lived in Indiana.

"You're traveling by yourself?" Leon asked.

"Not by myself," she answered. "Edrick is with me."

"That's not what I meant."

"You mean where is my husband?" she said, getting to the point. "He is dead. So my son and I travel alone."

Red shook his head. "That's not such a good idea. It can be pretty dangerous for a woman by herself."

"I can take care of myself." María smiled. To prove her point, she opened her bag and pulled out a pistol.

"Put that thing away," Red said, looking around nervously. "Don't ever show people what you're carrying. It could get you killed."

María put the pistol back in her bag and helped herself to a second doughnut. Edrick already had three.

"Maybe I can find a job in Indiana," she said hopefully. "My cousin said she would help me look. I'm a good cook, and I can clean too. Maybe I can get a job cleaning people's houses; that's what I did in Orlando."

"Are things bad in Orlando too?" Leon asked. He thought about the home he once had in Cocoa Beach. He had loved to jog along the beach at nighttime, feeling the salt air on his skin. Those had been good times, but they hadn't lasted.

María nodded. "Things are bad everywhere. Orlando too. The tourists don't come anymore, so most of the hotels and restaurants have closed. There isn't any work. No money. And the gangs are very bad, almost as bad as the ones in Puerto Rico. It's no longer safe to go out at night. Many people have died."

"What about Disney World?" Red asked, an expression close to horror on his face. "They haven't closed Disney World. Have they?"

"It is gone too," she replied.

Leon was shocked by the news. Although he was never a big fan of the theme park, finding it overpriced and over-crowded, he and Vanessa had taken their daughter there for her third birthday. They had even posed for a picture with Mickey Mouse. He couldn't imagine Disney World closing. It was an American institution, a symbol of hope and happiness. But maybe hope and happiness were also things of the past.

There was a lull in the conversation. Red turned to Leon. "What about you? What's your story?"

"Who said I had a story?" Leon asked evasively.

"It's written all over your face. And don't hand me any crap about visiting relatives. I want the truth."

He locked eyes with Red. There was something about the openness in the man's face that made Leon want to trust him. More than anything, he wanted to tell someone about what was happening to him, about the voice. Red was a former Earthie, a member of an organization that based their beliefs partly on the occult and mysticism. Maybe he would know what the voice was and could offer advice on what to do about it.

Leon opened his mouth to reply, started to take a chance on trusting a complete stranger, but then the moment passed and he changed his mind. What was haunting him was for him alone to deal with. His problem and no one else's.

"You're wrong," he said, grabbing his knapsack. "I don't have a story."

Leon stood up and turned his back on Red and the others. Making his way to the opposite end of the boxcar, he sat down by himself against the wall. By himself, alone, the way he had been for so many years.

CHAPTER
17

Night had fallen. The wind blowing across the Mississippi River was cold and damp. Amy shivered from the chill and tried to nestle down deeper into the pile of coal, but the little black rocks were hard and poked her in all the wrong places. Sleep was impossible, so she sat and watched the lights from the nameless little towns that drifted past, listening to the sounds of the river slapping against the shore. Some of the lights were street lamps. Others were the soft glows that came from inside homes, filtering through curtains out into the darkness. Pale amber lights that spoke of cozy living rooms where people gathered to talk, and kitchens filled with warm, comforting smells, like apple pie, fresh-baked cookies and pizza.

Amy longed to press her nose against the cool glass windows of the homes she passed, just to see who was on the inside and what they were having for dinner. Maybe the owners would invite her in and give her a cup of warm tea, with lemon, or a bowl of soup. Chicken noodle was her favorite. Her stomach rumbled and she frowned. Best not to think of food when there was nothing to eat except coal. But she couldn't help it; she was hungry and her thoughts kept returning to food.

When the tugboat stopped at Louisiana, Missouri, to unload two barges, Amy decided to jump ship. She was far enough away from St. Louis to feel reasonably safe that the policeman wouldn't get her. No sense in going any farther. One town looked the same as the next; they were all cold and inhospitable to a little girl on her own.

She waited until the tugboat tied up to the docks, then jumped from the lead barge onto the wooden pier. Not wanting to be seen by the tugboat's pilot, or any security guards that might be working the waterfront, she ran along the pier and disappeared into the shadows.

From the docks, she followed a narrow graveled lane leading into town. She expected the town to be a picturesque little village, but Louisiana had also been hit hard by the New Madrid earthquake. Many of the buildings suffered structural damage; some toppled completely. Many more had been destroyed in fires caused by ruptured gas lines. There had been sporadic cleanup efforts, but with little money to go around it would be a long time before all the damage was repaired.

It was quite late when she reached the center of the town's business district. The streets were deserted and ghostly quiet. In St. Louis she would never dream of being on the streets so late at night. It was far too dangerous. She wasn't sure if Louisiana was any safer. At least in St. Louis she knew what areas to avoid and where to find a place to sleep. But here she was in completely alien surroundings.

Although the thought of food was still heavy on her mind, Amy decided it would be too dangerous to try to find a meal this late at night. She had no idea where the restaurants were, or which Dumpsters had the best pickings. She knew from experience that some Dumpsters were considered the personal property of those living closest to them. She had heard tales of people getting killed for rooting through someone else's trash bin. No, it would be far safer to wait until the morning before she searched for food.

Ignoring her rumbling stomach, she began looking for a safe place to sleep. Not an easy job. Some of the buildings that looked deserted, and fairly rat-free, appeared to be in danger of falling down. They had been heavily damaged in the earthquake and one good kick would probably send them tumbling the rest of the way to the ground. The tiny park in the center of town was not a good choice either. There were plenty of trees, but no bushes to crawl beneath for safety. The concrete benches that sat in the open were also out of the question, as was the tiny wooden gazebo.

She was starting to feel a little frustrated when she spotted a small, white-frame church at the end of the street. Unlike the buildings on either side of it, the church appeared to have survived the earthquake with little damage, which was itself a miracle. Even better, the lights were on in the building. Someone was inside.

Amy had never gone in much for religion. It was hard to have faith when you were homeless and on your own. Still, she believed in God and said her prayers every night, even though she knew God was much too busy to bother with the problems of one little girl, especially a girl that didn't always tell the truth and had to steal occasionally in order to buy food. At least she hadn't killed the man who had tried to rape her, so God couldn't be mad at her about that. Or could He?

She hadn't killed the man, but she had tried to kill him, which was just as bad. Maybe God *was* mad at her. If so, then He might not help her find her mother. Amy thought about it for a minute and decided she ought to apologize for what she did, just to be on the safe side.

Crossing the street, she walked up the sidewalk to the front door of the church. She expected the church to be locked, for nobody left their doors unlocked anymore—not even churches—but was surprised when the knob turned easily in her hand.

Amy opened the door and stepped across the threshold, experiencing the same creepy feeling that always came over her when she entered a church. It always felt like someone was watching her, someone who could never be seen. She guessed all churches were like that; it probably had something to do with the way they were built.

The church wasn't very big as churches went, no more than twenty rows of pews on each side of the center aisle. Beyond the pews, weathered sheets of plywood covered windows that might have once held stained glass.

But even though the church was small, it still had the same atmosphere of mystery and calm that the big churches had, and the same smells of polished wood, candles and incense.

She started to ease the door closed, but the wind yanked it out of her hand and it slammed with a bang. The sound echoed like a giant heartbeat through the building, making the silence that followed much more noticeable. Amy held her breath, expecting someone to yell at her for making so much noise, maybe even order her to get out, but no one did. From the looks of things, she was quite alone.

Feeling more and more like a trespasser, she approached the altar to the left of the doorway. Several candles burned in their holders, which meant someone had been in the church recently. Taking a long wooden match from a silver holder, she lit one of the white candles. She was supposed to drop a donation in the tiny wooden box on the side of the altar, but she had no money and hoped no one would notice. Once the candle was lit, she proceeded down the center aisle to the main altar at the front of the church.

Amy knew she should have slid into one of the empty pews to talk with God, but she felt her sins were serious enough to warrant going all the way to the front. She stopped and kneeled at the tiny wooden railing, which served to separate the priest from his congregation. For a moment, she pretended it was a Sunday afternoon and she was about to take Communion. She could almost see the kindly-faced priest, every strand of his white hair perfectly combed, smiling down at her as he placed the thin, tasteless wafer on her tongue. The image didn't last. Amy didn't have any good clothes, so she had never attended a real church service. She knew only what others told her about them. Bowing her head, she prayed.

"Dear God, please help me find my mother. I know she's out there, somewhere. The people at the shelter said she was taken to a hospital after the earthquake, so I know she's still alive. She just has to be alive. Please help me find her so we can be a family again. Please."

Amy took a deep breath and continued. "And please, God, forgive me for what I did to that man in St. Louis. I wasn't try-ing to kill him. Honest. I just wanted him to stop what he was doing to me. I didn't want to die like Sissy Roberts. Please don't be mad at me; I'm truly sorry for what I did. Amen."

A hand touched Amy's shoulder. She jumped. Spinning around, she found a heavyset, gray-haired black woman standing behind her. The lady wore a faded blue dress and an old pair of black shoes, but she didn't look homeless. She just looked poor.

"No need to be sorry, sugar," the lady said, offering Amy a slight smile. "From what I just heard, you didn't do anything wrong."

"But I tried to kill a man," Amy said.

"Big difference between tried and done. Sounds like he had it coming anyway. Imagine a grown man trying to hurt a lit-tle girl." Her smile faded as she studied Amy. "You okay, sweet-heart? You need Sister Rose to take you to a doctor?"

"I'm okay." Amy nodded. "He didn't hurt me."

Sister Rose looked unconvinced. "Well, he must have scared you something bad to be in here this late. Where do you live? I'll take you home."

Amy looked at the floor. "I live in St. Louis, least I used to."

Sister Rose clicked her tongue. "Why, child, St. Louis is a long way from here. You'll just have to come home with me."

Amy raised her head. "But—"

"No buts about it. You're coming home with me. Looks like you could use a good night's sleep, and I won't have it on my conscious to have you go sleeping in the streets. Lord knows, I wouldn't be able to sleep a wink all night worrying about you. While we're at it, I'm gonna put some home cooking in you. You're as skinny as an alley cat." She sniffed and wrinkled her nose. "Smells like you could use some soap and water too. What you been doing, rolling in the mud?"

"It's coal," Amy answered.

Rose smiled. "You got a name, or do I have to make one up for you?"

"My name's Amy Ladue."

"Okay, Amy Ladue. You get your things, 'cause you're coming home with me."

Amy looked around. "I don't have any things."

"Then what are we waiting for? Let's go."

Amy didn't move. "Are you really a sister? Is this your church?"

The old woman laughed. "No, darling. This isn't my church: it belongs to God. Father Carmichael is the priest here, if that's what you mean."

Amy nodded.

"I'm a member of the congregation, been a member for fifty years, that's why everyone calls me Sister Rose. I come in at night to clean and do the little things that need to be done. Even got my own set of keys." She held up a crowded key ring for Amy to see. "Now, are you coming, with me, or do I have to lock you in here for the night?"

Amy couldn't imagine being locked up in a church all night. "I guess I'm coming with you."

"Good." Sister Rose beamed. Amy got up and followed the plump little woman around while she finished locking up the church. She even helped her blow out the candles before they left. Sister Rose said she couldn't leave them burning because they might start a fire. Closing and locking the front door, they walked down the sidewalk and turned left at the street.

Sister Rose lived only about five blocks from the church, in what was probably the poorer section of town. Small clapboard houses lined each side of a narrow cobblestone street. Even in the darkness, Amy could see that the houses were weathered and in need of a fresh coat of paint. But compared to the crumbling buildings she had left behind in St. Louis, the houses looked warm and inviting. Gingerbread houses.

The thought stopped Amy dead in her tracks. What if they really were gingerbread houses and Sister Rose was actually a witch? She had read the story of Hansel and Gretel and knew what witches did to children. She didn't want to be cooked in an oven and eaten. The thought passed as quickly as it came. Sister Rose couldn't be a witch, because she had been in a church. Witches melted when they stepped inside a church. Everyone knew that.

Noticing that Amy had stopped, Sister Rose turned to look at her. "You coming, or are you planning on standing out here in the cold all night?"

Amy smiled, embarrassed over the thoughts she had been thinking. "I'm coming."

Sister Rose's house was the last one at the end of the street. It was a simple wood structure, with a screened porch, surrounded by oak and elm trees. A sidewalk led up to the porch; above the porch door a light burned.

"You have electricity?" Amy asked, surprised.

"Electricity and running water too," Rose answered. She opened the porch door and ushered Amy inside, then unlocked the front door to the house. When she opened the front door something big and brown, and incredibly fast, came running out. The big brown thing barked once and then jumped on Amy, knocking her flat.

"No, Sammy. No!" Sister Rose yelled, trying to get hold of the dog's collar. The dog ducked his owner's attempt to grab him. Circling Amy, he jumped on her and covered her face with sloppy wet kisses. Frightened at first by the sudden attack, Amy quickly realized that the dog was just being overly affectionate. To keep Sammy from jumping on her, she hugged him around the neck.

"I hope he didn't hurt you," Rose said, grabbing the dog's collar. "He just loves children." She pulled Sammy away long enough for Amy to get to her feet.

"You stay down," Rose warned the dog in a harsh tone of voice. Sammy obeyed but was clearly unhappy about the command. He was even less happy when Rose ushered Amy into the house, leaving him alone on the porch.

"I'm sorry, I should have warned you. Sammy doesn't mean any harm; he just likes to love people in his own way." Sister Rose closed and locked the door. They stood in a tiny kitchen: yellow walls with faded white cabinets, a noisy old refrigerator, a small sink and a gas stove. In the center of the room sat an oval table. Amy's eyes were instantly drawn to the table and the loaves of homemade bread sitting on top of it. Fresh homemade bread. The overpowering fragrance filled the kitchen and invaded her nostrils, causing her mouth to water and making her stomach rumble. Sister Rose must have heard the rumbling.

"Land's sake, child. You must be starving. If your eyes got any bigger they'd fall out of your head." She opened one of the cabinets and removed a plate. "Was that your stomach I heard, or did we just have ourselves another earthquake?" She set the plate on the table, took out a knife and cut off several slices from one of the loaves. She removed a jar of homemade jelly from one of the other cabinets, setting it on the table next to the plate. "This oughta set you right."

Amy started for the table, but Rose held up her hand to stop her. "Wait. Manners first. Did you wash your hands?"

She shook her head.

"Bathroom's down the hall on the left. Now scoot."

Amy left the kitchen and followed the hallway, passing the living room and two tiny bedrooms. She found the bathroom, but it took her a minute to figure out how to switch on the light. A single bulb was mounted above the mirrored medicine cabinet and she had to pull a string to turn it on.

As Amy washed her hands, she studied her reflection in the mirror. Her auburn hair was tangled and streaked with coal dust and her face was almost black. Finished with her hands, she decided to wash her arms up to the elbows and get some of the dirt off her face. It was a big job, one that left a dirty ring in the sink. Amy scrubbed the ring the best she could, then dried her face, hands and arms. She turned off the light and went back into the kitchen. Sister Rose seemed genuinely surprised when she saw her.

"My, will you look at that. There is a little girl under all that dirt, and a pretty one too."

Amy smiled and felt a flush of embarrassment warm her face. No one had ever called her pretty before. Her mother probably had, but she didn't remember. Taking a seat at the table, Rose handed her the plate with the slices of bread on it and passed the jelly. She also set a glass of milk in front of her. Real milk, from a cow, not the powdered stuff that came out of a box.

"Are you rich?" Amy asked, amazed to be drinking real milk.

Sister Rose laughed. "Rich? No, child. I'm not rich. In fact, I'm poor. Been poor all my life."

"But how can you live in a house and afford milk?"

"Honey, when you're raised poor you learn to make do with what the good Lord gives you. I don't have a lot of money, but I don't owe anybody either. That's what gets people in trouble: they live beyond their means and pretty soon they owe everybody."

"Is that why there's so many homeless people?" Amy asked.

Rose nodded. "The earthquake and war are also to blame. When those things happened, one after another, the country went belly-up. Broke. Suddenly, everyone was poor. Many of those who still had homes standing didn't know how to act being poor. They didn't know how to save, spent more than they should, and ended up being homeless too. Now the people who were already poor, who never had anything in the first place, why it was just another day to them. Understand, child?"

Amy thought it over for a moment, then nodded. "I guess it's better to be poor than homeless any day." She took a drink of milk and then wiped her mouth with a paper napkin. "But why do the white people and black people hate each other so much?"

Rose cut a slice of bread for herself. "They don't all hate each other. Just some. Been that way ever since I was a little girl. Shoot, it's been that way ever since Jesus was around."

"But why?" Amy wanted to know.

"Child, you sure do ask a lot of questions." Rose smiled. "But that's okay; it means you've got a brain up there in your head. I don't know why whites and blacks don't get along. I think they're afraid of each other because fear is a part of human nature. It's natural for humans to be afraid of what they don't know. The old America was never quite honest with itself in admitting it had created a problem with the races. In the end all that hurt and anger and resentment got to be too much to ignore."

"I think wars are stupid," Amy said, spreading jelly on another slice of bread.

"Amen, child, amen," Rose replied. "Where's your family, precious?"

Amy shook her head. "We lost our home in the earthquake. My father was killed, at least that's what they told me. My mother was taken to a hospital. I don't know where she is, but I'm going to find her. I think she has namnesia and can't remember who she is . . ."

"You mean amnesia," Rose corrected.

"Right. Amnesia. I think she's got that and can't remember anymore. But I'm going to find her one day. She's a pretty lady, and a good cook too. I'm going to find her and then we'll live together again, in a real house. She'll take care of me and I'll take care of her." She stopped and looked to Rose for reassurance. "You believe me, don't you?"

Sister Rose leaned across the table and put her hand on Amy's. "Honey, if your mother is out there, I'm sure the good Lord will help you find her."

Amy seemed satisfied with the answer. "Right. I pray every night and I know that God will help me find my mother. Someday."

Rose leaned back in her chair and studied the little girl. She smiled. "I'm sure He will. But we can't have you finding your mother looking like you just lost a fight with an alley cat. You finish that last slice of bread while I draw you a hot bath. I think I might even have some clothes that will fit you."

Amy smiled a jelly smile as Sister Rose got up from the table and went into the bathroom. A few seconds later, she heard the sound of water running and knew that the bathtub was being filled. She couldn't remember if she had ever had a bath before; all they had were showers at the homeless shelters. She would have to ask her mother when she found her. And she would find her. Someday.

18

Rene Reynolds was not stupid. She knew her life was in danger. Randall Sinclair would not let her live knowing about his plans for the Neuro-Enhancer. The only reason she was not already dead was that he needed her. If the good doctor could not find the homeless man she had given the codes to, he would extract the information out of her. Slowly. Painfully. One numbered sequence at a time. She had no doubts that Dr. Sinclair would resort to torture or any other means to get what he wanted. And if they found the homeless man, they would no longer need her. She would be eliminated. It was as simple as that.

She thought of the man she had given the code disks to, feeling a twinge of guilt for putting his life in jeopardy. Randall Sinclair would not rest until he found him. His men would search the streets and back alleys of Atlanta, threatening, bullying. Sooner or later, the man, and the codes, would be located. Once found, he would be killed. So would she. But maybe death was a better choice than the imprisonment and torture that awaited her if the codes were never found. Then again, she had one other option.

Escape. She had to get away. Rene had to put as much distance between herself and Randall Sinclair as possible. Only then would she be safe. Unfortunately, escape was not an easy task to accomplish for a person locked in a cell and constantly guarded.

But you're not in a cell now.

Rene raised her head and looked around. Humiliated and angered by her confrontation with Dr. Sinclair only moments before, she hadn't been thinking clearly. Nor had she been paying attention to her surroundings. But now, as the same two guards led her back to her cell, she studied her environment, hoping to find a way to escape.

The hallway they traveled was narrow and well lighted, and presented little in the opportunity for freedom, especially since she was flanked by two armed men. At the end of the hallway, however, just beyond the elevators was a row of windows. The windows might offer an avenue to the outside, but she would need a ladder or rope to get to ground level. Unless . . .

Rene had looked out the windows in Sinclair's office. At the time she had been intent on finding out where she was, focusing her attention on the buildings across the street. Even so, she couldn't help but notice the tiny ledge beneath the windows. The ledge might run the entire length of the third floor. She would still need a way to get from the ledge to the ground, but Rene was hoping for a miracle.

They stopped before the elevators and one of the men pushed the button to summon the car. She was so intent on hatching plans for escape, several moments passed before she even noticed the door directly across the hall. And it wasn't until Rene heard the echo of footsteps on concrete that she realized what it was.

A stairwell.

Of course, stairs. She mentally kicked herself for being so stupid. There were always stairs in buildings with elevators, emergency exits in case of fire. The stairs would lead to the ground level, maybe even to a door to the outside. The door to the stairs had no lock; therefore, no key was required to open it.

As Rene studied the door, she felt a slight breeze caress her skin. Her heart fluttered. The breeze came from the direction of the door.

Air. She sniffed. *Fresh air.* Somewhere on ground level a door stood open, a door to the outside. The stairs led to that door, led to freedom.

Rene could barely contain her excitement over the discovery. If she could elude her guards, slip free for only a moment, she could race down the stairs and out the building. She wondered if someone guarded the stairs at ground level. She didn't think so. From what she had seen so far, she was the only prisoner.

Her thoughts of freedom were dashed by the arrival of the elevator. Reluctantly, she allowed herself to be ushered into the car. But as the elevator's doors slid closed, a slight smile touched the corners of her mouth. A thought had crossed her mind, filling her heart with hope once again. Maybe there was a way to escape after all. She had a plan.

Rene didn't protest her inhumane treatment, or try to question the guards, as she was led back down the hallway on the fourth floor. She was actually anxious to return to her cell, anxious to be alone. She was worried that her sudden change in character would arouse suspicion, but the two men who guarded her didn't seem to notice. If anything, they were probably thankful she was quiet for once.

She arrived at her cell, finding it to be exactly as she had left it. The sheets on the bed had not been changed; the room still stank. Obviously the maid's day off. Another tray of food had been brought. As always, the tray held a ham and cheese sandwich, an apple and a carton of warm fruit drink. She ignored the food, too keyed up to eat. It was all she could do to sit on the cot and appear despondent now that hope burned in her heart.

She was still sitting when one of the guards returned with a fresh change of clothes: a pair of denim pants, a matching shirt—navy surplus stuff—and a belt. No underwear. Rene waited a few minutes until she was certain the guard would not reappear, then she tried on her new clothing. The pants were a little too big, as was the shirt, but the belt and a two-inch cuff corrected the problem.

Slipping her shoes back on, she tossed her old clothes in the corner of the room and took a seat on the cot. Leaning back against the wall, she waited. If her plan was to work, then she had to be patient. She had to wait.

Out of fear of ridicule, and because she had witnessed them extremely rarely, Rene had never mentioned the Neuro-Enhancer's curious side effects in any of her reports. If she had, the medical and scientific community would have scoffed at the device, labeling her as a bona fide nut case. Support of the Enhancer would have quickly disappeared, along with any hope of obtaining the funds needed to market it. She had not even written them into her private notes. Therefore, Randall Sinclair had no idea that prolonged use of the Enhancer could develop psychic powers in certain individuals, and she was determined to make sure he never learned.

Rene slowed her breathing and willed her mind to relax, quickly reaching the same heightened state she did when using the Neuro-Enhancer. A tingling flowed down her body as thousands of neural regions in her mind were suddenly activated. When the tingling became almost unbearable, she again projected her thoughts.

This time, however, she did not focus her thoughts on a homeless man thousands of miles away. Nor did she just send them out at random. Instead she concentrated on the guard who brought her meals. Blocking everything else from her thoughts, she formed a picture of his face in her mind. With that image locked securely in place, she projected a command.

Help me.

Time passed. She began to tire from the strain. A headache formed behind her eyes; her mouth turned dry as cotton. Rene thought of the warm fruit drink sitting unopened on the table. Her concentration wavered.

She shook her head, pushing all thoughts of food and

drink from her mind. She had to stay focused. Her freedom depended on it. Her life. What seemed like an eternity slowly crept by. Finally, she was rewarded with the sound of a lock being turned. The draft which followed told her that someone had opened the door.

Rene didn't open her eyes, but she could tell that someone had entered the room and was standing just inside the doorway, watching her. Every nerve in her body could feel that presence. Her muscles tensed with anticipation, but she remained motionless, appearing to be asleep.

Closer. Come closer.

She heard the soft scrape of a shoe sliding across the floor, felt the gentle displacement of air. A pause. Uncertainty. The guard was being drawn to her, but he didn't know why.

Closer . . . closer.

Movement again. A shadow fell upon her.

Closer . . .

The guard leaned closer, perhaps to touch her, or to wake her. He never got the chance. Rene struck like a cobra, kicking him in the face as hard as she could.

The guard slammed back into the porcelain sink, going down hard. Before he could get back up, Rene was on top of him. She struck him in the nose with the heel of her hand, drawing blood, and then grabbed him by the hair. The man struggled and reached up to pull her off him, but Rene pounded his head against the porcelain bowl. Once. Twice. Three times. She didn't stop. Even when his eyes rolled back, she didn't stop banging his head against the sink until she was certain he was unconscious.

Rene released the guard's head, but remained sitting on his chest. Her heart pounded so hard she could barely breathe. She took several deep breaths and then slipped off him. Searching through the guard's pockets, she took his keys, wallet and a pocketknife. She also took the electric stun gun clipped to his belt, wishing it was a real gun instead.

Crossing the room, she pushed open the door and stepped out into the hallway.

CHAPTER
19

loser . . . come closer.

The voice came to him on silent wings, calling him from the darkness. Leon sat near the open doorway of the boxcar, feeling the night air upon his face, listening to the clickety-clack of the train as it made its way through the blackness of the land.

Unlike before, the mysterious voice did not slam into him like a speeding bullet. Instead, it floated to him ever so gently, softly. An angel's kiss. His intuition told him that the voice was not being directed toward him, not this time anyway. He was but an eavesdropper, listening to a mental conversation between the woman and someone else. He waited to see if the voice would be answered, if another person had the ability to project thoughts. Could there be more like her? He listened, but it was only her voice he heard. Hers and hers alone.

Even though she was not directing her thoughts toward him, Leon still heard them. A little fainter maybe, a little weaker, but he heard them all the same. For some strange reason, some peculiar twist of fate, he and the woman were now joined together mentally. He wondered if the connection would grow stronger with the passage of time and prayed that it would not.

The woman's mental calls already invaded his mind and haunted his dreams. If the connection grew stronger, would her feelings soon become his? What of her fears, her dreams and desires? Would her every waking thought infiltrate his mind, taking over, pushing aside the part that was him? If so, then surely madness would follow. That was why he needed to find her. If he didn't, then the voice would continue to haunt him, eventually driving him over the edge.

Closer . . . come closer.

He took the two computer disks out of his shirt pocket and studied them, wondering what vital information they contained. The disks were a clue to the woman whose voice he now heard, but it was a clue he could not unravel—not yet anyway.

Closer . . . come closer.

"I'm coming," he whispered. Slipping the disks back in his pocket, he stared into the darkness of the night. She was out there somewhere.

A sudden hand on his shoulder startled him. Leon jerked and reached for the knife in his knapsack.

"Easy, brother. I didn't mean to spook you." The hand released him and Red sat down beside him.

"You didn't," Leon lied.

"You want to talk about it?"

"There's nothing to talk about."

Red was looking at him, trying to study his face. His eyes shone with the reflection of moonlight. "A man doesn't sit alone and talk to himself unless he's crazy—which you aren't—or something's bothering him."

"I wasn't talking to myself,"

"I'm coming . . . I'm coming," Red said, repeating the words Leon had spoken.

Leon turned on Red, becoming angry. "Look, what I say and do is none of your business. You're not my guardian angel. I didn't ask for your help and I don't need it."

"You needed it the other night when you were hanging by your toes out the boxcar."

"Is that what this is all about? I owe you something?"

"You don't owe me a damn thing," Red said. "I just thought you could use a friend. My mistake." He started to stand up.

Leon reached out and touched his arm. "Wait. Don't go." Red sat back down. He didn't speak, giving Leon a chance to say what was on his mind. A few minutes elapsed before Leon said anything.

"You said you were a soldier?"

"I thought this was about you?"

"Tell me first. Which side?"

"Does it matter?"

"Yes."

Red sighed. "All right then. Yes, I was a soldier. And yes, I was with the pro-government forces. To answer your next question: yes, I fought in the uprising. You happy?"

"Did you kill anyone?"

"Yes."

"Tell me."

Red sighed again. "I was a platoon sergeant in the infantry. A ground-pounder. They sent my unit to Detroit . . . sent us to the biggest damn mess you'd ever want to see. Detroit was a war zone, a living, breathing hell. We took fire from day one, lost a lot of men. Seemed like everyone over the age of ten had a weapon of some kind. The snipers were the worst. You couldn't take two steps out in the open without someone popping a cap into your ass.

"It was bad enough we were getting our butts kicked, but a lot of the minority soldiers in our outfit refused to fight back. They laid their guns down rather than fire on people of their own race. Some of them even joined the other side. Men who were in my unit, men who were my friends, were suddenly the enemy."

He shook his head. "At least that's what our commanding officers called them—the enemy. But that was a lie, just like all the other lies they told us. There was no enemy, not really, no supreme evil about to take over the country. All there was were people, average everyday Americans trying to make their lives a little better. I finally got sick of the lies, sick of the officers telling me that I should shoot my neighbors, shoot my friends, and walked away from the whole bloody mess."

"You deserted?"

Red nodded. "In the middle of a firefight I laid my weapon down, took off my uniform, and walked out of there. I don't know how I made it without getting shot. Lucky, I guess. I kept walking until I was clean out of the state."

"What happened then?" Leon asked.

"I joined up with a religious group in Indiana, stayed with them for almost a year. But it wasn't for me. No matter how hard I prayed, how many times I confessed my sins, I couldn't come clean. Blood just doesn't wash off that easily. So I left them. Traveled around for a while, mostly in the South."

"And ended up becoming an Earthie," Leon added for him.

"You got it. But their teachings were just as flawed as those of the Jesus freaks. All they want to do is sit around and meditate, channeling their energy for the betterment of mankind. What a crock of shit. If they want to help other people, then they should share some of the food they've got stockpiled. You wouldn't believe how much they've got stored away. They're sitting fat while their so-called brothers and sisters starve."

Red stopped talking and turned to Leon. "I've said enough. Your turn."

Leon took a deep breath, thinking over what he would say. He wanted to tell Red about his job at NASA, about the magazine article that caused so much grief, the Senate investigation, everything. He wanted to lay his guilt and anguish at the man's feet, finally confessing to someone how badly he hurt deep inside, telling what it was like to have his heart ripped out every time he saw a cloud, a beautiful woman, or heard the laughter of a child.

Leon wanted to share the shame he felt when he mentally compared every little girl he saw to the memory of his daughter, gauging the differences in their height, their weight, the color of their skin, even how many teeth they had. And with each comparison the old wounds opened up, the pain flowing as thick and as fresh as the day he lost the child he loved so very much.

But he could not bring himself to speak of such things to a complete stranger. Even if he had the courage to talk of what lay heaviest upon his heart, the words would not pass through his constricted throat. Only a hissing of air would tumble past his lips, a hissing that spoke of his love for Vanessa and Anita, and of the sorrow and guilt he felt.

Instead of talking about his heartaches, baring his soul to a man he hardly knew, Leon spoke only about his encounter with the woman in the alley and the voice he now heard.

"And you're certain this voice you hear is the woman from the alley?" Red asked.

Leon nodded. "Sometimes I see her face too."

Red leaned back. "Wow, that's pretty heavy. No wonder you're talking to yourself. I'm surprised you haven't gone loony."

"I just might if I can't find her." Leon stared out into the night for a moment, and then turned to Red. "You used to be an Earthie. Don't they believe in clairvoyance and thought projection?"

"Believe in it? Yes. Can any of them actually do it? No. At least none of the ones I know. It's like the Bible thumpers who believe in God though they've never seen him."

"You're no help," Leon said, sarcastically.

"Hey, at least I gave you an honest answer. Any other Earthie would have talked your ears off about the great harmonic conversion, spirit guides and channeling." He grinned. "Maybe you're hearing a ghost."

"Why would a ghost tell me to go to Chicago?"

Red shrugged. "To tell you the truth, I don't believe in any of this mumbo jumbo, woo woo stuff."

Red might not believe in ghosts or spirits but Leon did, which was why he had been so upset when he first heard the voice. He thought it was Vanessa, calling to him from the great beyond. But he knew now that it wasn't his wife's voice. He was also certain that it wasn't a ghost he heard.

"It's not a ghost," Leon answered. "She's alive."

"Chicago's a big city. If she is alive, how are you going to find her?" questioned Red.

"I don't know. I'll worry about that when I get there." Leon started to ask some more about the Earthies' belief in thought projection, but he was interrupted by the train's whistle suddenly splitting the night. The whistle was immediately followed by the screech of brakes being applied. Looking out the open doorway, he saw that someone had lit a pair of torches and stuck them in the ground next to the tracks. The torches were crossed, forming a flaming X. Red also saw the torches and jumped to his feet.

"What's wrong?" Leon asked, concerned.

"There's a transient camp nearby," Red answered.

"So?"

"The torches are a warning for their brothers of the road. There's bandits up ahead."

"Bandits?" Leon also jumped to his feet.

"Bandits, robbers, thieves . . . call them what you want. They must have blocked the tracks. We've got to get out of here."

Leon looked around at the other passengers. "What about the others? We have to warn them."

"There isn't time. Hurry!" Red ran toward the other side of the boxcar. Leon started to follow, but as he turned away from the open door he spotted three men standing beside the tracks. Barely visible in the moonlight, they were dressed entirely in black, their faces hidden behind masks. The men watched the train as it slowly came to a stop.

Bandits!

Red had already reached the other side of the boxcar and was fumbling to slide the door open. Awakened by the train's whistle, some of the passengers were sitting up. Others were on their feet, alert to the fact that something was amiss. Leon was halfway across the boxcar when he spotted two familiar shapes in the darkness. He paused to grab the woman's arm and pull her to her feet.

"Bandits," he whispered.

María's eyes went wide, and Leon felt a tremor of fear pass through her body. She turned, grabbing her bag with one hand and Edrick's wrist with the other. Sensing something was wrong, the child made no effort to resist his mother's urgings.

Red was still struggling with the door when several bandits swarmed aboard the boxcar. Instantly everything turned into chaos. The bandits, armed with pistols and wooden clubs, fired a couple of shots into the air and yelled for everyone to raise their hands and keep still. But no one did.

Women and children screamed in terror, clinging to one another for protection. The passengers closest to the open doorway tried to run, colliding against and tripping over those behind them. One man lunged at one of the robbers and was shot dead, as was another man who pulled a knife from his belt. A third man jumped up to protect his wife, only to be viciously clubbed until he lay unconscious and bleeding on the floor.

The shootings and beatings sent a wave of panic through the other passengers. They were all on their feet now, pushing, shoving, trying to flee from the bandits in a boxcar grown terribly small. The darkness was choking. The bandits shouted for everyone to sit back down, but their orders were drowned out by the frightened cries of their victims.

"Help me!" Red said, struggling to get the door open. Reluctantly turning his back on the bandits, Leon stepped up to help. Together they forced the heavy metal door along the track, one inch at a time.

They had just gotten the door open enough to squeeze through when another shot rang out, close enough to leave a ringing in Leon's ears. He spun around and found one of the robbers only a few feet away. The man was on his knees, holding his stomach. Blood oozed from between his fingers and ran down his shirt. María stood in front of the thief, a smoking pistol clutched tightly in her hands. Leon watched as she squeezed the trigger again, shooting the man in the face. Satisfied, she turned around, grabbed Edrick's arm and hurried to join them.

They jumped from the opening to the ground. Red went first, followed by María and Edrick. Leon brought up the rear. Outside the night was filled with gunshots and screams as dark-clad bandits scurried over the train like hungry ants.

In front of the train, a barricade of burning logs had been laid across the tracks. In the glow of those logs, Leon could see a small group of bandits guarding the engine. They were armed with rifles, but made no move to either board the engine or rob those who drove the train. It was obvious that it was only the passengers they were interested in.

"This way," Red said, running toward the rear of the train. Leon and the others followed, trying to keep up. They had almost reached the last car when there was a metallic ping as something struck one of the boxcars, just above Leon's head. Turning, he saw several bandits slip from the darkness beneath the train and race toward them. Bright flashes of gunfire lit the night. Another bullet struck the boxcar next to María.

"Move, move, move!" Red yelled, urging them to greater speed. They raced along the tracks, stumbling over loose gravel and railroad ties, trying to outrun the men chasing them. María still clutched her pistol in her right hand, but dared not stop to shoot. She could only run along, dragging Edrick with her.

More bandits suddenly emerged from the darkness at the rear of the train. They were cut off, surrounded.

"The woods!" Leon said, grabbing María's arm and steering her away from the tracks toward the forest. Red grabbed Edrick's other arm. Together they fled for the protection of the trees.

They reached the forest and plunged headfirst into the darkness. Shots rang out behind them as the bandits realized they were getting away and attempted to stop them. The bullets struck all around, snapping branches and knocking bark from trees. Luckily, no one was hit.

"Keep running!" Red warned. "It's not over yet." He took the lead, weaving a path between the trees, forcing his way through a tangle of vines, branches and bushes. Behind them, they could hear the shouts of the bandits and the crashing sounds of pursuit. Those sounds soon faded, however, and eventually stopped. Even then, they continued running for another ten minutes or so before finally halting.

"I think we lost them," Leon said, listening carefully. Except for their heavy breathing, the night had grown strangely silent.

"I think you're right," Red agreed, struggling to catch his breath. "They won't follow us here when there's easy picking back at the train."

"Those poor people," María said as she hugged her son.

"Why didn't you warn them?" Leon asked Red, wondering about the man's lack of caring prior to the bandit attack.

"There wasn't time," he replied. "Besides, they would have panicked and crowded the door. None of us would have gotten out then."

Leon thought about what Red said and nodded. He was probably right. Had they told the others that they were about to be robbed, there would have been a panic. Even more people would have been killed. "Okay, where do we go from here?"

Red looked around. "We've got to head back to the tracks."

"Are you crazy?" Leon asked. "The bandits are still there. They'll kill us for sure."

"He's right," María added.

"But we can't go wandering through these woods at night. We'll end up lost. I need the tracks to steer by."

"Then we don't go walking around," Leon said. "We sit right here until daylight, or until the bandits leave. Whichever comes first."

"Sounds like a plan," Red agreed. He sat down on the ground, his back against a tree. "God, I'm thirsty. I wish we had some water."

María rummaged in her bag and pulled out several oranges. "How about orange juice?" She tossed one of the oranges to Red, another to Leon.

Leon thanked her for the orange. Taking a seat on the ground, he quartered the orange with his butcher knife and then passed the knife to Red. He bit down on an orange section, allowing the juice to run down his throat. As he ate the orange, he listened to the sounds around them. He could still hear an occasional gunshot, but they were too far away to be of any concern. They were safe, but somewhere in the distance people were being terrified, robbed, even killed. The sounds made his skin crawl.

20

The bath was hot and steamy, and scented with lilac bubble bath. Amy stood naked next to the tub, breathing in the flowery fragrance and feeling the steam caress her skin. Holding the tub's side for support, she slowly eased one tiny foot into the water and then the other. She gasped as she sat down, the hot water stinging her butt and turning her skin a rosy pink.

She picked up a bar of white soap from the soap dish and sniffed it. Unlike the bathwater the soap had no smell. Disappointed, she slowly rubbed the bar over her skin, gradually working up a lather. With the aid of a face cloth, Amy scrubbed the dirt from where it had gathered in the folds of her skin. Her elbows and knees were the dirtiest. She giggled when she cleaned the bottom of her feet and between her toes.

Finished with her body, Amy filled her right palm with herbal-scented shampoo and began to wash her hair. She shampooed twice to make sure all the coal dust was removed. She had just rinsed her hair with clean water when Sister Rose appeared.

Amy watched as Sister Rose scooped up the dirty clothes from the bathroom floor and left. She reappeared a few minutes later with an armload of replacement items.

"We're in luck. I had a couple of boxes of church donations in the back room." She placed the pile of clothing on the toilet lid. "Some of these should fit you. If they don't, then I'll just have to wash what you were wearing." She flashed a smile. "But I think the dirt is the only thing holding your clothes together."

Amy eyed the new clothing, but made no move to get out of the tub. She was enjoying her bath and didn't want it to end so soon. Rose shook her head. "Child, if you stay in there any longer you'll get wrinkles on your butt."

"I don't care." Amy laughed. "It feels good."

"Won't feel so good when that water gets cold," Rose replied. "Besides, I've made cocoa."

Cocoa? Real cocoa? Amy sat up straight. She had never had cocoa before. Excited, she pulled the plug and stood up. Rose handed her a towel and then left the room.

Drying quickly, she tried on some of the clothing, selecting a gray T-shirt and a pair of blue jeans that were only a little too big. They were boy's jeans, but she didn't mind. Amy also found socks and panties that were in much better condition than the ones she'd been wearing. Once dressed, she combed the tangles from her hair and ran water in the tub to remove the dirt ring. Hanging her towel over the shower rod, she turned off the light.

Rose waited for her in the living room. Two cups of hot cocoa sat on the small table in front of her. Amy sat on the couch beside Rose and accepted one of the cups. The cocoa was rich and sweet, and warmed her stomach in a delicious sort of way. The beverage hardly had time to cool before Amy finished it. She would have asked for more, but that would have been rude so she didn't. Instead she leaned back on the couch and listened to Rose talk about how things were a long time ago. Amy tried to pay attention to what was being said, but she felt her thoughts drifting and could only nod occasionally. Before she knew it, she was asleep.

* * *

Amy awoke later that night. She was still on the living room couch, but someone had thrown a blanket over her. Probably Sister Rose. The house was dark, quiet except for the occasional creak of the building settling in place and Sister Rose's snoring coming from the back bedroom. Amy lay on the couch, her eyes open, listening to the sounds. From somewhere down the street a dog barked. She thought of Sammy lying on the front porch and wondered if dogs had dreams.

Satisfied that everything was all right, Amy started to drift back to sleep. For a moment she wondered what had awakened her, but only for a moment as slumber raced to overcome her. She was just about to drift off when she remembered what it was. A voice. A woman's voice.

Help me.

She heard it again. Tossing the blanket off her, Amy sat up and looked around. In the darkness the unfamiliar room became scarier than it should have been. Shadowy pieces of furniture took on ominous, threatening shapes. Oversized chairs became toad-like creatures, while lamps reached for her with scarecrow fingers.

Help me!

Amy was too terrified to move. Someone cried out for help, which meant that danger lurked nearby. She started to grab the blanket and cover her head to hide but stopped. What if it was Sister Rose who called for help? How could she ignore the cries of someone who had treated her with such kindness? She couldn't. It wouldn't be right.

Easing off the sofa, she slowly navigated her way through the crowded living room. She banged her shin on an end table and nearly knocked over a lamp before reaching the hallway that led to the back bedrooms. The door to Sister Rose's room was open; Amy stood in the doorway and listened.

"Sister Rose?" she called softly.

The bedroom was pitch-black and draped in silence. Amy couldn't tell if Rose was in the room or not. Feeling like an intruder, she stepped across the threshold and entered the tiny bedroom. As she inched forward something began to materialize out of the darkness. A bed. There was a dark shape on the bed.

She was almost to the bed when the shape moved and began to snore again. Her heart jumped with fright, but then she relaxed. Sister Rose was sleeping soundly; no harm had come to her. The voice that awoke Amy was not hers.

Retreating from the bedroom, Amy slowly made her way to the front of the house. She checked to make sure the front door was locked. It was. Her jingling of the latch produced a whine from Sammy and a scratching at the door.

"Shhhh, Sammy. It's all right," she whispered. "Go back to sleep."

Turning away from the front door, she went back into the living room and sat down. No one else was in the house, so the cry must have come from outside. Someone was in danger, but she didn't know who. Or where. Amy also didn't know what she could possibly do to help that person.

In St. Louis such cries were a regular nightly occurrence. They were also ignored. Getting involved in other people's problems was a good way to end up hurt. Or dead. Amy didn't know if the same rules applied to small towns, but she imagined they did. Besides, the call for help had already stopped. Either the person had been helped, or . . .

A shudder danced down her spine. She didn't want to think of the other possibility. It made her remember the bald-headed man in St. Louis and how close she had come to being a victim. She pushed the images from her mind and thought instead of happy things: bubble baths, fresh bread, hot cocoa.

Help me!

Amy jumped up and looked around, her heart pounding wildly. Someone was in the living room with her. But that couldn't be. The living room was small. There weren't any places to hide. Still, she was certain the voice had come from the same room.

A chill feeling of terror settled deep in Amy's stomach as she suddenly realized that she didn't hear the voice with her ears. She heard it with her mind. The person who called for help wasn't outside, or in the living room. They were in Amy's head. She forced herself to stand motionless and listen for the voice. A few seconds ticked slowly by before she heard it again.

Help me!

It was a woman's voice, loud and clear, calling for help. The woman sounded like she was in the same room with Amy, but she wasn't. Instead she was somewhere deep inside the little girl's head.

Amy tried to attach a name to the voice she heard. She thought of the few friends she had, but the voice didn't belong to any of them. Nor did it belong to any of the workers she knew at the shelters, neither the nice ones nor those who weren't so nice. It wasn't Sister Rose's voice either.

Who then? Who? Whose voice could it be that called her, asking for help?

Amy's eyes went wide. Was it a ghost she heard? She looked around the room, hoping with all her heart that she wouldn't see a ghost. Not that she believed in ghosts. Not really. All the same, she didn't want to see one. But the room remained empty. Amy breathed a sigh of relief.

But if it wasn't someone she knew—and if it wasn't a ghost—who could it be? Who could be so linked to her that they could magically call for help? Amy thought it over, and came up with the answer.

"Momma?"

Of course. Who else could it be? After all these years Amy's mother must have finally regained her memory. She knew her daughter would be looking for her, so she was reaching out to her, calling her. Amy didn't know how her mother was doing it. Maybe God was helping her.

That must be it. Amy had gone to the church and lit a candle, said a prayer. God must have forgiven her for cutting the bald-headed man. He had answered her prayers, putting Amy in touch with her mother.

"Where are you, Momma?" Amy turned around and around. She couldn't tell where the voice was coming from, had no idea in which direction to look.

Help me!

"I will, Momma. I will." Amy ran around the room, trying to follow a voice she could not see. "Where are you? Tell me where you are."

Her mother must have heard, for she answered her. It truly was a miracle.

Chicago.

Amy stopped. Chicago. Her mother was in Chicago. She had to go there. Tonight. Now!

Hurrying from the living room, Amy entered the kitchen and turned on the light. Her shoes sat by the door, where Sister Rose had put them. She quickly pulled them on.

She started to open the front door but stopped. It wouldn't be right to leave without saying goodbye, especially after all Sister Rose had done for her. But Sister Rose was still sleeping; Amy didn't want to wake her.

Looking around the kitchen, she found a pen and a piece of paper. Amy scribbled a quick note, thanking Sister Rose for everything and saying that she was on her way to Chicago to find her mother. She signed her name at the bottom of the note, then added an apology for stealing a loaf of bread. Putting the pen down, she picked up the loaf of bread and opened the door.

Sammy greeted her as she stepped out onto the porch. He tried to jump on her, but Amy told him to lie down. Crossing the porch, she opened the door and hurried down the sidewalk. Amy was a block away before she realized she was being followed. Sammy came bouncing down the street, dancing around her, wanting to play.

"No," Amy said, lowering her voice to sound more grown-up. "Go home." The dog only cocked his head and wagged his tail. "I said go home!" He still refused to obey.

She tried ignoring Sammy, hoping he would get tired of following her and go home on his own. But four blocks later he was still at her heels. Angry now, Amy wheeled and kicked at the dog, missing him by inches. Sammy barked and jumped playfully out of the way.

"I said go home!" she yelled. Sammy stopped and dropped his head, dejected, wondering what he had done wrong. She started to yell at him again, but his pitiful look stopped her. Instead, she bent down and gave him a hug.

"I know you want to come with me, Sammy, but you can't. You belong to Sister Rose. It wouldn't be right if you came along . . . she'd think I stole you."

She straightened back up. "Besides, it might be dangerous and I don't want you getting hurt." Sammy cocked his head, as though trying to understand what she was saying.

"Go on home now, Sammy. Go home." He only sat there. Amy backed away slowly. The dog watched her, but made no attempt to follow.

She turned and ran, not stopping until she reached the end of the block. Sammy still sat in the middle of the street and watched, perhaps waiting for her to call him. She didn't. Amy turned her back on the dog and kept walking, turning her back on a possible companion. She was alone again, as always, and Chicago was a long way off.

CHAPTER
21

The road stretched like an endless black ribbon through the barren countryside, passing deserted townships and crumbling farmhouses where the ghosts of shattered lives still dwelled. A great sadness clutched the heart of Jacob Fire Cloud as he stared out the dirt-streaked windshield of the pickup truck, wondering what had happened to those who once made the empty towns and farms their homes.

Had the men answered the call of sabers rattling and marched off to war, their heads held high, their chests filled with foolish pride? Did they set aside their plows and bid farewell to their wives, girlfriends and children? Was it a final farewell? Of those who left, how many had returned? How many now lay buried in unmarked graves? If the houses could speak, what stories might they tell? What sadness would they share?

Maybe the people of the farms and villages had simply packed up their belongings and left, joining the parade of wandering homeless that walked the highways in search of greener pastures and a better life.

Even on the loneliest stretches of road, there always seemed to be someone walking: individuals, couples, entire families. Loaded down with backpacks and baggage, they shuffled their feet wearily beneath the blistering sun, eyes focused on some imaginary oasis in the distance—an oasis where a better life might be had, a place that didn't know of suffering, hunger or war.

And when they could walk no more, when their feet grew weary of mile after endless mile, they stopped and erected their tents, cardboard shacks and shanties of weathered plywood, proclaiming to the rest of humanity: "I am here, and here I will stay."

That voiceless cry swept through the countryside like a beacon. One tent became two, and two soon grew into many. Villages and communities popped up where none had existed before, spreading across the prairie like a rash. New cities formed. Metropolises not of gleaming high-rises, all glass and chrome, but of plywood and canvas. They were places where the have-nots could finally find peace, friendship and the chance to start over.

Unlike in the cities of old, the citizens of the new America were forced to rely on one another for survival. There were no strangers among the once homeless, no slackers or the terminally lazy. And while robbery was often accepted as a means of survival on the open road, it was not tolerated within the boundaries of the new communities, at least not among the citizens who lived there. A person did not dirty his own nest. Those who broke the rules were dealt with quickly and often severely.

Weary of watching the land darken with the coming of night, Jacob turned and looked at his traveling partner. Danny Santos had run out of things to say several miles back and now drove in silence, tapping the fingers of his right hand on the steering wheel in rhythm to a song only he could hear.

In the past several hours, Jacob Fire Cloud had learned a lot about the talkative young man. Danny was full-blooded Filipino, but he had never been to the Philippines. Nor did he speak the language. He knew little about his culture, other than the few food dishes his mother had taught him how to prepare. Born and raised in southern California, he now lived in Montana.

Danny's wife was also from California; he had showed Jacob her picture. She was a white woman, very pretty, with long blonde hair and green eyes. They had been married for seven years and had two sons, ages five and six. Like their father, both boys had brown hair and dark skin.

From their conversation, Jacob also learned that Danny had been making deliveries only for a year or so. Before that, he had worked in a factory. This was the first time he had driven out of state. His wife had argued against him making such a trip, but they needed the money so he had accepted the job. The company that hired him provided the pickup; they also provided the assault rifle. Danny had never shot anyone, let alone killed anyone, and was hoping he wouldn't have to do so. After seeing the bodies of the men Jacob had killed in self-defense, he was having serious doubts about doing any more cross-country deliveries.

Luckily for Danny, this particular trip was almost half over. Omaha was only about a hundred miles away. In two hours he would arrive at his destination, unload his shipment of electronic components, and then spend the night at a state-run hostel—a safe haven for cross-country drivers. Only those with the safety and luxury of armor-plated vehicles with sleeping compartments spent the night beside the open road.

Danny would start back home in the morning. Jacob would be on his own then with only a rusty bicycle to get him the rest of the way to Chicago.

Jacob sighed. The White Buffalo Woman waited for him in Chicago, her life threatened by unknown forces. Even now he could hear her pleas reaching out to him, begging him to help her before it was too late. Time was running out. Not just for the White Buffalo Woman, but for all mankind. The Great Shaking drew near.

"Last stop before Omaha," Danny said, pointing out the window. Up ahead, a small village of tents and wooden shacks was set up in a field near the highway. Most of the village sat in darkness, but a few of the tents and shanties were illuminated by the glow of tiny campfires. A couple of larger fires burned alongside the road, their dancing flames illuminating a barricade of wood and wire and the armed men who guarded it.

Like the local, state and federal governments of old, America's newest communities also had their ways of securing income. Instead of taxes, however, many claimed the sections of roads that passed by their borders and tolled them accordingly. The tolls applied only to those with motor vehicles. After all, if you could afford to ride then you could afford to pay. Sometimes the state stepped in to shut down such illegal operations, but since the toll was usually only a coin or two, or an item of trade, they were usually left alone.

"Better slip those pistols under the seat," Danny said. "No sense spooking the locals."

Jacob did as suggested, concealing the pistols they had taken off the robbers. "What about my pistol . . . and the assault rifle?"

"Naw. They're okay. We'd appear suspicious if we were completely unarmed," Danny replied as he slowed the pickup.

The barricade stretching across the road was constructed of a half dozen or so wooden sawhorses, connected together by several rows of barbed wire. It appeared rather flimsy, and they could have driven right through it if it weren't for the men standing guard next to the barricade. Armed with shotguns and military assault rifles, the guards could stop what the barricade did not.

Danny pulled off the road and stopped.

"You stopping?" Jacob asked the obvious.

Danny nodded. "I figured this might be a good place to stretch our legs. Maybe get a little food. You hungry?"

"You buying?" Jacob asked.

"Maybe."

"Then I'm hungry."

"Leave your pistol on the seat. No one will steal it." Jacob slipped the revolver out of his belt and laid it on the seat. Rolling up the window, he climbed out of the pickup. Danny locked the doors and also climbed out. One of the guards approached them.

"Turn around," the guard ordered. Danny and Jacob did as they were told, allowing themselves to be frisked for concealed weapons. Satisfied they were unarmed, the guard stepped back and told them they could turn back around.

"Where are you headed?" the guard asked.

"Delivering supplies to Omaha," Danny answered. "Thought we'd stop and stretch our legs, maybe get a bite to eat."

"What kind of supplies?"

"Electronic components: gauges, switches, that sort of thing. The city is trying to repair a couple of water-treatment plants that got damaged during the war."

The man nodded, satisfied with the answer. "Toll's fifty cents, but we'll take anything of value."

Reaching in his pocket, Danny pulled out two quarters and handed them over. The guard nodded and pocketed the money.

"I'll move the roadblocks when you're ready to go, and I'll keep an eye on your truck in the meantime."

"What about my bicycle?" Jacob asked.

"I'll keep an eye on that too." The guard smiled. "If you're hungry, there's food for sale in the camp. We also sell gas if you need some."

Danny thanked the man for the information, assured him that they were interested only in food and started toward the village.

The village was small as far as roadside villages went, with probably less than a hundred people living in a variety of shacks, tents, tipis and lean-tos. A small stream entered the village on the north side, providing a source of fresh drinking water, irrigation for the vegetables in a community garden, and a place for bathing and washing clothes. When the stream left the village, it carried with it raw sewerage from a row of latrines.

In the center of the village an acre or so of land had been left unoccupied to form an open square, which was used for social gathering and as a place for merchants to sell their goods. Several vendors were set up, selling and trading everything from scrap metal to jugs of homemade blackberry wine. Jacob and Danny passed up the wine booth and headed for a food stand instead.

A slender, middle-aged woman sat beside an open fire, roasting thin strips of meat on wooden sticks. On a sheet of rusted tin beside her were stacks of corn tortillas, made by spreading a thick corn gruel over the bottom of a frying pan and then heating it over the fire. She looked up with interest as the two of them approached.

"You hungry?" she asked. "I've got fresh rabbit. My oldest son just killed it today." She slipped a tiny piece of meat off one of the sticks, tore it in half, and offered it to them. Jacob and Danny both sniffed the meat before trying it.

"It's not rat. It's rabbit." To prove her point, she pointed at a small plastic bucket containing the heads of two wild rabbits.

"How much?" Danny asked.

"Two dollars a stick," the woman replied.

"What! Two dollars!" Danny exclaimed. "That's outrageous."

The woman's face darkened with anger. Reaching behind her, she picked up a rock and tossed it to the young man. "You don't like my price? Go kill your own fucking rabbit."

Danny dropped the rock and started to walk away. "Let's go. We'll buy our food somewhere else."

Jacob didn't move. He cocked his head and looked at the woman.

"What are you looking at?" the woman asked, directing her anger at him.

"Who's sick?" he asked.

The question caught her off guard. "What?"

"Who's sick?" he repeated.

"Who said anything about being sick. No one's sick."

"You're lying," he said calmly. "I can smell the sickness on you. I can see it in you. Who's sick?"

The woman's hardened exterior crumbled. Pain showed in her eyes. "My youngest son . . . but how did you know?"

Jacob ignored the question. "May I see him?"

"Why? Are you a doctor or something?"

"Perhaps."

The woman looked at him for a moment longer, then nodded. She stood up and gestured for Jacob to follow her. "This way."

Jacob and Danny followed the woman through the twisting passageways between the makeshift homes to a mildewed canvas tent. Inside the tent a small fire burned. Beyond the fire, three sleeping bags were stretched upon the ground. On one of the sleeping bags lay a boy about twelve years old.

Jacob could tell the child had a fever just by looking at him. His face was flushed and, even though the evening was quite warm, he lay shivering beneath several tattered blankets. Crossing the tent, he laid his palm on the boy's forehead. The child was burning up.

Jacob turned and looked at the boy's mother. "How long has he been like this?"

"He took sick yesterday morning," she answered.

"Have you given him anything?"

"Only water. We don't have any medicine, and he can't keep food down. I keep hoping the fever will break, but it hasn't." She wiped the tears from her eyes with a trembling hand. "He's bad off, isn't he? Real bad. I just know it. Is he going to die?"

"Yes." Jacob nodded. Without another word, he stood up and left the tent.

"Wait! Where are you going?" the woman called after him. "Can't you help my son? Please, won't you help him? Please?"

The old Indian walked back through the village, returning to the pickup. Danny hurried to catch up with him.

"What are you doing?" Danny asked.

"Leaving," Jacob replied, leaning against the truck.

"Leaving?"

"Yes, leaving, You said the food was too expensive, so we leave."

"What about her son?"

"What about him?"

"Aren't you going to help him?"

Jacob looked Danny up and down. "What makes you think I can help him?"

"You're an Indian. You guys know all about medicine and healing people. Don't you have some kind of herb you can give him, or a dance you can do?"

"Even if I did there is no time. I have to get to Chicago."

"The hell with Chicago," Danny said, angry. "That boy's going to die if someone doesn't do something for him."

"Many more may die if I don't get to Chicago." Jacob looked past Danny. He sighed and nodded. "All right. I will help him."

Jacob walked around to the back of the pickup and untied his medicine pouch from the handlebar of his bicycle.

"See, I knew you had something that would help him," Danny said. Jacob ignored the comment.

They walked back through the village to the tent. The woman was still inside, hovering over her sick son. She turned with a start as they stepped back inside.

"I thought you left," she said, her tone harsh.

"I changed my mind," Jacob said, stepping past her. He turned back toward Danny, who still stood in the doorway. "Either come inside or get out, but close the flap." Danny stepped inside, closing the tent's flap behind him.

Jacob kneeled beside the sick child; the boy's mother stood just behind him. He pulled back the covers and felt the boy's clothes. He was soaking wet.

Jacob turned to the mother. "What is your name?"

"Lea . . . Lea Montgomery."

"And his?"

"Jeffery."

Jacob nodded. "Lea, we need to get your son undressed."

Lea stepped forward and helped Jacob remove the boy's clothing. Jeffery Montgomery shivered uncontrollably as his T-shirt was removed, followed by his pants, socks and underwear. Jacob carefully examined the naked child, paying particular attention to his underarms and genital area. He found what he was looking for in the child's left armpit. A small brown dot. A deer tick.

Pinching the tick between his thumb and index finger, Jacob slowly pulled it loose. He held the tick out for Lea to see. "This is what makes your son sick. He has the tick fever."

"How did you know what to look for?" she asked.

He tossed the tick into the fire. "You said your sons hunted rabbits for you. To hunt, one has to leave the village. It has been a dry year, the winter was mild, a good year for bugs."

"Can you help him?"

"Maybe. Maybe not. I don't know," he said. "Give me room."

Lea backed up, watching as Jacob untied the three leather cords that secured his medicine bundle. Opening the bundle, he removed two small leather pouches and set them on the ground beside him. One of the pouches was filled with sage, the other with tobacco. He also took out an abalone shell, his pipe and a medicine fan made from five tail feathers from a golden eagle.

Opening the smaller of the two leather pouches, he placed a pinch of desert sage in the abalone shell and lit it with his lighter. He waited until the sage was burning good, then blew out the flame and passed the smoking herb back and forth over the sleeping boy to purify his body.

"What's he doing?" Lea asked, whispering to Danny. When he didn't answer, she addressed the question to Jacob.

"What are you doing?"

Jacob ignored the woman's question. He had enough on his mind without having to stop to explain his actions. Instead he silently said a prayer and then slowly filled the bowl of his pipe. Once it was filled, he turned his attention to Lea.

"Bring me a bowl of hot water, or a cup, something you can drink from. Set it just inside the doorway, but do not come in. I must not be disturbed if you want your son to be healed." She nodded and then hurried from the tent to fetch the water. Jacob turned to Danny. "Get out."

Danny's mouth dropped open in surprise. "Why? I'm not hurting anything. I want to watch."

Jacob frowned in disapproval. "This is not a free show. Your being in here will keep the spirits from coming. Please leave."

Danny opened his mouth to protest, but stopped. Disappointed, he pushed the flap open and left.

Jacob waited for the flap to fall back in place before continuing with the business at hand. He sat on the ground beside Jeffery and lit his pipe, offering it to the Great Spirit, Grandmother and the four directions. He blew several puffs of smoke at the sleeping boy, praying for the sickness to leave his body.

As he prayed and smoked his pipe, Lea Montgomery opened the tent's flap and placed a cup of hot water on the ground. She hesitated long enough to glance at Jacob before leaving again. Jacob ignored the cup, concentrating instead on the words he whispered. He visualized the child's sickness as a living entity, an evil beast that inhabited his body. When the last of the tobacco was smoked, he waited for the ashes to cool and then sprinkled them over Jeffery's body. Leaning forward, he shook the child, waking him.

Jeffery Montgomery turned his head and looked at Jacob. His eyes were bloodshot from the fever. They also had a hollow, vacant look to them, as though they were nothing more than windows to an empty room. Jacob frowned. That was not good, not good at all. The sickness had pushed the child's spirit back, driving it deep down inside the body to a place that was hard to reach even for a medicine man. If the boy's spirit had traveled too far away it might be reluctant to return to the frail body that housed it. He might not be able to bring it back and the boy would surely die. He could only try.

Setting his pipe on top of his medicine pouch, Jacob stood up and crossed the room. He picked up the cup and tested the water's temperature. The water was hot but not boiling. Perfect. Carrying the cup with him, he sat back down and searched through the contents of his medicine pouch.

While his supply of herbs was limited, he did have the ingredients he needed. A pinch of feverfew and red clover, a piece of yarrow root and a few other ingredients with healing powers went into the cup. Jacob stirred the mixture with his index finger and set the cup aside to steep. While he waited, he relit the sage in the abalone shell and fanned the smoke over Jeffery with his eagle feather fan. When the last of the sage burned out, he lightly rubbed the fan over the child's body, starting at the top of his head and working downward. Jeffery watched him, but Jacob doubted if the boy even knew what was going on.

Setting the fan aside, he slipped his hand behind the boy's neck and raised him to a sitting position. Jeffery groaned and tried to slip free, but Jacob held him tight. Still holding him, he picked up the cup and brought it to the child's lips.

"Drink," Jacob ordered. Jeffery tried to resist, but he was too weak to put up much of a fight. His lips parted like pieces of dead flesh and the greenish liquid flowed from the cup into his mouth.

The boy gagged and tried to spit out the mixture, but Jacob reached around with the hand that held him upright and covered his mouth. He waited until he saw Jeffery swallow before removing his hand. He forced the child to take another sip, and then another. Half the cup was empty before Jacob allowed Jeffery to lie back down.

Jacob Fire Cloud wiped a hand across his sweating forehead. The tent was unbearably hot, but that was good. The heat would help drive the sickness from the boy's body. Unfortunately, Jacob had no sickness or demons that needed to be sweated out. And he didn't need to shed any extra pounds either; he was thin enough as it was. He would probably be even thinner before he was through. The child was still a long way from being out of danger.

Several hours passed before Jeffery showed any signs that the medicine was working. Jacob was sitting by the boy's side, starting to nod off from the heat, when he heard him groan. He opened his eyes and listened. The boy groaned again and coughed. Jacob smiled. Good, Jeffery's spirit was starting to fight the sickness.

He leaned over and placed his hand on the child's forehead. Jeffery still had a temperature, but he wasn't nearly as hot as before. "That's it." Jacob smiled. "Fight it. You can do it. Your spirit is strong."

Jeffery opened his eyes and looked at him. The boy's eyes were still bloodshot, but they were no longer glazed. Jacob saw life in them. Jeffery's spirit had returned.

Getting to his feet, he bent over and picked up the naked boy in his arms. Now was the most important time, also the most dangerous. Jeffery's spirit was back, but it was not yet firmly attached to the boy's body. It might decide life was too much trouble and try to leave again. A shock was needed to firmly anchor the spirit in place.

Jacob pushed aside the tent flap and carried the boy outside. Jeffery's mother and Danny were sitting a few feet beyond the doorway. They both jumped up when they saw him and the child.

Lea rushed forward. "How is he?"

"He is not out of danger yet," Jacob warned, stepping past her. "Get a blanket and come with me."

He hurried through the village carrying the boy, weaving his way between tents and shacks. Danny and Lea followed. At the square he paused to get his bearings and then turned right. Jacob found the stream, which is what he was looking for, but he located it near where the row of latrines was set up. The water was brown and fouled with sewerage.

"Where is the clean water?" he asked, frustrated.

"This way. Upstream." Lea grabbed his arm and led him to the place set aside for public bathing. Here, someone had used stones to damn the creek, creating a wide pool about four feet deep. Jacob wasted no time wading out into the pool. Reaching the center, he tossed Jeffery into the water, completely submerging him.

"What are you doing?" Lea shouted from shore. "You'll drown him." She started to wade out to stop Jacob, but Danny restrained her.

Jacob ignored the woman's cries as he lifted Jeffery's face from the water so he could breathe. Shocked from the cold water, half drowned, the boy coughed, then let out a scream of pain. His eyes opened. Clear eyes. Angry eyes. He beat at the hands that held him, scratched, struggled to get free. Jacob smiled but held on. Only when the boy quit fighting did he let go. Jeffery stood in the middle of the pool, naked, chest heaving, face twisted in rage. But he stood on his own. His spirit had returned.

Jacob nodded and turned away from the boy, wading back to shore. Lea Montgomery watched him approach, uncertain, waiting for a word or sign that her son was going to be all right.

"The fever has broken," Jacob said. "Your son will live, but he still needs to rest for a day or two." He smiled. "And he needs a blanket." Lea looked past him and saw her son standing naked in the pool. Wading out into the pool, she wrapped the blanket around the boy and hurried him away.

Jacob and Danny returned to the Montgomerys' tent surprised to find it empty. Lea must have taken her son someplace else. Entering the tent, Jacob gathered together his belongings.

"Now what?" Danny asked, watching him.

"We leave," Jacob replied, tying his medicine bundle closed.

"What about food?"

"Eat later. I have spent enough time here." Jacob stood and left the tent. Danny followed. They were almost back to the road when they heard someone calling them.

"Wait! Wait!"

They turned and saw Lea racing after them, carrying a brown paper sack. She ran up to them, breathless.

"I didn't know you were leaving. I wanted to thank you." She thrust the paper sack into Jacob's hands. "It's not much, I know, but it's all I have to give."

Inside the sack were six wooden skewers of rabbit meat. Jacob would have refused the offering, knowing that she might go hungry because of it. But to refuse such a gift would have been an insult and hurt the medicine that comes from the act of giving.

"Thank you," he said, accepting the gift.

"I wish there was more I could do for you," she said, awkwardly.

"No, this is enough." He stepped back from her to allow the conversation to end on a gracious note, not wanting her to feel that more was owed. "We must go now. Make sure your son rests for a few days."

"I will," she said, smiling. "Thank you." She turned and started back through the village, stopping once to turn and wave. They waved back.

Danny waited until Lea was out of sight before unlocking the pickup. He started to climb in when Jacob stopped him.

"Wait. There is something I forgot." Jacob pulled a copper bracelet off his right wrist. "Catch her. Tell her to give this to her son. It will help him get well faster."

Danny took the bracelet and raced to catch Lea. Jacob waited until he was out of sight, then hurried around to the passenger's side and climbed into the truck. Once in, he reached beneath the seat and pulled out the pistols they had taken off the thieves. He unloaded each of the guns, slipping the bullets into his pants pockets. He also unloaded the assault rifle. He had just slid the pistols back under the seat when Danny returned.

"She said to thank you," Danny said, climbing behind the wheel.

Jacob nodded and handed the young man one of the meat sticks. "This is thank-you enough."

Danny took the stick and started up the truck, waiting until the roadblock was removed and they were waved through. Back on the road, they each ate two of the rabbit sticks, saving the other two for later.

"That was a nice thing you did back there," Danny said between mouthfuls of stringy meat. "That kid might have died if you hadn't helped him. You're an all-right guy in my book."

Jacob was busy chewing and only nodded.

They reached Omaha less than two hours later. Danny's delivery destination was a warehouse on the west side of the city. Jacob waited in the truck while Danny and two other men unloaded the wooden crates of electrical components. He didn't have to wait long.

"Well, that's that," Danny said, climbing back into the truck. He started the engine and drove away from the building. Turning left on the street, they headed back in the direction of the highway.

"Guess I'll be starting back," the young man said. "Where do you want me to let you off?"

"Chicago," Jacob replied.

Danny smiled. "Sorry, but this flight doesn't stop there."

Jacob pulled his revolver and pointed it at him. "Yes it does."

Danny's smile melted like ice cream on a warm summer day. He slammed on the brakes and made a grab for the .45 beneath the seat.

"I took the bullets out when I sent you to give Lea the bracelet." Jacob grinned. "I emptied the other pistols too—and the assault rifle. Go ahead. See for yourself."

Danny's mouth dropped open. He picked up the .45 and released the clip. The pistol was indeed unloaded. "Why . . .

you . . . no good . . . I take back all the nice things I ever said about you—every last one of them."

Jacob shrugged. "I don't care."

"So now what?" he asked. "You going to shoot me? I should have known better than to give you a ride. I never should have trusted you. My wife always said I had shit for brains. She was right. I'll probably lose my job over this. We'll lose our house. I'll never—"

Jacob held up his hand. "I'm not going to shoot you, not unless you keep babbling. You make my ears hurt."

Danny stopped talking.

"All I want is to get to Chicago. Once I get there, you and your truck are free to go."

"What's so important about Chicago?"

"I'll explain on the way. Will you help me?"

"Do I have a choice?" Danny asked.

"No."

"That's what I thought." He tossed the empty .45 onto the floor. "Look's like we're going to Chicago."

Jacob just smiled.

CHAPTER
22

Fear twisted Rene's intestines into tight little knots, turned the lining of her mouth into cotton. Breathless, she ran down the hallway, painfully aware of the echoed footsteps of her own passing. The worn carpeting did little to muffle the sounds, which reverberated off the walls and ceiling, sounding like a herd of elephants following behind her.

She fled past a dozen doorways, praying that none would open and no one would step into the hallway to stop her. She reached the end of the corridor. To her left were the elevators. To the right stood the gray metal door that opened onto an inside stairway.

Turning her back on the elevators, she stepped up to the metal door and placed her left ear against it listening for sounds from the other side. The metal door felt cool against her flushed skin, like a breath of winter on a hot summer day.

She had to wait for the thunderous pounding of her heart to slow before she could hear anything. Each second that passed seemed a painful eternity. Finally, her heartbeat eased enough to allow her to hear what lay beyond the door.

At first Rene imagined she heard someone slowly creeping up the concrete stairs, reaching a sinister hand out to snatch open the door upon which her ear rested. She almost jerked her head back before realizing the sounds were nothing more than the hum of fluorescent light fixtures vibrating through the walls and doorway. The stairway beyond the door was empty.

Rene cautiously inched open the door, breathing a sigh of relief when she saw that no one waited for her on the other side. The landing was empty, as were the stairs beyond it.

Closing the door slowly behind her, she stood on the landing and listened for a minute. She heard no sounds. No voices. No footsteps. Nothing to indicate that anyone else was around. The building was as silent as a cavernous tomb. Rene wasn't fooled, however; she knew a building so large was rarely empty. There would be guards, custodians, maybe even a maintenance man or two.

The thought of someone lurking in the darkness made her uneasy and caused her legs to tremble. Still, she could not stay where she was forever. Sooner or later someone would notice the absence of the guard she had knocked unconscious. They would find him and come looking for her. God only knew what they would do when they found her. With no other choice she started down the stairs.

She took the stairs one step at a time, careful not to make any noise. At the third-floor landing she paused, uncertain of her actions. Two more flights of steps and she would reach the ground level. Freedom awaited her there. More than anything Rene wanted that freedom. She wanted to run screaming into the night, alert the authorities about what had happened to her. But freedom would have to wait a few minutes longer. There was something she had to do first, something she had to get.

Rene would not leave without the Neuro-Enhancer. The device was her life's work. It had taken years of research, years of trial and error to invent the Enhancer. If Dr. Sinclair's men had stolen all the records, it would be next to impossible to build another one—not that she would have the heart to start again from scratch.

She would rather die than allow Randall Sinclair and his cronies to own the Neuro-Enhancer, which is exactly what would happen if she got caught before she could find it and make good her escape. Even so, she would not leave without first trying to get the Enhancer back.

She listened at the door, which opened onto the third floor. Not hearing anything, she eased it open and peeked out. The hallway was empty.

Thank God.

Rene had just stepped into the hallway when she was startled by the sound of a door slamming on the stairway below. The slam was followed by the echoing tap-tap of footsteps on the concrete steps. Someone was coming.

Panic-stricken, she turned and looked over her shoulder. She couldn't see anyone, only the empty gray stairs, but the footsteps drew nearer, came her way.

Danger.

She didn't need the mental warning to tell her danger approached; her ears alone could do that. Rene slipped into the hallway and closed the door behind her, careful not to let it bang.

Danger . . . danger . . . danger.

"I know. I know," she whispered, looking around for a hiding place. Directly across the hall were the elevators, but she didn't dare summon one of the cars for fear someone would be on it when it arrived. Instead she ran down the hallway, turning left at the first corridor. Randall Sinclair's office was three doors down on the right. The office now represented more than a chance to retrieve her stolen property: it meant safety. The only problem was getting inside.

The door was locked, as she knew it would be. Fortunately the lock was in the doorknob and not a deadbolt. Reaching into

her pocket, Rene pulled out the pocketknife she had taken off
the guard. The knife had only two blades, but with a little fumbling she managed to slip the longer one between the door and
the frame. Working the blade back and forth, she was able to
catch the edge of the latch. A few twists to the right and the
door popped open.

Hurrying across the threshold, Rene closed and locked the
office door. She stood there in the darkness, her cheek pressed
against the door, waiting to see if anyone was coming. But the
footsteps she strained to hear never came. Whoever it was, they
had gone the other way.

That was close. Too close.

Stepping away from the door, Rene fumbled for a light
switch, found it and switched on the lights. She turned to face
the empty room. If the Neuro-Enhancer was still in the office it
was probably locked away somewhere, maybe in the desk.

Rene crossed the room to the desk. The drawers were
unlocked, but none of them contained what she was looking for.

"Where would he hide it? Think, girl. Think."

She stepped away from the desk and looked around the
room. The Neuro-Enhancer was much too valuable to leave
lying around. Dr. Sinclair would have hidden it, or locked it
away. But what if he took it home with him?

Rene shook her head. She wouldn't have risked carrying
the Neuro-Enhancer to and from work. Neither would Randall
Sinclair. Too many things could happen to it. No, he would keep
it in his office. But if it wasn't in his desk, then where was it?

A safe.

Of course, that would be the logical place to keep something worth millions. She had kept the Neuro-Enhancer in a
safe; so would Randall Sinclair. There had to be a hidden safe
somewhere. Maybe it was behind one of the paintings, or
behind some of the books in the library.

She started toward the closest painting, but was interrupted
by the sound of voices coming down the hallway.

Danger.

Again she didn't need her newly acquired sixth sense to warn her of trouble. Rene spotted the tiny wires running along the door frame and knew she had tripped a silent alarm. The voices came closer, stopping just on the other side of the door. Someone tried the knob. Thank God, she had remembered to lock the door behind her. There was a pause, then she heard the jingling of keys.

No . . . No . . . No . . . No . . .

Rene sprinted across the room, unhooking the stun gun from her belt as she ran. She jammed the gun's electrodes against the lock and pulled the trigger. Someone on the other side of the door screamed as 100,000 volts of electricity shot through the metal lock. The scream was followed by the thud of a body hitting the floor. She smiled. That would make them think twice about using a key.

Clipping the stun gun back on her belt, she ran behind the desk and snatched up a metal waste paper can. Turning, she took two steps and threw the can as hard as she could at one of the plate glass windows. The glass shattered, exploding into a thousand tiny fragments. Careful of the remaining shards, Rene climbed through the window. She had just stepped out onto the ledge when the door was kicked in.

"Get her!"

Two men charged into the room, jumping over the body of a third man lying prone in the hallway—obviously the same man she had zapped with the stun gun. Rene caught only a glimpse of them as she hurried along the ledge. She didn't look back, nor did she look down. Hugging the face of the building, she tried to become invisible in the darkness. But that was impossible. The building was white; her clothing and skin were dark. Even in the night she would stand out, easily seen from above or below.

Rene had to slow down to climb around a protruding gutter. Precious time wasted. Once past the obstacle, she cast a quick glance behind her. No more than thirty yards behind her a shadowy shape slithered along the ledge in hot pursuit. The sight of the man following her made Rene's heart jump and nearly caused her to miss her footing. She slipped but did not fall, a short scream escaping her lips. Her scream caused the man who followed to hesitate, but only for a moment.

At the corner of the building an emergency escape ladder led to the ground below. She climbed down the ladder, taking the rungs two at a time. Once on the ground she was forced to make a quick decision. Her instincts told her to run away from the building, to seek help from someone, anyone, in the streets. But on foot she would be easily caught; what she needed was a ride. So instead of fleeing the property Rene circled the building, trying different doors until she found the one to the parking garage.

Inside the garage were six vehicles: four trucks and two cars. Rene hurried from vehicle to vehicle, trying doors and checking for keys in the ignition. Unfortunately, they were all locked and none of them had keys. She had just checked the last vehicle, a large cargo truck, when three men entered the garage through the same door she had.

Rene ducked down just in time. She stood hunched on the driver's-side running board, on the opposite side of the truck from the three men. She watched through the truck's windows as they entered the garage, obviously searching for her. Her heart began to hammer as they checked the vehicles closest to the door, slowly working their way in her direction.

Looking around, she frantically searched for a way out. But there was none, other than the door through which she had entered and the vehicle exit to the street at the other end of the garage. Nor was there any other place to hide. She could do nothing but crouch behind the truck, knowing the three men would eventually search that vehicle too. When they did they would find her.

What then? Imprisonment? Torture? Perhaps even murder? She didn't want to find out. Whatever was in store for her wouldn't be pleasant. Not pleasant at all.

Still looking for a way to escape, she was almost caught off guard when headlights suddenly swept the wall in front of her. Rene pressed her body even tighter against the truck she hid behind as a car entered the garage, parking only two places from where she hid. The three men searching for her looked at the car as it pulled in, and then turned their attention back to the search.

Now! Now! Now! Now's your chance!

Rene's brain screamed the commands, forcing her body into action. Staying low, she jumped off the running board and circled around the front of the truck. She watched as the driver of the car put the vehicle into park and killed the engine. He opened the door and started to climb out, but Rene was upon him. Before he could defend himself, or even cry out, she jammed the stun gun against his throat and pulled the trigger. The man let out a wheezy gasp and collapsed like a bag of old laundry.

Snatching the keys out of his hands, she climbed into the car and started the engine. Her adrenaline pumping, she accidentally pushed too hard on the accelerator, causing the motor to rev.

The three men at the opposite end of the garage heard the noise and looked her way. "Hey!" one of them yelled.

She shifted into reverse, tires squealing.

"Stop her!"

Rene straightened the car out and slammed the gearshift into drive. The three men ran toward her. One of them drew a pistol.

She stomped on the gas pedal. Tires squealed and the car lunged forward. The man with the gun fired. She ducked as a spiderweb of cracks formed across the windshield. He fired twice more, and then jumped out of the way to keep from being run over.

Rene flew past the three men and took the corner on two wheels. She came dangerously close to crashing into the wall, but managed to regain control of the car. Shifting from second into third, she shot out of the garage into the street. Free.

PART IV

"Violence as a way of achieving racial justice is both impractical and immoral. It is impractical because it is a descending spiral ending in destruction for all. . . . It is immoral because it seeks to humiliate the opponent rather than win his understanding; it seeks to annihilate rather than to convert. Violence is immoral because it thrives on hatred rather than on love. . . ."

—Martin Luther King, Jr.

CHAPTER
23

Leon and the others emerged from the forest in the chill gray of the early morning dawn. They reached the railroad tracks and turned right, heading south. The train they had ridden the night before was long gone, as were the bandits. All that remained as evidence of the previous evening's violence were the logs that had been used to block the tracks, and they had been pushed off to the side out of the way.

They had walked only about a mile when they came upon a small transient camp nestled among the pine trees of the forest, about fifty yards from the railroad tracks. The camp was barely visible from the tracks and they might have walked right on past it were it not for the aromas of coffee and campfires, which hung heavy in the air.

Within the crowded confines of the camp lived twenty to twenty-five single men, mostly middle age or older, and a few families. They were the same people who had erected the burning torches the night before to warn about the bandits. Leon was worried about stopping at the camp, afraid the bandits might return, but Red assured him that they would be safe. Leon hoped he was right.

Although their visit came as somewhat of a surprise to the camp's residents, the transients quickly made them feel welcome by offering to share coffee and food with them. Breakfast consisted of fried bread and bowls of stew. The stew simmered in a large iron kettle that hung over a fire in the center of the camp. Leon and the others were told to take as much stew as they wanted, but they took only one bowl apiece.

"How can you be sure the bandits won't come here?" Leon asked between mouthfuls of stew.

"Because a transient camp serves the needs of all people," Red replied. "They're neutral territory."

"All people? Bandits too?"

Red nodded. "Everyone is welcome here; they're all treated equally. The bandits know that. If they come here they'll be welcomed and treated with respect, just as we were. It's all part of the official transient creed."

Leon looked around the camp. To him it looked like a hundred other refugee settlements he had seen: buildings made of plywood and scrap material, ill-clothed people surviving the best they could. "This place is just like all the others."

"Ah, but that's where you're wrong." Red smiled. "These people aren't homeless. They're transients."

"What's the difference?"

"The difference is they'd be doing this no matter what shape the country was in. This lifestyle hasn't been forced upon them; they've chosen it. They're the last of the free spirits, wandering across the land, riding the rails. They never put down roots, call no place their home."

"You make it all sound so romantic." Leon laughed. He pointed at one of the tiny buildings. "Never put down roots, huh? What about the shacks?"

"Temporary lodging at best. The owner stays for a while, then moves on. Somebody else moves in."

"And the bandits?" Leon asked. "How many of them live here?"

"Not many," Red replied. "This place is way too calm for bandits. No wild parties allowed."

"I suppose that's another rule from the transient creed."

Red nodded. "You're starting to catch on."

Finishing his stew, Leon carried the ceramic bowl over to a bucket of water to wash it. Once it was clean, he returned the bowl to a stack of dishes sitting on an old picnic table. Red also finished eating and joined him by the table.

"That's some of the best stew I've had in a long time," Leon commented.

"Yeah, it's pretty good," Red agreed. "It's kind of a tradition with these camps. There's always a pot of stew cooking for visitors. The recipe varies from place to place, with each camp trying to outdo the other."

Leon cast a glance toward the stew pot. "I wonder what they put in it?"

"Oh, a little bit of this. A little bit of that." Red pointed at a stack of empty cans sitting in front of a nearby shack. "And a little bit of those."

Leon felt his stomach do a slow roll. The empty cans Red pointed at were dog food cans. "You're kidding. Dog food?"

"They say beggars can't be choosers, and most of the transients I know are definitely beggars. Relax, it won't kill you. Might even put some meat on your bones. You never heard a dog complaining, have you?"

"If one did it would probably end up in the pot." Leon looked away from the cans and saw María and Edrick finishing up their bowls of stew. He hoped, for their stomachs' sake, they wouldn't see the dog food cans and put two and two together.

Leon and Red spent the next hour talking with the residents of the camp. From their conversations, they found out that an express freight train carrying farm equipment and machinery was due through in the next hour or so. Leon's heart jumped when he learned that the train was heading north, non-stop to Peoria, Illinois.

"I've got to get on that train," Leon said, excited.

Red shook his head. "That train will pass by here at fifty miles an hour. There's no way you can hop it."

"But I've got to try."

"You ever try to grab hold of a train going that fast? It'll pull your damn arm right out of the socket."

"But this is a transient camp. These guys catch rides all the time."

"Not expresses." Red patted him on the shoulder. "Besides, there'll be another train along tomorrow."

Leon explained that he couldn't wait another day. The voice that called him was urgent, frantic. He felt the woman's life was in danger and time was running out. If he was to help her it would have to be soon or not at all. Fortunately, he had a plan. He suggested that they drag one of the logs used by the bandits back onto the tracks to slow the train or bring it to a stop. He would then be able to climb on board.

"Will you help me?" asked Leon.

"What do I have to lose?" Red shrugged.

Red and Leon hurried back to the straight stretch of track where their train had been stopped the night before. Not wanting to be left alone among strangers, María and Edrick also tagged along. Good thing too, for it took all four of them to drag one of the unburned logs up onto the track. Once finished, they sat around and waited for the express. They hadn't long to wait.

"It's coming!" Edrick cried, running along the railroad tracks. Leon had asked the boy to walk back along the tracks, acting as a lookout. He now ran along the rails, yelling to the others. "I see the train! I see the train!"

They hurried away from the tracks, hiding behind a clump of bushes at the edge of the forest. Edrick had just joined them when the train appeared out of the south like a one-eyed steel dragon. Leon felt the excitement building in him and took a deep breath to steady his nerves. The train bore down on them, racing straight at the log that lay across the tracks.

"It's not stopping," he said. Disappointment surged through him, and then a twinge of fear. What if the train hit the log at full speed? Would it jump the tracks? The thought of a two-hundred-ton locomotive going airborne made him more than a little nervous.

"Wait," Red said. "The engineers haven't seen the log yet. They'll stop; you can bet on it."

Suddenly there was a whistle blast and the metallic screaming of brakes being applied. The train slowed, coming to a complete stop a few feet in front of the log barricade. From the concealment of their hiding place, Leon could see the train's engineers looking toward the forest. They had obviously received word of last night's robbery and were being cautious. Several minutes passed before three men climbed down out of the engine to remove the log. Leon started to slip from his hiding place.

"Not yet," Red whispered, grabbing his arm. "They'll see you. They wouldn't be too happy knowing they had to stop just so you could hop a ride. Wait until they get going again."

"What about you?" Leon asked. "You guys going?"

Red shook his head. "Not this time. María and Edrick want to rest for a day before doing any more traveling. It wouldn't be right to just leave them, so I said I'd stick around. Besides, I'm in no hurry to get anywhere."

Leon understood. Under different circumstances he would have done the same thing.

With the log clear of the track, the engineers climbed back aboard the engine. There was a hiss as the train started to roll again.

Red stuck out his hand. "I hope you find your mystery woman."

"Thanks," Leon said, shaking hands. "I will." He gave María and Edrick a quick hug and then slipped out from behind the bush. "Maybe we'll bump into each other again."

"I wouldn't be a bit surprised." Red grinned.

Leon smiled and then raced to catch the train. It still wasn't going very fast so he was able to slide open a door on one of the boxcars and climb in. Once in, he leaned out the doorway to wave a final goodbye. Red and the others waved back. He stayed in the doorway until they faded from sight, and then turned away. He was going to miss them.

Stepping away from the door, Leon waited for his eyes to adjust to the boxcar's dark interior. The boxcar was empty; he was the only passenger. It was just as well, he really wasn't in the mood for company. Sitting down along the wall, he thought about what might be waiting for him at the end of the line in Chicago.

Next stop Peoria, Illinois. He was almost there.

CHAPTER
24

Fog blew off the river and drifted chill and damp into town, carrying with it the smells of the Mississippi: fish, rotting wood, vegetation and black bottom mud. The fog rolled ghostlike across the streets, pooling in the low-lying areas, coating houses, trees and cars in misty gray cotton candy. The town appeared as a ghost town, a Brigadoon from the past, empty, quiet. A place where spirits walked. A village not for the living.

Amy Ladue walked through the deserted, foggy streets, following a voice only she could hear. She turned right, left, and right again as she headed toward the river, answering the call of a siren's cry. A siren with the voice of her mother. The words of that voice were emblazoned in neon across her brain. *Help me . . . I'm in Chicago.*

Reaching the river, she turned left again and followed the shoreline. The fog was thicker near the water. It welcomed Amy in its wet, clinging embrace as it soaked through her clothing, plastering her hair flat against her head. She shuddered slightly from the chill but pushed on, her sight fixed on the iron skeleton, which rose from the mist like the bones of some prehistoric beast.

The bridge that spanned the Mississippi River at Louisiana, Missouri, still stood, its structure untouched by either earthquake or war. The road passing over the bridge, U.S. Highway 54, was still used by those with the luxury of motor vehicles and by farmers with horse- and mule-drawn carts. On this particular evening it was also used by a little girl searching for her mother.

Amy crossed the bridge and entered the state of Illinois. Just beyond the bridge a rusted, bullet-ridden sign told her that the town of Pike lay just up the road. She couldn't see the town, even when she put her hand over her eyes and squinted. The fog lay as a thick blanket over the land. She could see only the road and a few feet to either side of it.

She had just passed the sign when sounds of movement came from the darkness to her right. The rustling of tall grasses and leaves, the snapping of sticks. Amy froze, afraid, suddenly aware of how truly alone she was. She cocked her head and listened, trying to identify the sounds. But she was a city girl, used to the sounds of an urban metropolis. The country was different, with different noises. Some, like those she heard now, were terribly frightening, conjuring up images of wild animals and slobbering beasts.

Amy turned and looked behind her, regretting that she had sent Sammy away. The dog could have protected her from whatever was lurking in the darkness. Too late now. Sammy was probably sound asleep on Sister Rose's front porch dreaming doggie dreams. She was alone.

The sounds drew closer. Crackle. Crackle. Snap. Amy took a step back. Glancing around, she searched for something to defend herself with but found nothing. She remained unarmed, vulnerable.

As she watched, the fog parted to reveal the source of the noise. It was a dog. A big dog. Not a friendly, smiling, tail-wagging pooch, like Sammy, but a half-starved, matted-fur mongrel with fangs bared and evil yellow eyes.

The dog stepped onto the road and stood with its legs spread and head lowered. It growled at her, a growl that came from deep within its throat, threatening, menacing. A growl that meant business.

Amy took a fearful step backward. The dog lowered its head, the yellow eyes tracking her like twin gun sights. The growling grew louder.

"Nice doggie," she said, knowing that the dog was anything but nice. A ridge of fur stood up along the mongrel's back, making it seem less like a dog and more like a werewolf.

A second dog emerged from the darkness and flowed out onto the road. And a third. Three dogs, all wild, part of a pack. Savage. No one's pets. Living off the land. Hunting as a group. Killing as a group. Killing . . .

Amy swallowed hard, feeling her throat tighten with dread. The other two dogs—one brown, one black—crept forward to join the first. They also growled at her and bared their teeth. Big teeth. Sharp. Teeth capable of ripping great chunks of flesh and breaking bones. Amy's flesh. Her bones.

Amy began to tremble as she realized there would be no talking nice to the animals before her. Nor would a threat work. She could stomp her feet and yell all she wanted, it would make no difference. If anything, a sudden movement would only anger the dogs, cause them to attack.

Don't be afraid. Don't show fear. Dogs can tell if you're afraid. They can smell your fear. But Amy couldn't help it. She was afraid. Terrified.

She looked around for a place to run, somewhere to hide where she would be safe. Amy knew she couldn't make it back to town, even if she ran her fastest. The dogs would be upon her before she could reach the bridge. They would sink their teeth deep into the back of her legs and drag her down. Eat her all up.

She thought about running for the forest. Maybe she could find a tree to climb, get high enough off the ground to be safe. But even if she could outrun the dogs to the forest, she would still have to find a tree she was able to climb. She'd never make it.

Nowhere to run. No weapons. She could only stand there as the dogs slowly moved toward her, watching as they spread out, working as a team to circle her. Amy wanted to scream, but she had no voice. She wanted to wave her arms, but they were frozen to her sides. She could only watch knowing that death was moments away.

Suddenly, a noise came from behind her—faint but growing louder. It was the clackity, clackity, chug, chug of an engine. The dogs must have heard the noise too, for they paused, frozen in place like a photograph. A painting of terror.

The sound of the engine came closer.

Clackity, clackity, chug, chug.

The glow of headlights appeared in the darkness, piercing the night and cutting through the swirling vapors of fog. The road was suddenly basked in the brilliance of light—sweet, wonderful light that pushed back the night and silenced the growl of the three mongrel dogs. They stood for a moment, confused, perhaps even a little fearful, caught in the piercing brightness of the light. And then with hateful glares they abandoned their prey and fled into the darkness beyond the road.

Amy whispered a short prayer of thanks and stepped to the side of the road as an old farm truck rattled into view, emerging from the fog like something out of the past. The truck's headlights caught her in their brightness and blinded her, freezing her in place like a helpless little fawn. The vehicle slowed to a stop; its engine chugged, coughed and backfired. Someone inside the truck's cab leaned over and rolled down the passenger window. A voice came from the darkness.

"Hey there. You need a ride?"

Amy didn't move, made no attempt to reply. The voice reached out to her again.

"I'm talking to you. Do you need a ride?" A flashlight was switched on, illuminating the interior of the truck. In the dim glow she could see the man behind the voice. He was old and gray-headed, his thin face cracked and wrinkled from years of toiling in the hot sun. Amy thought the man might be a farmer, even though she had never met a real farmer before.

"Make up your mind. I don't have all night," the man called. "You need a ride or not?"

Amy was leery to accept the farmer's offer, her memories of the bald-headed man in St. Louis still fresh in her mind. But if she turned down the ride, she would be alone again . . . alone with the dogs.

"Where are you going?" she asked, finding her voice.

"I'm taking a load of corn to Peoria," came the reply.

Peoria? Amy tried to pinpoint the town of Peoria in her mind. She had seen maps before, even a map of Illinois, but hadn't paid much attention to them.

"Is that near Chicago?" she asked, unable to remember where in Illinois Peoria was, if it was even in Illinois.

The old man whistled in surprise. "Honey, you've got a long walk if you're thinking about going all the way to Chicago. A very long walk. What you going to Chicago for? You lose something?"

Amy nodded. "My mother."

The old man looked at her for a few seconds, then said, "Peoria's about halfway to Chicago, if that's what you want to know. You'll be a lot closer there than where you're standing right now."

Amy thought it over. Halfway to Chicago. She would be almost there. "Okay, I'll ride."

The old man opened the passenger door and motioned for her to climb in. Amy was taking a risk, but she would rather take her chances with a farmer than with the dogs. Besides, her mother needed her.

Climbing up into the cab of the truck, she closed the door behind her. The farmer shifted the gears, the engine coughed twice and they started down the road.

Once inside the truck she turned to look at the old man. He didn't appear dangerous; at least she didn't think he did. He looked more like somebody's grandfather and probably was. As Amy studied the man, she became aware of the smells inside the truck, his smells, farm smells: the deep, earthy aroma of hay and manure, the lingering fragrance of tobacco smoke. She noticed the tips of several cigars protruding from the breast pocket of his overalls. There was also an odor that was like gasoline but different.

"Didn't anyone tell you it's not polite to stare."

Caught off guard, Amy quickly lowered her eyes. "I'm sorry," she said.

"Apology accepted." He laughed. "You got a name, or did you lose that in Chicago too?"

"Amy Ladue," she said, raising her eyes.

"Amy. That's a pretty name," he said. "My name's Roy Fletcher."

"Are you a farmer?"

"Yup. Been a farmer all my life." He pulled a cigar from his breast pocket and lit it with a lighter. A cloud of pungent smoke filled the cab. Amy wrinkled her nose but didn't cough.

"How about you?" he asked. "You a farmer too?"

She shook her head, but then realized that he was watching the road and hadn't seen her. "No. I'm from the city."

"Chicago?"

"St. Louis."

"And your mother lives in Chicago?"

She nodded and then quickly said yes.

"What part of Chicago?"

"I don't know," she answered, suddenly wishing he would change the subject. "I've never been there before."

"But you're going there now? All by yourself?"

"Yes."

Roy turned and looked at her, perhaps wondering if she was telling the truth. Maybe he thought she was lying to him, but she wasn't. Her mother really did live in Chicago. Amy knew it, but she didn't want to explain how she knew. To keep from answering any more questions she changed the subject.

"Are farmers rich?"

He snorted, then laughed. "Rich? That's a good one. No, darling, farmers aren't rich, at least none that I know of."

"But you've got a truck."

"This old thing? Hell, I've had this truck for years. It would have up and died long ago if I didn't spend all my time tinkering with it. When the gas prices went through the roof I fiddled with the engine some, made it where it would run on cornahol."

"Cornahol?" Amy asked.

He puffed his cigar. "That's what I call the stuff; they've probably got other names for it. It's like gasoline only I make it out of corn, sort of like the shine whiskey my grandfather used to make."

"Can you drink cornahol?" Amy asked.

Roy laughed again. A pleasant, healthy laugh. Amy liked the sound of it. "I reckon you could drink it if you wanted to," he replied. "I never do. Anything that will keep this old truck running, and clean grease off my tools, can't be good for you. But maybe I should try some. Maybe it would make me run as fast as this truck. What do you think?"

Amy giggled, picturing the old farmer running down the road, his belly full of cornahol, a cloud of exhaust smoke coming out of his butt. Still smiling, she leaned against the door and stared out the window, watching as the willowy wisps of fog danced past the truck. Outside, the night was chill and spooky; inside the truck everything was warm and cozy. She yawned, listening to the rumble of the truck's engine and Farmer Roy humming a song she didn't know. Before they had gone another mile down the road she was fast asleep.

* * *

She awoke with the sun in her eyes, awakened from a dream by the truck bouncing over a rough patch of road. Amy didn't know where she was at first and this caused her to have a mild anxiety attack. Her heart pounding, she sat up and looked around.

"Sorry if I woke you," Roy said, offering her a smile. "The road's kind of rough through these parts." Amy relaxed a little and smiled back.

"That's okay." She rubbed sleep from her eyes and stared out the windshield. The land was flat and featureless, empty fields dotted with an occasional tree or farmhouse. "Where are we?"

"We're on State Road 100, just north of Beardstown."

That information didn't really tell her anything. Farmer Roy must have read her thoughts, for he added, "We're about halfway to Peoria."

"Oh," Amy said, trying to work the math out in her head. They were halfway to Peoria, and Peoria was halfway to Chicago, which meant that a fourth of her trip was through. Only a fourth? She frowned. Chicago was still a long ways away.

"You want some breakfast?" He tapped the paper sack on the seat beside him. "There's a thermos of coffee in there and some buttermilk biscuits, if you're interested. I made them myself."

Amy passed on the coffee, but she did take one of the biscuits. They were a little stale, but still tasted good. She would have had more than one, but it was kind of hard eating them dry and she didn't like coffee. She had just forced down the last of the biscuit when she noticed a string of small ponds in a field off to the right.

"Oh, look. Fish ponds," she said, pointing out the window. "I wonder what kind of fish they have."

"Dead ones," Roy replied. "Those aren't fish ponds, darling. They're bomb craters."

"Bomb craters?"

He nodded. "Yup. One of the worst battles of the war was fought right here in these fields. Nearly ten thousand soldiers lost their lives in just one week of fighting. Can you imagine that? That's more soldiers than there are people in most of the towns around here."

"What happened?" Amy asked, trying to imagine so many soldiers fighting at the same time.

"Sweetheart, I really don't like talking about it—damn fool thing, war—but since you asked I'll tell you. The fighting started when General Dixon's men seized control of the Mississippi River between Clarksville and Quincy—"

"Who's General Dixon?" Amy interrupted.

"General Wyatt Dixon was the leader of the minority soldiers; they're the ones who wanted to change the government, make it where all people were treated the same—no matter what color their skin was. His army was known as Dixon's Militia. Pretty tough bunch of boys, if you ask me. They had a lot of heart.

"Anyway, the Militia had seized control of the river and they weren't letting anything through. Now this didn't sit too well with the old government. The Mississippi River is an important supply line, always has been, always will be. They didn't like having that supply line closed off, so they sent in several army units to reopen it.

"The first battle took place just south of Hannibal, Missouri, at Lock and Dam No. 22. The government tried to knock out the Militia's positions with air strikes, but the Militia fought back with tanks, rockets and artillery. The battle lasted for thirty-six hours and was one heck of a fight. There were so many explosions going off the night sky looked like the Fourth of July. When the battle was over the Militia still had control of the river."

Roy pulled a new cigar out of his pocket and lit it. "The government wasn't about to give up just because they lost one battle. No ma'am. They figured if the army couldn't get the river back the navy could, so they sent a bunch of warships up the river to fight the Militia."

"What kind of warships?" Amy asked.

"Six Coast Guard cutters and two dozen U.S. Navy river patrol boats. Damnedest thing you'd ever want to see. Kind of funny in a way. Here's all these boats sailing up the river like it was some kind of parade, their decks filled with soldiers."

He laughed. "My neighbors and I went down to the river to watch the ships go by, packed ourselves a picnic lunch and took turns waving at the soldiers. Not that we were for the government, mind you. Truth was most of us didn't care who won the war. We figured once the fighting was over things would be pretty much the same as they were before, no matter which side came out on top. Best not to get in someone else's fight if you can avoid it. Know what I mean?"

Amy nodded.

Roy patted her on the head and continued. "Anyway, it wasn't a secret that the United States Navy was heading up the Mississippi. We knew it. The people upriver knew it too. So did the Militia. They waited until the boats were almost to Clarksville, then floated several hundred barrels of gasoline down the river to meet them. When the barrels reached the boats, the Militia blew them up with explosives—set the river right on fire. The damn thing burned for days."

"They set the soldiers on fire?" Amy asked, horrified.

Roy turned and looked at her. "That's the kind of thing that happens in war. Terrible things. But both sides did stuff like that; it wasn't just the Militia."

"Did all the soldiers on the boats die?"

"A lot did, but not all. Those that didn't get burned up retreated across the river into Illinois, joining up with other units. If the Militia would have let the government soldiers go, things might have turned out different, but they smelled victory and went after them. They chased them all the way to Beardstown. That's where the government soldiers decided to make a stand. They dug in just north of the town and waited for the Militia to catch up with them. While they were waiting, they called in another air strike. The jets caught the Militia out in the open, in these fields you see here, dropping napalm and high-explosive shells on them. Bombs are a lot like bullets, they aren't particular about who they kill. A lot of government soldiers also got blown up by the bombs, so did a lot of innocent civilians.

"I had a nephew who owned a house not too far from here, had himself a pretty wife and a new baby girl. When the fighting broke out he packed up his family and tried to get away, but they never made it. They were killed by some idiot flyboy, with one too many bombs to drop, who couldn't tell the difference between a tank and a pickup truck."

Roy coughed and spit out the window. "Damn fool thing, war. My nephew wasn't even a soldier and didn't want nothing to do with no race war. He was white, like me, but his wife was Chinese. He died because of someone else's hatred. Him and his family are buried out there in one of these fields, but I don't know where. I can't even place flowers on their graves."

He finished talking and an uneasy silence settled over them. Not knowing what else to do, Amy slid next to the old man and placed her hand lightly on his arm. She didn't speak, because she didn't know what to say. Instead she sat there, quietly watching out the window as they drove along. Off to the left, a burned-out tank sat rusting in an empty field. Amy saw that someone had stuck a white cross in the ground in front of the tank, a memorial to the insanity of war.

CHAPTER
25

Leon Cane was tired beyond words, and there was a dull ache in his lower back from too many hours spent riding in a boxcar. He could still feel the swaying and rattling of the train, even though he had gotten off several hours ago. He now sat in a clearing amidst a clump of oak trees, a few hundred feet back from the road, not far from the Illinois River. Just up the road was the town of Bartonville, population 8,962. Beyond that was the city of Peoria.

He had decided to get off at Bartonville rather than ride the train on into Peoria. Larger cities could be dangerous, especially to someone who didn't know their way around. He would rather take his chances in the country. Besides, on the southern outskirts of Bartonville was an open-air farmers' market where produce and vegetables were bought, sold and traded. Luckily, the train had slowed near the market's center because of congestion. When it did Leon abandoned his free ride.

Walking through the market, he had purchased a small onion, three small tomatoes and a large catfish with what little money he had left. The fish and vegetables were now impaled on a stick, slowly roasting over a small fire. Leon leaned forward and turned the fish over. It was almost done. Good thing. He was starving and the smell was driving him crazy.

Talking with some of the locals at the market, he had found out which train to catch to get to Chicago. Unfortunately, he would have to hop the train at a junction just north of Peoria, which meant extra walking. Already exhausted, and with darkness setting in, he had decided to find a place to bed down for the night. The voice in his head still tugged at him, urging him onward, but there was nothing he could do until morning. The mystery lady would just have to wait.

Leon had just leaned back against the tree when he heard the crunch of footsteps on dry leaves. Turning, he discovered he had company.

A little girl watched him from the shadows beneath an elm tree. She was Caucasian, with long auburn hair, and looked to be somewhere around ten or eleven years old. She also looked hungry, appearing to be more interested in Leon's fish than in him. Maybe the aroma of his dinner had drawn her. That worried him. If she had smelled his fish cooking, someone else might too.

The little girl didn't say anything, or make any attempt to come closer. She only watched. Leon didn't say anything either. But when the fish was finished cooking he divided it into two pieces. One half he kept for himself; the other half he placed on a flat rock next to the fire. The girl watched him with interest.

"Your half is getting cold," Leon finally said, glancing up from his meal. The girl stared at him for a minute longer and then slowly approached, her movements reminding him of a timid little squirrel. She picked up the fish, placing two ears of corn on the rock in exchange. Leon looked at the corn and smiled. "Fair trade," he said. The little girl nodded and began to eat her piece of fish.

Neither of them spoke as they ate, each too busy devouring the delicious white meat of the catfish. When they finished with the fish, Leon shared the onion and tomatoes. The little girl accepted the tomato wedges, but passed on the onion. He then spread out the campfire and laid the two ears of corn on the burning embers to roast. Leon also remembered that he had a couple of slightly stale doughnuts in his bag and offered her one. She countered his offer with a loaf of homemade bread wrapped in an old T-shirt.

"Why, this is quite a feast!" Leon said, sniffing the loaf of bread.

"Yes, a feast," she replied, biting into a doughnut.

Leon pulled the butcher knife from his knapsack and saw fear dance into the girl's eyes. She took a step backward. He quickly held up his other hand. "Don't be afraid, I just want to slice a piece of bread . . . if that's okay." She relaxed a little, then nodded.

"It would be bad manners to tear a piece from such a fine-looking loaf," he continued, cutting off a slice of bread. "Would you like a slice?" She shook her head no.

He returned the knife to his knapsack and handed back the loaf. "It's also bad manners to have dinner with someone and not know their name. Names are important," he added, remembering what Red had said to him. "I'm Leon Cane. And you?"

"Amy Ladue," she answered, speaking around a mouthful of doughnut.

"Pleased to meet you, Amy." He tried the bread. "This is wonderful. Did you make it?"

She shook her head. "Sister Rose made it. She's not really my sister, that's just her name. She's a lady I met on the other side of the river."

"The Illinois River?"

Again she shook her head. "The Mississippi."

"The Mississippi? That's quite a ways from here. You walk all the way by yourself?"

"Not all the way. I got a ride with Farmer Roy. He's the one who gave me the corn. I rode on a barge before that."

Leon was surprised. Obviously, he wasn't the only one who had been doing a bit of traveling. He wasn't sure how much of the girl's story could be believed, especially the part about riding the barge, but he had a feeling she was telling him the truth.

"Where are you from?" he asked.

"St. Louis," Amy answered. "I mean that's where I used to live, but I'm going to Chicago to live with my mother."

A flicker of doubt crossed Leon's mind. If Amy had a mother, why would she be traveling alone? No one in their right mind would let their kid travel by themselves, especially nowadays. Despite the fact that her clothing looked fairly clean, he suspected she might be one of the growing number of homeless children forced to make it on their own.

"What about your father?" he asked, daring to delve deeper into the child's personal life.

"He died in the earthquake," she answered. "I thought my mother was dead too, but I found her again. She had namnesia and didn't know who she was."

"Amnesia," Leon corrected.

"Right. Amnesia." Amy nodded. "My mother called me and now I'm going to Chicago to be with her. She has a big house, with a swimming pool. And I'll get to go to school."

Leon was now convinced Amy was making everything up, because he knew all public schools had been closed. Since phone service was also pretty much a thing of the past, there was no way her mother could have called her. Still, he didn't say anything. Who was he to spoil the child's fantasy? If she wanted to pretend that her mother owned a big house in Chicago, then let her. He went along with the story, humoring her with a nod when a nod was needed, allowing Amy to rattle on about her mother, their nice house and the school she would be attending. One thing for sure, she was quite a storyteller.

The two of them talked late into the night, falling asleep near the glowing embers of the fire. They probably should have taken turns standing watch, but Leon felt they were far enough from the road to be reasonably safe. And truthfully he was just too damn tired.

He awoke early the next day, with the morning dew still heavy on the grass and the first rays of sunlight just starting to peek through the trees. Stretching the kinks from his back, he sat up and looked around. The forest was alive with the melody of songbirds greeting the dawn. In the tiny clearing he saw a female cardinal, two blue jays and a robin. He also spotted a pair of rabbits. He thought about how good roast rabbit would taste for breakfast, but only for a moment. He had no way to hunt the rabbits—no gun, no bow, not even a slingshot—and he wasn't about to make a fool out of himself by trying to chase them down.

Turning his attention away from the rabbits, he watched the sleeping form of Amy Ladue. The child lay on her side, facing him, her chest slowly rising and falling. His daughter would have been around the same age had she not died. Maybe even the same size . . .

Stop it. Leon shook his head, pushing back the images that threatened to flood his mind. *Your daughter is dead.* Blinking back tears, he turned his attention back to Amy.

The little girl's presence presented something of a problem. Even though they had just met, she obviously felt safe around him and would probably attempt to latch on to him for protection. Kids were like that. Leon felt sorry for her, but he was in no position to assume the responsibility of looking after a child. Any child. And even though they were both heading to Chicago, he did not want Amy to be with him for fear of endangering her.

Endanger? Was he heading into danger? Most certainly. Though it was silent for now, the voice that called him was from a woman in serious trouble. He too might be in trouble once he reached Chicago.

Leon sat back and thought about the situation. He was almost to Chicago and he didn't even have a plan. He had been so preoccupied with just getting to Chicago that he hadn't even thought about what he would do once he got there. What could he do? He had no gun, no weapon other than a rusty butcher knife. The men who abducted the woman would be armed and extremely dangerous.

You'll probably get yourself killed.

He smiled. Maybe, but he had no choice. He was drawn to the voice as a moth was drawn to a flame. But Amy had a choice. He would not endanger the child. She would just have to find some other adult to latch on to.

Getting to his feet, Leon quietly gathered together his belongings. Amy continued to sleep soundly. She would probably be upset when she awoke later and found him gone, but he was only thinking of her. She would be better off hooking up with someone else, someone safer to be around. Besides, she was not his daughter; therefore, he owed her nothing.

With knapsack in hand, he left the clearing and started walking toward the road. He'd gone only about fifty yards when he stumbled upon two bodies lying in the tall weeds. Leon jumped back, horrified.

"Oh, my God!"

The victims, a young black man and woman, had each been shot once in the forehead at close range. They lay on their backs, their eyes open and glassy, staring sightlessly up at the morning sky. In addition to being shot, they had also been gutted and skinned, like animals, all but their hands, feet, heads and genitalia. Their naked, skinless bodies were pink and bloody, like something fresh from a womb. Swarms of flies crawled over the bodies, feeding off the bloody flesh and laying their eggs in the meat. Sickened by the sight, Leon turned away and threw up.

He had heard about Skinners from others on the street, whispered stories told around late night fires about evil men who hunted and murdered people of color, selling their skin for illegal medical skin grafts. In some cases the internal organs were also taken and sold. Leon had always thought the stories to be mere fantasies, brought on by alcohol, drugs or a primitive urge to create bogeymen where none previously existed, but now he knew otherwise.

Terror blew icy kisses up and down his spine as he thought about how close the Skinners had been to his campsite, perhaps even performing their hideous act while he and Amy slept. He knew the victims had not been murdered here, for the gunshots would have awakened him. But they might have been skinned here, and that was bad enough. The bodies hadn't been there the day before, so it had happened sometime during the night, which meant the Skinners might still be in the area.

Leon's peaceful little campsite didn't seem so peaceful after all. Nor did it seem very safe. Turning away from the bodies, he hurried back to the clearing. He wasn't sure if Skinners hunted anyone other than black people, but he didn't want to take the chance. He could not leave Amy alone, sleeping, with the possibility of such fiends still lurking in the area.

He reached the clearing and slowed down, trying desperately to calm himself. He didn't want to frighten the girl, but it was all he could do not to snatch her up and run screaming into the woods. Taking a deep breath, he leaned over Amy and gently shook her.

"Amy, wake up."

She opened her eyes, seemed confused for a moment, then sat up and looked around.

"Grab your things. We have to leave." He spoke softly, but there was a tremor of fear in his voice that he couldn't disguise.

"Why? What's the matter?" Amy asked, sensing something was wrong. She tensed, looking about the clearing.

"Nothing's wrong," Leon lied. "But if you don't hurry, we'll miss the train to Chicago. You don't want to keep your mother waiting. Do you?"

He had found the magic words. Amy jumped up and quickly gathered her belongings together. Not wanting her to see the mutilated bodies, Leon chose a different path through the woods to the road. Like it or not, once again he had a traveling partner.

CHAPTER
26

Rene Reynolds wanted to go to the police, but she didn't know where to find a police station. Even if she did, they would be of little help. Most police departments operated on strictly a cash-only basis. She had no money to pay them, no identification card to even prove who she was. Driving a stolen car only added to the problem. Instead of being a victim, she would probably be considered a criminal. The police would lock her up until the owner of the car could be located, delivering her back into the hands of Dr. Sinclair or one of his men.

With going to the police out of the question, her only chance for safety lay in putting as much distance as possible between Dr. Sinclair and herself. She drove through the empty boulevards of Chicago, past run-down tenement buildings and deserted office complexes, choosing streets entirely at random, constantly checking the rearview mirror to see if anyone was following. So far, no one was.

She was completely and utterly lost, trapped in a city she did not know, traveling down avenues that were both dark and dangerous. She passed the same park twice, and the same abandoned brewery three times. On a narrow, one-way street she had been chased by four club-wielding men who sprang at her from darkened doorways. They had shouted obscenities and threats of violence as she sped away to safety.

After nearly two hours of panicked driving, she reached the outskirts of the city. She headed west, following a deserted, nameless highway, careful of the enormous potholes, which suddenly appeared out of the darkness and threatened to swallow her car. An hour later she turned south on a narrow two-lane blacktop road, speeding along between open fields and patches of deciduous forest.

It was just before dawn when the car's temperature gauge began to climb into the red. She ignored it and kept going. Thirty minutes later the engine seized up and died. The car coasted to a stop.

"Damn . . . Damn . . . Damn!" Rene slapped the steering wheel in frustration. She turned off the ignition, then tried to start the car again. The engine growled but would not turn over.

Angry, she got out and walked around to the front of the vehicle. A cloud of steam rose from the engine; the air was filled with a choking chemical smell. In the pale light of the coming day she could clearly see the two bullet holes in the car's grille. The man who had shot at Rene in the garage had missed her but killed the radiator.

Tears of anger and frustration filled her eyes. She wiped them away with clenched fists and stood trembling in the center of the road. She was in the middle of nowhere, broke, without food, water or transportation, a thousand miles from home, hunted by a crazed maniac of a doctor. Things couldn't possibly get any worse.

But as she stood there, Rene suddenly remembered a phrase her father had been fond of saying: *things are always darkest before the dawn.* Just thinking of that phrase, thinking of her father, helped to lift her spirit and calm her anger. He was right. Instead of looking at everything in the negative, she should be seeing the positive side of things. She was stuck in the middle of nowhere, true, but it was better than being stuck in a jail cell. She had escaped from Dr. Sinclair, even if it meant leaving behind the Neuro-Enhancer. She had no money, again true, but neither did a lot of people and they survived. Maybe she could find help somewhere, at a farmhouse perhaps. At least she had gotten out of Chicago. And if Rene didn't know where she was, neither did Randall Sinclair.

Knowing that Sinclair's men would recognize the car, she decided to abandon the vehicle and start walking. Rene had gone only a mile or so down the road when she heard the sound of an approaching vehicle. Turning around, she saw a blue and white cargo truck coming down the road. The truck was a government transport, probably hauling goods and supplies from one city to the next. She couldn't imagine what it was doing out in the middle of farm country. Maybe the driver was taking a shortcut.

Danger!

The warning shot through her mind like a rocket. She spun around expecting to see someone sneaking up on her, but no one was there. The fields beyond the road were also empty. It was just her and the—

The truck! She turned back around. The cargo truck was less than a quarter mile away, bearing down on her.

Danger . . . danger . . . danger.

The warning echoed through her head like a jackhammer. She took a step backward. The truck began to slow.

Why was it stopping? Government drivers didn't pick up hitchhikers. It wasn't safe. Too many robbers used women and children as a ploy to get a driver to stop. Even Rene knew that. So why was the driver stopping?

Danger. Danger. Danger.

Rene stepped off the road and down into the ditch. The truck slowed to a stop, bringing with it a wave of black terror so strong it was almost a physical blow. The feeling engulfed her, turned her legs to jelly and froze her bowels.

She stood, transfixed, staring at the vehicle's dirt-smeared windshield. Inside the truck's cab sat three Caucasian men; dirty, rough-looking men. They were not soldiers, wore no uniforms of any kind, so they couldn't be government drivers. The truck must have been stolen, or else it had been painted to look like a government transport. The three men stared at her, their eyes keen with interest.

DANGER!

The wind suddenly shifted, blowing from the direction of the truck, carrying with it a foul, sickly-sweet odor. The stench of something dead.

Rene coughed. For a brief instant she wondered if the driver of the truck had hit an animal on the road—a dog, or maybe a cow—but then she heard a moan of agony so terrifying it caused the tiny hairs on the back of her neck to stand straight up. It was not the cry of an animal. Neither dog, cat nor wounded beast could produce such an unholy wail. The cry was human, and it came from inside the trailer.

"Dear God," she gasped, horrified by the sound she heard, realizing that the smell of death that clung to the truck also came from the trailer. She had just made the connection when the driver of the truck favored her with an evil smile, and pointed the barrel of a rifle in her direction.

DANGER . . . DANGER . . . DANGER . . . RUN!

Rene turned and fled, scrambling up the ditch and into the field beyond. She expected to hear a gunshot, knew the driver was going to shoot her, but didn't care. Better to be shot in the back than face the nameless horror lurking within the darkness of the trailer. But instead of a gunshot, she heard the sound of a door opening. Throwing a glance behind her, she saw two men scramble out of the truck's cab and run across the road after her.

No. No. Please, not again.

She raced across the empty field, her footsteps kicking up dirt and crunching the stubs of last year's corn stalks. Elbows pumping, Rene ran like a frightened rabbit escaping the jaws of a hungry hound. Had there been someplace to hide she would have done so, but the field was flat and empty like much of the countryside in Illinois. She could only run and hope that the two men who chased her would soon tire.

She would also tire, but not before the men. Fear gave her the energy to sprint across the field at heart-bursting speed. She was smaller, faster, could easily outrun them. If she did not trip, stumble or fall, she would get away.

Her hope of escape was dashed, however, by the crack of a gunshot. A small puff of dirt sprang from the ground in front of her. Two more shots, two more puffs of dirt. Rene again glanced behind her. Neither of the men chasing her carried guns; it was obviously the driver who was doing the shooting.

Another shot rang out. Rene veered to the right, and then back to the left, trying to present a difficult target to hit. Left, right, then left again, never straight, always changing directions. Two more bullets struck the field ahead of her and kicked up dirt, but none hit her.

Running in a serpentine pattern was costing Rene her lead. If she continued to weave back and forth the two men would overtake her. But she had no choice. If she ran in a straight line she risked being shot. Or did she? A thought crossed her mind.

She had been running straight when the driver first shot at her, yet he missed. The field was wide open; there were no trees in the way. She should have been an easy target. Come to think of it, all the shots had landed in front of her.

Oh, God. No.

She had been so stupid. The driver wasn't trying to hit her; he had missed on purpose. He was only trying to slow her down. They wanted to take her alive.

But why? Who were these men? What did they want with her? There could be only one answer: they were Randall

Sinclair's men. Their orders must be to find her and bring her back, unharmed if possible.

But what about the moan she had heard, and the smell of death that clung to the truck? These couldn't be Sinclair's men. They had to be something far more sinister than the doctor's hired thugs. And far more dangerous.

Rene's troubled thoughts spurred her to even greater speed. No longer worried about being shot, she ran in a straight line again, desperately trying to regain the lead she had lost. But the extra running had sapped her energy. She was tired; her legs felt like lead. A painful stitch had also developed in her side, making each step sheer agony. She tried to swallow, but her mouth was too dry to form saliva.

At the far end of the field stood a small grove of oak trees. If she could reach the trees, she might find someplace to hide. Hope surged through her, for she was almost there. But that hope flickered and died moments later when she spotted the dark scar of a fence stretching across the field.

An old three-strand barbed-wire fence separated the field from the woods. The fence had probably been put up by a farmer to keep cattle from wandering out of the pasture, or to keep deer and other wild animals out of the crops. That same fence now prevented Rene from reaching the safety of the trees.

There would be no time to crawl under the fence or climb over it. In the few seconds it took to do either the two men would catch up with her. So instead of trying to get through the fence, Rene suddenly turned right and ran parallel to it, desperately seeking an opening or break in the wire.

The men who chased her must have anticipated such a move, for one of them turned before she did in an attempt to cut her off. Rene could not outrun the man, nor could she stop or change directions since his partner was still behind her. That left only one avenue of escape still open.

She ran straight for a few more feet then turned left, racing toward the fence. Rene dove at the fence, attempting to crawl beneath the bottom strand of barbed wire. She was halfway under the fence when she heard crashing footsteps and someone grabbed her legs.

Rene kicked and struggled, dug her fingers into the dirt and tried to crawl beneath the strands of barbed wire. She slipped free, only to be grabbed again and pulled back beneath the fence. She cried out in pain as a barb on the bottom strand of wire tore her shirt and ripped a bloody furrow down the center of her back.

She came up swinging, striking one of her attackers in the face. Jumping to her feet, Rene tried to pull the stun gun from her belt but was tackled to the ground.

"What have I done? Let me go! Leave me alone!" Her cries fell on deaf ears. The men pushed her face into the dirt and forced her arms behind her back, fastening them in place with a thick plastic tie.

Rene lay on the ground, gasping for breath. She wanted to close her eyes and make the world go away, but the men wouldn't let her. They grabbed Rene by the arms and dragged her to her feet, marching her back across the field in the direction of the truck.

She moved in a white-hot haze of pain. Overheated from running, her body felt like a blazing furnace. Sweat poured down her face and rolled into her eyes, blinding her, ran salty and stinging into the cut on her back. The muscles in her legs quivered with fatigue, her feet stumbling as she was dragged along.

Rene turned her head and looked at the men who held her, wondering what evil they had in store for her. The men were dressed alike, each wearing combat boots and white coveralls that were splattered with what looked like dried blood. Heavy leather belts encircled their waists, from which hung large, curved hunting knives. The handles of the knives, as well as their sheaths, were also stained with crimson splotches.

They arrived back at the truck, the driver waiting with rifle in hand. Rene voiced a plea for water, but her request was ignored. Instead the driver trained his rifle on her as the other two men searched her, confiscating the stun gun and pocket-knife. She was then dragged around to the back of the truck and forced to kneel while one of the men opened up the trailer's double doors.

Shaken from the ordeal, and about to pass out from heat exhaustion, she was staring at the ground when the trailer's doors were unlocked and opened. Her thoughts as unfocused as her gaze, Rene didn't look up until she heard a moan of pain similar to the one heard before. She looked up—and screamed.

Inside the narrow trailer were at least sixty men, women and children—all African-American—packed together so tightly there was barely enough room to sit down, let alone move around. There was no air-conditioning in the trailer, no windows or vents of any kind. The air that spilled out when the doors were opened was stifling hot and reeked with the odors of urine, vomit and death.

Rene screamed again as the two men hauled her to her feet. She tried to fight back, but she no longer had the strength to resist and could only groan in despair as she was bodily lifted aboard the trailer and forced to sit with her back against a large wooden crate. An iron manacle was clamped around her left ankle. A length of chain fastened the manacle to an iron ring on the trailer's wall. She turned her head and saw other rings, other chains, hundreds of them.

Rene stared in disbelief at the manacle fastened around her ankle. She was a prisoner again, and this time there would be no escaping. She wanted to scream, wanted to attack the men who stole her freedom, but she was unable to gather the strength needed to mount such an assault. Her body, weak from physical exertion and fright, refused to obey even her simplest commands. She could only sit there and watch as the ring of iron snapped in place, feeling a numbing cold seep slowly into her back.

Cold? It was definitely not cold in the trailer. Rivulets of sweat poured down her face as testimony to the stifling heat.

Not only was there no air-conditioning, but there were no fans, not even a window.

But Rene still felt a chill. It came from the wooden crate her back rested against, a crate that was refreshingly cool in the unbearable heat of the trailer. Curious, she turned her head and looked into the crate, seeking the source of the coldness. What she saw chilled her, all right—chilled her to the bone.

Inside the crate were steaming blocks of sterile ice and layer upon layer of human skin, black and bloody, carefully peeled from the body of some poor victim. Resting on top of the skin was a small plastic container filled with blood. Floating in the blood were two human livers and a kidney.

Rene stared at the contents of the crate and then at the bloody clothing and knives of the two white men, her mind reeling with horror as she realized what they were.

Skinners! Dear God, they're Skinners!

Climbing down out of the trailer, the Skinners stepped back and slammed the doors closed, casting Dr. Rene Reynolds into the darkness of hell.

CHAPTER
27

He could find no joy in the beauty of the summer afternoon. The blue sky and fields of wildflowers did little to comfort him. Earlier in the day, Leon Cane had discovered the murdered bodies of a man and woman—murdered and skinned. Since then an uneasiness had settled deep in the pit of his stomach, steadily growing until it gnawed at him like a hungry rat. It was almost as if a feeling of dread was carried upon the wind. A feeling thick enough to taste.

Amy must have felt something too. She stuck close by his side as they walked down the center of the road, practically clinging to him. She hadn't seen the bodies, so maybe she was only being affected by his nervousness. Leon had once read that children were more sensitive to things than adults, often able to pick up feelings and emotions from their surroundings. If so, then what she was picking up made her afraid.

They had just rounded a curve in the road when he heard the sound of an approaching vehicle. The sound came from behind them, the heavy roar of a truck engine. Leon couldn't see the truck because of the curve, but he didn't have to see it to be afraid of it. It was almost as if a wave of pure terror preceded the vehicle. For some strange reason, he knew that danger was coming their way.

Leon looked around, searching for a place to hide. The truck was almost upon them. Any second it would come around the curve. Visions of ebony black death machines driven by laughing skeletons flooded his mind. He turned and spotted the weed-filled ditch that ran along the opposite side of the road.

"Hurry!" he yelled, grabbing Amy's hand and pulling her across the road and down into the ditch. The sound of the truck was louder, closer.

Amy must have known what he wanted, for she dove into the ditch and burrowed beneath the weeds like a rabbit. Leon did the same, flattening himself out the best he could, peeking through the tall weeds at the road.

The truck appeared, a dark blue cargo truck with bold white lettering. A government transport. Leon caught a glimpse of the man driving the truck and felt the evil that enveloped the vehicle. Then he felt something else.

As the truck zoomed past, Leon knew she was inside it, the woman whose voice he heard—the woman from the alley. Her terror was like a physical blow and he nearly cried out from the force of it. Instead it was Amy who screamed.

"Mother!"

Amy started to jump up, but Leon grabbed her legs and dragged her back down.

"Let me go!" she yelled, kicking to get free. Her foot struck him in the mouth. He tasted blood but held on. Only when the cargo truck was nothing more than a receding dot in the distance did he let go. Amy scrambled out of the ditch and ran to the middle of the road.

"Mother! Wait!" she yelled.

Leon jumped up and chased after the little girl. He grabbed her by the shoulders and spun her around. "Amy, what's wrong?"

She tried to tear free of his grasp. "My mother's in that truck."

"Your mother?" Leon asked, remembering what she had told him the previous night.

Amy nodded.

"How do you know she's in the truck?" he asked.

"She called me," Amy said. "I heard her."

Could it be possible they both heard the same voice? He kneeled down in front of Amy, speaking to her softly. "How did your mother call you?"

She looked at him, but didn't answer.

He tried again. "Sweetheart, this is important. I want to help. How did your mother call you?"

"You won't believe me."

"Yes I will."

Amy touched her forehead. "In here. My mother talks to me here."

Leon was stunned. He wasn't the only one who heard the voice of the mystery woman. Amy also heard the voice, only she believed it to be her mother who called. He wanted to question the child further, to find out what the voice said to her, but there wasn't time. If they both heard the voice, then the woman must surely be in the truck that had just passed. She was also in danger. He turned and looked down the road. The cargo truck had disappeared, but a black pickup was coming from the opposite direction.

"Amy, listen to me," he said. "Do you want to help your mother?"

She nodded.

"Good, then I want you to do exactly as I tell you."

He instructed her to sit by the side of the road, with head lowered, while he tried to flag down the oncoming pickup. Stepping to the center of the road, Leon waved his arms and pointed at Amy. The driver started to swerve around him, then spotted the little girl and stopped. Through the dirty windshield,

Leon could see that the driver was a young, dark-skinned man, probably Hispanic or Filipino. With him was an old man with long gray hair. An Indian.

"Can you help us?" Leon asked, stepping up to the passenger window. "My little girl is bad off."

The driver looked at him suspiciously. "Your little girl?"

"She is now. Her father's dead. I promised him before he died that I would take care of her."

"What's wrong with her?" asked the driver.

"I don't know. She's got a bad fever. Please, I need to get her to a doctor." As he spoke, Leon spotted an assortment of pistols lying on the seat between the two men. He also saw a revolver sticking out of the old Indian's belt. His mouth went dry.

Leon's plan had been to get the two men to step out of the truck, then pull his knife and rob them of their vehicle. But with the guns that plan was now out of the question. Unsure of what else to do, he kept talking.

"Yeah, she's real sick. She can't keep anything down, been throwing up for two days now. I think she's dying."

A look of concern crossed the driver's face.

Good. Good. Keep talking.

But the old Indian didn't seem to be buying the story. He stared at Leon, a slight smile touching the corners of his mouth.

He knows I'm lying.

"Maybe you could take a look at her," Leon continued, stalling for time, trying desperately to come up with a plan. "I don't know what to do."

The driver opened his door and started to climb out of the truck, but his companion laid a hand on his arm and stopped him.

"The girl is not sick," said the Indian.

Leon felt his stomach tighten. "What do you mean not sick? Of course she's sick. Real sick, maybe even dying. Go see for yourself."

The old man studied him for a moment, glanced at Amy, and then turned his head and looked back down the road. It was the break Leon was hoping for. Before either of them could react, he reached in through the open window and snatched the revolver from the Indian's belt.

"Put your hands up," Leon ordered, stepping back from the truck. The men hesitated until he cocked the revolver's hammer. "I just want your truck. Keep your hands where I can see them and nobody will get hurt.

"Okay, old man, climb out of there and walk around to the back of the pickup." The Indian did as he was told. Leon pointed the revolver at the driver. "Now you."

The young driver climbed out of the truck, livid with anger. "I can't believe this is happening!" he yelled. "Hijacked twice in one trip—and with the same damn gun! I'll get fired for sure." He turned and glared at the Indian. "This is all your fault; I never should have given you a ride. I suppose he also wants to go to Chicago to rescue the White Buffalo Woman. I guess he hears voices too."

Leon's mouth dropped open in surprise. *Voices? Chicago?*

Ignoring the complaints of his companion, the old Indian continued to stare down the road. He finally turned around and looked at the driver, and then at Leon.

"He hears the voice," the Indian said. "And so does the little girl. But the White Buffalo Woman is no longer in Chicago; she is in the truck we just passed."

Leon was shocked. "You hear a woman's voice too?"

The old man nodded. "It is the voice of the White Buffalo Woman. She has come here to save us. But we can talk of these things while we drive"—he smiled—"if you don't shoot us first."

Leon stared at the old Indian for a moment longer, then slowly uncocked the pistol and handed it back. He wasn't sure why, but he felt he could trust the man. Maybe it was because he also heard the voice.

"I'm sorry," Leon said. "I was desperate."

"I would have done the same," replied the Indian. "Let's go."

Leon called Amy and the four of them squeezed into the pickup truck. Once they were in, the driver turned the pickup around and chased after the cargo truck.

As they sped down the road, each of them explained their side of the story. The old Indian's name was Jacob Fire Cloud; he was a Lakota medicine man. He had come all the way from South Dakota, following what he claimed to be the voice of the White Buffalo Woman—a sacred prophet of the Indian people, or something like that. Jacob said that the Buffalo Woman had been reincarnated to stop the third shaking from happening. As Leon understood it, this Great Shaking was some kind of Armageddon.

Amy still insisted it was her mother she heard. But as the men continued to talk about the voice, she grew strangely quiet. And when Leon asked her if she ever saw a face with the voice, she refused to answer. He suspected she was having doubts about whose voice it really was, but he didn't want to push the issue.

Of the four of them only Danny Santos did not hear the voice, which was probably a good thing. While the others urged him to drive faster, anxious to catch up with the cargo truck, Danny used his wits and stuck to a safe speed limit. Realizing that something pretty amazing was going on, he quit complaining about being hijacked and focused his attention on figuring out the phenomenon.

"I understand why Jacob might be picking up this woman's thoughts," Danny said, slowing to take a curve. "Indians are all the time meditating, going on vision quests, things like that. Strange voices are a part of their culture. But why do the rest of you hear her and I don't?"

Leon tapped the computer disks in his shirt pocket. "I think I hear her because she physically touched me. Amy probably hears her because she's young. Experts say children are often more sensitive to things than adults."

Jacob nodded in agreement and patted Amy on the head. "Little ones can see and hear things their elders cannot."

"If that's true there might be hundreds of kids who hear the voice," Danny said.

That was something to think about. If Amy heard the woman's voice, how many others also heard it? There could be hundreds, maybe even thousands. Leon turned and looked out the window, almost expecting to see an army of children marching across the countryside, following the voice of an invisible Pied Piper.

Even though Leon was convinced they all heard the same voice, he still couldn't figure out how the woman got into their heads. Was she an Indian goddess, as Jacob claimed, someone with superhuman powers, or just the mother of a lonely little girl? Unfortunately, all arguments and theories would have to wait; they had finally caught up with the cargo truck.

"Slow down!" Leon warned, leaning forward in his seat.

Danny eased off the accelerator. "Speed up. Slow down. Make up your mind."

"He's right," Jacob agreed. "There is danger here. It is best to stay back and not be seen." Danny dropped back, keeping the truck in sight but trying not to appear as if they were chasing it.

They followed the truck for several hours, eventually crossing the Mississippi River into Iowa. Just across the border, the truck turned into a long driveway, which led up to what looked like a sizeable farming operation. But as the pickup drove closer, they could tell this was no ordinary farm. For one thing there was no equipment to be seen, or livestock of any kind. And the half-dozen large white buildings that sat on the property were surrounded by a tall cyclone fence topped with razor wire. In addition to the fence, they spotted several armed men patrolling the grounds.

Danny drove past the farm and turned off onto a narrow gravel lane. He brought the truck to a stop in the shade of an oak tree and switched off the engine. "Doesn't look like a farm to me," he said.

Leon nodded. "Looks more like a prison."

"Now what?"

Leon sat and stared out the window. The cargo truck had disappeared behind one of the buildings, so he focused his attention on the fence and the guards. He counted close to a dozen armed men moving about the property. No telling how many more were inside the buildings. A dozen guards, maybe more. No way he could sneak past them and locate his mystery woman, at least not in the daytime.

"Well?" Danny asked.

"We wait until dark, and then I'll try to sneak in there," Leon said.

Danny looked at him with genuine surprise. "Are you out of your mind? You'll get yourself killed for sure. I don't know what that place is, but it sure isn't a farm. You get caught sneaking in there and they'll be serving your balls for dinner."

"I didn't come all the way from Atlanta just to give up now," Leon replied.

"I didn't say give up," Danny argued. "But it's suicide going in there alone. Wait until we can come up with a better plan, or get some help."

"There isn't time to wait!" Leon jabbed a finger against his forehead. "You don't hear the woman's voice, so you don't know what kind of danger she's in. But I hear her voice; it's like a scream of pain. Her time is running out. If we wait too long she could die."

"If you don't wait, then you could die," Danny said.

Leon turned to face the young man. "I died a long time ago, my friend. A very long time ago. I have nothing to lose."

Danny shook his head. "I don't understand."

He took a deep breath. "Two people I loved very much were killed because of something I did, something I said. When they died part of me also died—the part that makes me a man, makes life worth living. Two people died because of something I did; I will not allow this woman to die because of something I didn't do."

Leon leaned forward and picked up the .45 automatic that was lying on the truck's floorboard. "You mind if I borrow this?"

"Won't do you much good." Danny nodded toward Jacob Fire Cloud. "The old man took the bullets out."

Leon turned and looked at Jacob. "You really did hijack him, didn't you?"

Jacob smiled and dug into his pants pockets, fishing out a handful of bullets. He sorted out the .45 cartridges and gave them to Leon. "I will go with you."

"Oh, no you won't," Leon said, loading the pistol.

"But it is the White Buffalo Woman. I must go."

Leon understood Jacob's desire to accompany him, but one person had a much better chance than two of slipping in unnoticed. Armed guards meant serious business. Leon would be signing his own death warrant if he got caught. He could not allow the old Indian to do the same.

"Listen, if she's in there I'll find her. I promise," Leon said. "But I have to go alone."

Jacob looked at him for a moment, then nodded. He reached beneath his shirt and pulled out a necklace, slipping it off over his head. The necklace was a simple leather cord, adorned with turquoise beads and a bear claw. He handed the necklace to Leon.

"The bear is strong medicine," Jacob said. "He will keep you safe."

Leon accepted the necklace, slipping it over his head. He didn't really believe in Jacob's magic, but he was willing to accept any help offered, spiritual or otherwise. Slipping the pistol into his belt, he climbed out of the pickup. The others followed.

Danny had chosen a good place to park. They were far enough away from the farm that it was doubtful anyone would spot them, not unless someone just happened to be looking their way with a pair of binoculars. As an added precaution they stayed in the shadows beneath the oak tree, sitting quietly as they waited for the arrival of darkness.

Jacob Fire Cloud sat by himself, chewing on the end of his unlit pipe, while Danny kept Amy occupied by telling her fairy tales and playing games of tic-tac-toe with her in the dirt. Leon watched them as they played, amused at how quickly they had taken to each other, relieved that there was now someone who could look after the little girl in case something happened to him. It was one fewer thing for his mind to be troubled with.

Sitting with his back against the pickup's right rear tire, Leon thought about what dangers lay ahead for him. For the others the hours seemed to pass by slowly, but for Leon the night came much too fast.

28

Every second was an eternity of mind-numbing horror, every moment an endless nightmare. Cast into the steamy hot darkness, Rene Reynolds gasped for air, struggling against the nausea that racked her body, fighting to keep from vomiting. With every breath she took her nose filled with the wretched stench of death and sickness. The odor plugged her nostrils and sent wet tentacles slithering down her throat, twisting her guts into tiny knots. She had gotten sick, drenching her clothing with the curdled contents of her stomach, adding to her misery and the foul odors that choked the air.

And in the inky depths of darkness and despair, she had prayed for death to come take her life. But no winged messenger of the apocalypse came to answer her beckoning call. No angel of mercy, with grinning skull and sharpened sickle, appeared to end her suffering. Even death would not set foot in such a miserable place as that which existed in the back of the cargo truck. So Rene was doomed to linger among the living, aware of every sway of the truck, each tiny bump in the road, and the continuous passage of time. Slowly. Slowly. Almost stopped. Tick-tock. Tick-tock.

Overcome by sickness, stifling heat and the hopelessness of her situation, she felt barely alive when the truck slowed and finally came to a screeching stop. A few minutes later the doors opened and fresh air rushed in.

Air, blessed air, cool and sweet, breath of the gods. The air washed over her, smothering the fire in her skin and reviving her. Rene breathed deeply, filling her lungs with the first clean breath she had taken for hours. Voices reached her ears, pushing through the fogginess that clouded her mind, pushing back the darkness. She raised her head and looked around.

She was on a farm. What farm and where she could not say, but a farm nonetheless. Rene saw several large livestock buildings, and a tall grain silo that rose above the ground like a giant penis. Beyond the buildings, open fields stretched as far as she could see.

Those golden fields were unreachable, however, for separating them from the farm was a cyclone fence topped with razor wire. Inside the fence walked men armed with automatic weapons. Several more armed men stood at the back of the truck, staring at her. Rene saw no warmth in any of their eyes, only the cold, uncaring gaze of a guard.

The armed men watched, weapons at the ready, as the driver of the truck climbed into the trailer and began removing the manacles of the prisoners. Since Rene was the closest to the door, her shackles were removed first. The plastic tie binding her wrists together was also cut. She was told to jump down out of the trailer, but the long time spent in a cramped position had taken its toll on her. She could not feel her legs, and when she tried to jump down she fell sprawling to the ground.

Rene wanted only to lie there until the circulation returned to her legs, but she was grabbed by the arms and yanked to her feet. Staggering, about to fall, she was led away from the truck and made to stand, waiting while the other prisoners were unloaded. Once everyone was out of the trailer, they were forced to huddle in a group while several men rinsed them off with garden hoses. Rene welcomed the crude shower, washing the vomit from her clothes and drinking as much water as she could catch in her hands and mouth.

Once clean, they were marched several hundred yards to one of the large livestock buildings. No one spoke during the march; everyone was much too afraid to say anything. Even Rene was at a complete loss for words.

They entered the building through a door on the end, the harsh brightness of the afternoon replaced by a dark and gloomy interior. Her eyes adjusting to the sudden change in lighting, Rene was horrified to see that the building was already occupied by dozens of African-American prisoners. They lined the two longest walls, their legs shackled to the wall by short lengths of chain. Dressed in the tattered remnants of filthy clothing, they sat around, or slept, on a dirt floor covered with a thin layer of moldy straw.

None of those already imprisoned in the building showed any interest in the new arrivals. Most didn't even bother to look up as Rene and the others were led past them to an empty place along the wall, an area obviously left open for new prisoners.

Prodded and threatened by the guards, they were ordered to sit against the wall while iron manacles were fastened around their right ankles. Rene would have asked to use the bathroom, just to keep from being chained up again, but she spotted several metal buckets stationed at strategic intervals along the wall and knew that's what they were used for.

The guards left after chaining them, only to return a few minutes later carrying wooden trays loaded with bowls of food and cups of water. The bowls contained an almost flavorless, porridge-like substance. While it may not have been much in the way of taste, it was probably very high in calories judging by the obesity of some of the other prisoners.

Oh, my God.

Rene jammed a fist against her mouth to keep from gagging as she realized why such a high-calorie food would be on the menu in their prison camp. Fat people meant more skin, and more skin meant more money. The Skinners were deliberately fattening up the prisoners, like cattle before a slaughter.

Determined not to gain an ounce if she could help it, Rene decided to eat only a small portion of the porridge, just enough to keep up her strength. But in addition to being bland and flavorless, the porridge also left a bitter aftertaste in her mouth. Suspecting the food might be drugged, she waited for the guards to look the other way and then quickly dug a hole in the ground and buried her serving. Less than an hour later, Rene's suspicions proved correct when her fellow prisoners slipped into a catatonic state.

Knowing the guards would force-feed her if they found out she had not eaten the porridge, Rene pretended to be drugged too. She sat with her back against the wall and stared off into the space, observing the coming and going of the guards out the corner of her eye. Only when she was certain no one was watching did she allow herself to look around.

Later that afternoon, her act almost unraveled when three men entered the building. Two of the men she had never seen before, but the third looked familiar. Rene nearly cried out in surprise when she recognized the third man as Dr. Randall Sinclair.

Dressed in blue jeans and a dark green shirt, Dr. Sinclair walked down the center of the building, looking over the prisoners. Rene barely had time to slump and let her face drop into her hands before he looked in her direction. Her heart thudding madly in her chest, she held her breath and prayed she had not been recognized. She breathed a sigh of relief when the doctor walked on past.

Dr. Sinclair was already to the other end of the building, and about to go back outside, when she spotted a padded gray case tucked beneath his left arm. Her case. Inside was the Neuro-Enhancer.

Rene was in shock, stunned. Dr. Sinclair's presence could only mean he was involved in the Skinners' operation. Maybe this was the place where he obtained the materials for his numerous skin grafts. Then again, maybe he was running the farm. Either way, he was here and he had brought the Enhancer.

She glanced around. There were no guards in the building, though one might show up at any moment. Knowing she was putting herself at risk, Rene stood up and faced the wall. Above her was a small window, gray and grimy with years of accumulated dust. Standing on her tiptoes, she wiped a corner of the glass clean and peered out the window.

At first she didn't see anything, only two of the other anonymous white buildings. Her heart sank. Dr. Sinclair must have gone the other way. But then he came into view. He was alone now, heading for the closest building. Rene watched as he entered the building; she was still watching when he came back out a few seconds later. When Randall Sinclair reemerged from the building he no longer carried the Neuro-Enhancer.

He left the Enhancer inside.

Hoped surged through her. The Neuro-Enhancer was in the very next building. So close, yet impossibly far. If she could only get free, she could grab the Enhancer and get away. If all else failed, she would destroy the device so Dr. Sinclair could not have it.

Rene was so wrapped up in her thoughts that she almost didn't hear the door open. As it was, she barely had time to drop back down into a sitting position as a guard entered the building. With the guard came the realization of just how hopeless her situation really was. She was a prisoner, chained to a wall like an animal. There was no way she could get loose or get to the Neuro-Enhancer, no chance of getting free.

Rene started to cry. Freedom: the word meant so much to those who didn't have it.

29

D arkness came on leathery wings, draping the night sky in ebony velvet, filling the air with the cries of crickets and frogs. There was no moon; the only light came from the twinkling of a million stars. Beneath those stars Leon Cane made his way cautiously across an open field. Armed with only a .45 automatic, he moved like a shadow, a ghost in the night, silent in his passing. Reaching the razor-wire fence, he paused to study the farm beyond.

Here there were lights, set on poles and fastened to the sides of buildings, places where he could easily be seen. There were also guards. Not nearly as many as he had seen earlier in the day, but guards nonetheless. He counted four, but knew there were probably more. Kneeling in the darkness, Leon watched the guards until he became familiar with their movements and then focused his attention on the six livestock buildings.

Four of the barnlike structures lay in darkness. Lights burned in the other two. The woman he sought would proba-bly be in one of the darkened buildings, but which one? There was no way of telling without searching each and every one of them. Maybe he would get lucky and find her in the first one he checked. Maybe not. If only there was some way to narrow down the search a little. He smiled. Perhaps there was.

He had come all the way from Atlanta, drawn to a woman he did not know, following a voice that he could not explain. Though the voice was now silent, he still felt a tingling in the very fibers of his being, like the caress of invisible fingers along the inside of his spine. He could still feel her.

But where?

Leon focused his attention on the closest of the buildings, but felt nothing to make him believe she was in that one. He studied the second building. Again nothing. He concentrated on the third livestock building for a minute and was about to pass over it when something touched him. Call it a feeling, a hunch, the voice of his consciousness, whatever, he was certain the woman he sought was somewhere inside the third building.

Now that he found the woman there was still the problem of getting to her. Could he make it past the guards without getting caught? He didn't want to think about what would happen to him if he was discovered; it was not a pretty picture. And what if the building was locked, or if there were alarms? Leon forced such thoughts from his head, for they brought the metallic taste of fear to his mouth. He was scared enough as it was.

Waiting until the area was temporarily free of guards, Leon moved closer to the fence. A quick check for transformers and insulators turned up negative. The fence was not electrified, but it was topped with three strands of razor wire, which would rip him to shreds if he attempted to climb over it. Even if he wore protective clothing, which he didn't, there was still the danger of being seen as he climbed the fence. Such an unwelcome intrusion would probably be greeted with a hail of gunfire. So if he couldn't climb over the fence, he would have to crawl under it.

Leon moved along the fence until he found a natural depression in the ground. He looked to be sure no guards were in the area, and then tore away the weeds and began digging handfuls of dirt from under the bottom of the fence. Luckily, the ground was soft from years of farming so it took only a few minutes to scoop a hole large enough to squeeze beneath the fence. Checking again for guards, he crawled under.

Once under the fence, he ran for the closest of the white buildings, hiding in the deep shadows along an unlit wall. His heart pounding in fear, his mouth dry, Leon waited for sirens or alarm bells to sound. None did; he had not been seen.

Breathing a sigh of relief, he crept along the wall to the corner. He was about to peek around the building when footsteps alerted him that someone was coming. He barely had time to press himself flat against the side of the building as a guard walked past. Had the guard looked to his right he would have spotted Leon, for he was half in and half out of the shadows. But the man was more interested in the cigarette he smoked than any intruder, never once turning his head to either side as he walked away. Leon waited until the guard passed by, then slipped around the corner to the other side of the building.

From the first building he ran to the second, again hiding in the shadows until he was certain that the coast was clear. Even with no guards in sight Leon was reluctant to leave the shadows of the second building, for the area between the second building and the third was brightly lit by a floodlight sitting high atop a telephone pole. Once he stepped out into the open he would be in the light, easily seen by anyone looking his way.

The light on top of the pole was also positioned in such a way that it reflected off the side of the third building. There were no shadows on the side of the building that faced him, no place to hide if a guard happened to wander by. Once he stepped into the open, Leon would be exposed until he made it inside the third building. And if the door happened to be locked he was doomed, for there would not be time to retrace his steps back to the safety of the shadows before another guard showed up.

Here goes nothing. Mystery lady, I hope you're in there.

Leon pulled the .45 from his belt and switched off the safety. He took one final look around and sprinted toward the third building. He reached it without being seen, but he wasn't out of danger yet. Framed against the brightly lit wall, he hurried to the end of the building and peeked around the corner. No one was between him and the door. He made a run for it.

He had just reached the door when he heard voices approaching from the other side of the building. Someone was coming!

There was no time to make it back to the safety of the shadows along the second building. He didn't even have time to make it to the corner. The voices came closer. Two men. Any second they would appear from around the opposite corner. He was caught!

Terror nearly tore a scream from Leon's lips. He clenched his teeth, cutting the cry off in his throat. He grabbed the handle of the door and twisted.

Please open . . . please open . . . please . . .

The handle turned; the door was unlocked. Frantic, he pushed open the door and slipped inside, closing it behind him.

He stood in semidarkness facing the door, afraid to move, afraid to even breathe. He was certain that he was caught. Someone must have heard him when he closed the door, nearly slamming it. He waited for the handle to turn, waited for the guards to enter after him to investigate the cause of the noise. He would kill the first man that stepped through the door and likely be killed by the second. He faced the door, waiting for death.

But to his surprise the men kept walking. He heard their footsteps and snippets of their conversation as they passed the door, and then they were gone.

Leon's legs trembled so badly it took a tremendous effort just to remain standing. He wanted to sit down, but didn't. Instead he stood motionless, taking deep breaths to steady his nerves and slow his racing heart. He couldn't believe that he hadn't been caught. Either he was terribly lucky, or the guards were terribly inefficient. Maybe they were just overconfident in their own security. Whatever the reason, he was grateful. His composure somewhat recovered, Leon lowered his gun and turned around, shocked by what he saw.

Oh, my God.

The interior of the building lay cloaked in shadows, lit only by two amber lightbulbs at opposite ends. Still, it was not dark enough to hide the horrors that lay before him. Once a home for horses and cattle, the livestock building now housed people. Lots of people.

About a hundred men, women and children—most of them black—were scattered along the length of the building's interior. Half-naked, dressed in filthy rags, they were shackled and chained to the walls like slaveship cargo. Some of them slept on the dirt floor, their bodies cushioned by only a thin layer of straw; others sat around in silence, their backs to the wall, appearing to be almost oblivious to their plight. Leon stared at the prisoners, sickened by the sight.

Slaves! Oh, dear God, they're slaves!

He remembered images he had seen in history books, black and white photographs that captured the suffering of his ancestors. But these were no photographs; the people were real. Slavery had again reared its ugly head in America.

Horrified, Leon moved through the building, carefully stepping over and around the people in his way. Some of the ones that were awake turned their heads in his direction, but most looked off into space with glassy, wide-eyed stares. He had seen such stares before, on the streets of Atlanta, among those who lived their lives in the haze of drugs and alcohol.

No wonder the guards are so careless. There's nothing to guard. Prisoners that have been drugged and chained are no threat, no threat at all.

He was almost to the end of the building when he felt a familiar tingling at the nape of his neck. Turning, he noticed a woman watching him with keen interest.

Leon felt his breath catch. Even in the shadows there was no mistaking her. She was the woman from the alley, the one whose voice had led him here. He had found her. She must have recognized him too, for her eyes widened in surprise.

30

They stood in darkness by the pickup truck, looking toward the farm, expecting at any moment to hear gunfire or the wail of alarms. But the night remained strangely quiet, the silence weighing heavily upon each of them.

Jacob Fire Cloud pulled his pipe from his shirt pocket and placed it in his mouth, but did not light it. Even the tiny flame of a match could give their hiding place away. Instead he puffed on the unlit pipe to calm his mind and give his hands something to do.

"Do you think he made it?" Danny Santos whispered. Jacob could barely see the young man in the darkness. Danny stood in front of the pickup, while Amy sat on the ground next to him.

"I do not know," Jacob answered. "There have been no shots, so I do not think they caught him."

"Isn't there something we can do to help?" Danny asked. "This waiting is starting to get to me."

"Yes. You can pray." Jacob slipped his pipe back into his pocket and walked around to the back of the pickup truck.

Lowering the tailgate, he climbed up and rolled his bicycle toward the rear of the truck. Seeing what he was doing, Danny hurried around behind the truck.

"What are you doing?" Danny asked.

Jacob lowered the bike to the ground and then climbed down. "I am going for a ride."

"What? Are you nuts?"

Jacob smiled. "My son thinks so."

"You can't go riding around out here. It's too dangerous. What if someone sees you? What if Leon comes back?"

"You ask too many questions," Jacob said, climbing onto his bicycle. "Do not worry, I will be back soon. Here, you may need these." He handed Danny the bullets he had taken out of the assault rifle. "Take care of the girl while I am gone."

Jacob pushed off and started pedaling down the narrow dirt lane, leaving Danny to stand by the truck and stare after him. It wasn't until the old man disappeared into the darkness that he mumbled, "You could have at least told me where you were going."

Closing the tailgate, Danny grabbed the assault rifle off the seat and loaded it. Feeling a little less vulnerable armed, he walked back over to where he had left Amy. The little girl was gone.

"Oh, dear Jesus."

Panic surged through him. If Amy had decided to take off, he would never find her in the dark. Worse yet, if she had decided to follow Leon, then her life was in danger.

"Amy," he whispered.

No reply.

He tried again, a little louder. "Amy!"

Only the crickets and the tree frogs answered his call.

"Damn . . . damn . . . damn." Danny circled the truck, straining his eyes to see in the darkness. He didn't know what to do. What could he do? What would he do if one of his sons was missing? He stopped, the thought bringing a painful lump to his throat.

He was a father; it was his job to protect his children. He would die before allowing anything bad to happen to either one of his sons. But Amy had no father, no one to look out for her.

You do now.

Danny knew what he had to do. He had to go after Amy, try to find her before someone else did. That meant leaving the truck. What if Leon returned before he got back? He might have found the woman he was looking for. Jacob said the woman was very important, a savior of some kind. It was vital that she be taken to safety.

He pulled the truck's keys out of his pocket and tossed them on the seat. Let Leon and Jacob take the woman to safety; he was not about to leave Amy behind. He would find her if it took all night.

Luckily, it wasn't necessary that he search for her. As he turned away from the truck, he spotted a tiny shadow standing not too far away. He hurried to where Amy stood.

"You gave me quite a scare, young lady," Danny said, controlling his anger. "Didn't you hear me calling you?"

She nodded.

He stepped closer. "Then why . . ."

Even in the darkness he could see that she was crying. Tears glistened like diamonds on the little girl's cheeks, and her body shook with tiny sobs. Concerned, he kneeled down in front of her.

"What's the matter, Amy?" he asked. "Why the tears? Are you scared?"

She shook her head.

"What then?"

Her lower lip trembled. "I thought I heard my mother's voice; I thought she had found me. But Leon was right, it's not my mother. It's some other lady."

"You'll find your mother," Danny said, trying to comfort her.

She shook her head. "No. I've looked everywhere, but I still can't find her. I don't know where she is . . . I don't have anybody."

Danny felt a great sadness squeeze his heart. He looked into Amy's eyes, moved deeply by what he heard, touched by the spirit of a lonely little girl. No one should be so alone, especially not a child.

"Amy, honey . . ." He faltered and started again, trying to find the right words to say. "Amy, I know my wife and I can't possibly take the place of your real parents, but if you want you can come live with us—at least until you find your mother. I have two sons you can play with . . ."

Amy sniffed. "Sons?"

"That's right," he said. "Two boys, ages five and six. They could be your brothers, and you could be their older sister. How about it, Amy? My wife and I have always wanted a daughter . . ."

"Brothers?"

Danny nodded.

Amy was silent for a moment, perhaps thinking over the offer. "Will you take care of me?" she asked.

"We'll take good care of you."

"And will you love me too?"

Danny felt tears well up in his eyes. "We will love you with all our hearts. That's a promise," he said. "Amy, will you be a part of our family?"

Amy looked at him, searching for the answer to a question only she knew. She must have found what she was looking for. "Yes," she whispered. "I'll come live with you."

Danny Santos felt his heart break. He grabbed Amy in his arms, hugging the little girl tight against his body, feeling her soft breath upon his face, feeling her tears running warm and wet down his neck. Amy hugged him back, accepting the offer that he made, accepting his love. They were family now, father and daughter, brought together by the mysterious calling of one woman's voice. Danny smiled. Jacob Fire Cloud was right; the woman was magical. Strong medicine.

CHAPTER
31

"You. You've found me," Rene Reynolds said, surprised. "But how?"

Leon placed an index finger against his temple. "You tell me. I've been hearing your voice all the way from Atlanta."

Her mouth dropped open. "You heard me? That's incredible. I wasn't sure it would work, but it did."

"What did?" Leon asked.

"The Neuro-Enhancer. It's a—" She shook her head. "Never mind, I'll explain later. Do you still have the disks I gave you?"

Leon tapped his shirt pocket. "Yes, but we can exchange gifts after we get out of here."

She rattled the manacle chained to her leg. "I can't."

Kneeling in front of her, Leon quickly examined the iron ring that encircled Rene's ankle. The manacle was held closed with a simple padlock, which wouldn't be too hard to pick provided he had the time and the right tool to do so. Unfortunately, he had neither. The opposite end of the chain was anchored to the wall with a heavy metal bolt. Again he would need a tool that he didn't have.

"I've got to find something I can use to pick this lock," he said. "A piece of wire. A screwdriver. Something small."

"There isn't time," Rene argued. "The guards might return at any moment. We're both dead if they catch you in here."

Leon threw a glance toward the front door. "How often do they come?"

"I don't have a watch so I'm not sure." She was trembling. "Maybe once every twenty minutes."

"How long since they've been in here?"

"Ten, fifteen minutes ago."

Leon stood up and looked around, frantically searching for something he could use to help free Rene. Only a few minutes until the guards showed up, not nearly enough time to pick a lock. If only he had a pair of bolt cutters, or a hacksaw, something he could use to cut the padlock from the manacles. But there were no tools lying around, nothing but an old terry cloth towel.

He stopped, an idea springing to mind. Grabbing the towel, he wrapped it around the barrel of his pistol.

Rene scooted back from him, her eyes widening. "What are you doing?"

Leon squatted down in front of her. "I don't even know your name, but I came all the way from Atlanta to help you. Will you trust me?"

She looked at him for a moment, then nodded. "Rene."

"What?"

"My name's Rene."

Leon took her right leg and straightened it out, twisting her ankle so that the manacle's lock lay flush against the ground. With the towel still wrapped around the pistol, he placed the barrel of the gun against the lock and pulled the trigger. The lock exploded, the towel muffling the gunshot and preventing pieces of jagged metal from flying up and injuring either of them. He smiled. "Pleased to meet you. My name's Leon."

He tossed aside the broken pieces of the lock and removed the manacle. Rene was free, but the towel had only partially muffled the gunshot. Someone walking by the building might have heard the report.

"Let's go," he said, pulling Rene to her feet. He took her hand and started toward the front door, but she tore free from his grasp.

"Wait," she said. "There's something I have to get first."

Leon stopped, feeling his freedom slipping away. "What?"

"The Neuro-Enhancer."

"There isn't time," he argued. "Someone might have heard the shot. We've got to make it under the fence before they discover that you've escaped."

"You don't understand," she said. "The Neuro-Enhancer can cure diseases, even cancer. All of them. But there's only one; it's a prototype. They stole it from me and I have to get it back."

Leon could hardly believe what he was hearing. "You're saying that you've got a machine that can cure cancer?"

Rene nodded. "Cancer. Diabetes. Everything. I'm not leaving without it. Not this time. If you don't want to help me, fine, I understand."

Help me.

Her words were like a slap to the face, conjuring up painful memories from Leon's past: Fire. Screams. The distant wail of fire engines. For a brief instant it was no longer Rene that stood before him but Vanessa, his wife, calling to him, begging him to help her. He could almost feel the heat from the flames and smell the stench of burning flesh. Vanessa had asked for his help but he had failed her, and in doing so his life had been cursed to an eternity of loneliness and guilt. But maybe, just maybe, this was a chance to redeem himself, to free himself forever from the failure that haunted him.

He took a deep breath and nodded. "Okay, you win. We'll do it your way."

Turning away from the front door, Leon followed Rene to a second entrance at the back of the building. Placing his ear against the door, he listened for a moment, didn't hear anything, then opened it a few inches and peeked out. Rene squeezed next to him and pointed at one of the other livestock buildings.

"There," she said. "That's where I have to go."

The building Rene pointed at did not sit in darkness, as did the one they were in. On the contrary, lights shone brightly from several of its windows.

"You're out of your mind," Leon whispered. "It's too far; we'll never make it. Besides, it looks like somebody's home."

"I don't care," she replied. "The Enhancer is too important to leave behind."

Leon studied the distance to the other building. It was only about a hundred yards, but all of it was in the open. There were no shadows, no places to hide. But they couldn't stay where they were either; it was only a matter of minutes before the guards would return to check on the prisoners.

"All right," he said. "We'll do it, but not until I say. And once we start running, we don't stop until we reach the back side of the building. The side facing us is too exposed; we'll be seen. If anyone spots us, we forget the whole thing and keep running. Head for the fence. You understand?"

Rene nodded.

He inched the door open farther and stuck his head out, looking quickly left then right. He didn't see any guards, but that didn't mean that one wouldn't show up at any moment. "Okay," he whispered. "Let's do it."

They opened the door and ran toward the other building. Leon was fast, but Rene was faster and reached the building ahead of him. She slipped around to the back side, waiting for him in the shadows. He joined her a second or two later, his heart pounding.

Staying in the shadows, they crept along the wall until they reached a narrow door. Leon tried the knob, but it was locked. Pressing his ear against the door, he listened carefully. He didn't hear anything, but that didn't mean the building was unoccupied. There was only one way to find out.

Stepping back, he raised his right leg and kicked the door near the latch. Even with tennis shoes on the sound of the kick was loud. Too loud.

"What are you doing?" Rene whispered, alarmed. "Someone will hear you."

He stopped and looked at her. "Would you rather I ask one of the guards for a key?"

She shook her head. Leon smiled and kicked the door again. A crack formed in the wood near the latch. He threw his weight against the door. The wood splintered and gave; the door opened.

Leon dropped into a crouch as he entered the building, trying to make himself as small a target as possible. Arms extended in front of him, he gripped his pistol tightly in both hands as he scanned the room for occupants. Rene followed him like a shadow, closing the door behind them, peering over his left shoulder at what he saw.

The first thing Leon noticed as he stepped across the threshold was how cold the building was inside. Extremely cold, almost freezing. The frigid temperature was the result of a row of air conditioners mounted along one wall. The second thing he noticed as he entered the building was the bodies.

Dear Jesus. Leon lowered the gun, his hands beginning to shake.

Eleven naked bodies lined the wall opposite the doorway, seven men and four women. They hung from steel hooks like sides of beef in a slaughterhouse. And like sides of beef they had all been gutted, their internal organs removed. They had also been skinned, all but one. Leon stared in shocked disbelief at the naked, pink bodies, suddenly realizing the purpose behind the farm and wishing he was anywhere else in the world but where he stood.

The farm was not a prison camp, nor was it a slave planta-tion. Those chained within the building were not prisoners or slaves; they were livestock, waiting to be butchered for their skin and internal organs.

"Skinners," he whispered, his throat constricting with fear.

Directly across the room from the bodies stood three stain-less steel mortician tables. The tops and sides of the tables had been wiped clean, but the wooden floor beneath them was cov-ered with splatters of dried blood and tiny pieces of flesh. Under each table sat a white plastic bucket. Leon didn't know what the buckets contained, nor did he want to find out. He had already seen enough to turn his stomach.

"You knew about this?" he asked, turning to Rene.

She tore her gaze away from the bodies. "I knew. There was skin and body parts in the truck they brought me in.

"No wonder Randall Sinclair doesn't want the Neuro-Enhancer to become public knowledge," she added. "He's mak-ing a fortune."

"Randall Sinclair. Why do I know that name?" he asked.

"You may have read about him," Rene replied. "He devel-oped a skin fusion process to treat skin cancer."

Leon's mouth dropped open. "The zebra man? He's behind all this?"

She nodded. "This must be his source of donor material."

Leon was stunned. He had read about Dr. Sinclair in numer-ous medical journals. The man was highly respected in the sci-entific community, having performed hundreds of successful skin fusion operations. A chill marched down Leon's spine as he realized that for every Caucasian patient the "highly respected" doctor treated a black man or woman had been murdered.

Leon had seen a lot of injustice in his life. There was no way to grow up as a black man in America without being exposed to it. Racial prejudice was a painful reality that he, like every African-American, had to learn to deal with almost from birth. Vanessa and Anita had provided Leon with a true sense of belonging in this world, an island of peace in an ocean of anguish. The love that Leon had for his family was what had sustained him, and when they were taken from him on that fateful night, it was as if his soul had been ripped away. Since their deaths he had been protecting himself the only way he knew how—by disconnecting from the world.

His strategy of isolation had served him until this moment. Standing there with Rene, he knew he was a witness to something unspeakably evil, some dark force that had at its core the malignancy of hate and intolerance that had ultimately destroyed a nation. He was being confronted by an evil so unconscionable that its manifestation was powerful enough to bring Leon back from the dead.

"There's got to be a way to stop him," he said, feeling his face become flushed with the rage of a lifetime.

"There is," Rene replied. She passed between the mortician tables and hurried to the other end of the building. Leon followed close behind. The back side of the building was sectioned into four small rooms, two on each side of a narrow hallway. They had probably once been stables, but someone had boarded them up and added doors.

Leon tried the first door, but the room was locked. The second door opened, but the room contained only cleaning supplies, empty buckets and stacks of plastic sheets. The third room contained similar items. He was about to give up when Rene opened the fourth door and found what she was looking for.

The Neuro-Enhancer sat safely in its padded case, in the middle of a large wooden table. Leon watched as Rene opened the case and removed the Enhancer. She turned and held the device up for him to see.

"This is it," she said proudly. "This is the cure for the human race. Think of it. No more sickness. No more disease. And no more Dr. Sinclair. With this device a person can train their mind to heal their body." She smiled mischievously. "This is also how I got inside your head."

"I knew it wasn't anything mystical." He looked closely at the Enhancer. "Were you wearing it when you called me?"

She shook her head. "No. It isn't necessary."

A troubled thought suddenly crossed Leon's mind. If the Neuro-Enhancer did everything Rene claimed, it was worth millions. No one would leave something so valuable just lying around unguarded, not unless there was a good reason to do so. Not unless it was a . . .

A trap.

A soft click was the only warning they had. It was the sound of a latch being turned, a door slowly opening. Rene must have also sensed something was wrong, for her eyes went wide with fear.

"Danger," she said, her voice barely a whisper.

All the rooms were unlocked, all except the first one.

Leon lunged across the room and grabbed Rene around the waist, pulling her down behind the table. He didn't have to hear the footsteps to know they had been set up. They had walked into a trap as blindly as an insect flies into a spider's web.

Two guards, both armed with pump shotguns, appeared in the doorway at the same time. Neither one bothered to aim. Instead they held their weapons at waist level and fired, filling the air with buckshot. Had the guards been a few seconds quicker, Leon and Rene would have been blown to pieces.

Shielding Rene's body with his, Leon returned fire from beneath the table. He could see the guards only from the waist down, but it gave him all the target he needed. His first shot missed, but his second and third struck the guard standing to the left of the doorway in the groin, tearing a scream from his throat and knocking the man's legs out from under him.

The second guard lowered his aim and fired again. The shotgun's deadly pellets clipped one of the table's legs and struck the floor about a foot in front of Leon. Splinters of wood bounced off his shirt and embedded themselves in his hands.

Damn. Leon aimed at the guard's legs and squeezed the trigger three times, emptying his pistol. *Damn. Damn. Damn.*

The .45 slugs ripped through the guard's knees, causing his legs to crumple beneath him like an accordion. Leon was up and moving before the guard hit the floor. He dove at the man, striking him in the head with the barrel of his gun, knocking him unconscious.

Leon dropped the pistol and grabbed the man's shotgun, turning to aim the weapon at the other guard. He needn't have bothered, however, for the man had passed out from the pain of being shot twice in the groin.

"That was close. Too close," Leon whispered, speaking to himself. He picked up the other shotgun and turned around, motioning for Rene to come out from under the table. He knew the gunshots had been loud enough to be heard. They had to get away while they still could, before an army of guards showed up to stop them.

Grabbing the Neuro-Enhancer, Rene stepped over the wounded guards and hurried from the room. Leon followed her down the hallway toward the front door. They had just reached the mortician tables when the piercing wail of sirens split the night.

Rene froze, the Neuro-Enhancer clutched tightly to her chest. Suppressing a shudder, Leon slipped between the hanging bodies to a small window on the opposite wall. Looking out, he saw that the darkness was now lit by several floodlights. In the glare of those lights he could see the hurried movements of armed guards.

"They've got us," he said, racing back to Rene's side. He offered her one of the shotguns. "I don't know if you can shoot, but now would be a good time to learn."

She shook her head. "Give me the code disks."

Leon was confused. "What?"

"The disks," Rene repeated. "You said you had them. Give them to me."

"Why?"

"There isn't time to explain, but it might be our only chance of getting out of here." She held out her hand. It was shaking.

Leon glanced back toward the window, and then turned to face the door. There was no way they could make it to the fence without being caught or shot. It was only a matter of time until the door opened—a matter of minutes, or seconds.

"Okay, okay." He laid one of the shotguns on the table and pulled the computer disks out of his shirt pocket. "I hope you know what you're doing."

Rene took one of the disks and slipped it into the Neuro-Enhancer. Taking a seat on the table, she carefully placed the copper headband on her head. "Five minutes, that's all I need."

"Five minutes!" he exclaimed. "Are you crazy? We don't have five minutes. We may not have five seconds!"

She ignored him and switched on the Neuro-Enhancer, turning the power all the way up. The instrument hummed like an angry bee as it sent hundreds of tiny electrical charges to her brain's neurons. She looked at Leon, smiled, and then closed her eyes.

"Damn," he said, turning back toward the door. Five minutes. They didn't have five minutes. They would be lucky if they had two minutes before the guards found them. He had only the two shotguns, a few shells in each, not nearly enough firepower to make much of a stand.

He took a deep breath and braced himself, waiting for the door to open, ready to shoot anyone who attempted to come inside. Leon knew he was about to die. They were terribly outnumbered and outgunned. He should have been scared, but he wasn't. Death held no fear for someone whose life wasn't much worth living, someone whose spirit had already died a long time ago. If anything, it offered the hope of eternal rest and the chance to again be with those he loved.

Leon heard the sound of running footsteps coming closer. Shouts. He placed his index finger lightly on the shotgun's trig-

ger, thinking how he was about to rejoin his family in the here-
after. He smiled. *It won't be long now. Not long at all. Daddy's
coming.*

He was still facing the door, his back to Rene, when he felt
a strange tingling sweep up his spine, causing the tiny hairs
along the base of his neck to rise. Curious, he turned around to
see what was happening.

Rene sat on the edge of the mortician's table, her eyes
closed. The muscles in her arms and legs quivered, and her skin
rippled. He watched, spellbound, listening as the Neuro-
Enhancer's hum rose in volume until it sounded like the battle
cry of a thousand angry hornets.

He started to take a step forward when a mental scream
ripped through his brain like a fiery meteor. With the scream
came a barrage of emotions so powerful, so terribly over-
whelming, that they tore a cry from his throat.

"Noooo . . . !"

Anger, hatred, rage; the emotions slammed into him like a
fist, staggering him. He dropped the shotgun and stumbled
back, almost falling, clamping his hands to his head in a vain
attempt to block out the attack.

Images flashed through his head at high speed like a
demonic slide show. Mental pictures of wars and murders,
mutilated bodies and mass destruction.

Oh, God. Oh, God. Oh, God . . . The images came faster,
blurring together into a vision of what hell must truly look like,
filling him with the unquenchable desire to lash out at someone, anyone, seeking revenge for a thousand atrocities, a million shattered and ruined lives.

And then it was over, the assault on his mind ending as
quickly as it began.

Leon slowly lowered his hands. Rene's arms and legs no
longer twitched; her muscles no longer rippled. A feeling of
awe settled over him as he realized that she had just used the
Neuro-Enhancer to send a message more powerful than one

ever sent before. But the message was not for him; he was but an eavesdropper. Who the message was for he did not know, but Leon thanked God that he wasn't the recipient. He had just taken a step toward Rene when she swooned.

Rushing to her side, Leon caught her before she could fall off the table. He removed the copper headband from her head and held her. She was limp, weak, her eyes unfocused. The mental message she sent must have physically drained her, leaving her as helpless as a kitten. He wondered how long it would take before she recovered, for each second they lingered increased the risk of being caught.

"Come on. Come on. Wake up." He rubbed her arms and legs, trying to get the circulation flowing. Her skin was cold and clammy to the touch. He was starting to worry that Rene had done some permanent mental damage to herself when she opened her eyes and looked around.

She was still weak, but at least she was conscious again and able to sit up on her own. Letting go of her, Leon turned off the Neuro-Enhancer and placed it back in its padded case. He had just closed the case when the night was shattered by a barrage of gunshots.

"What the hell?" Leon turned and ran to the window, amazed by what he saw. Outside a battle raged, but it was not a war fought between opposing armies. On the contrary, it was being fought by members of the same side. It was the guards who fought; they fought one another.

Unable to believe his eyes, he watched as the guards battled each other with guns, knives, even their bare fists. And as he watched, Leon realized that it was Rene who had started the war. She had used the Neuro-Enhancer to project her thoughts and emotions with enough force to affect the minds of the guards, causing them to turn on one another.

"Incredible," he whispered. "Absolutely incredible." Turning away from the window, he hurried back to where Rene still sat.

"Can you walk?" he asked.

Rene nodded, but nearly fell when she tried to stand up. Holding her around the waist, Leon tucked the Neuro-Enhancer beneath his arm and grabbed the shotgun off the table.

"Okay, let's go."

He led her across the room to the door, pausing to check for guards before stepping outside. He needn't have bothered, however, for the guards were much too preoccupied with fighting one another to worry about the two of them.

Moving from building to building, using the shadows for concealment when possible, they made their way slowly toward the opening in the fence. By the time they reached the fence Rene had recovered enough of her strength to walk on her own. Once through the opening, they hurried across an open field. Behind them, the night was filled with gunshots and screams.

They arrived back at the truck a few minutes later, only to discover that they had unwelcome company waiting for them. Dr. Randall Sinclair stood near the pickup's front bumper, quietly smoking a cigar, a submachine gun clenched tightly in his right hand. A few feet away on the ground sat Danny Santos, bleeding from a gunshot wound to the shoulder. Amy stood beside Danny, holding his hand, crying softly.

"Hello, Dr. Reynolds." Sinclair smiled. "How nice of you to drop by. As you can see, I've been expecting you." He pointed his gun at Leon. "Please, toss that shotgun over here."

Leon did as he was told.

"You son of a bitch," Rene hissed.

"Oh come now, Dr. Reynolds. You didn't think I would be stupid enough to leave the Neuro-Enhancer just lying around, did you? I recognized you earlier and knew that you would try to get it back. I'm still trying to figure out how you managed to escape in Chicago. Obviously, you are a woman of many talents. According to my guards, you are also quite dangerous."

He puffed on his cigar and continued. "One of my drivers reported that he was followed today by several people in a pickup, including a black man. I had a suspicion it might be your friend coming to rescue you." He nodded at Leon. "Looks like I was right. I assume you brought the codes?"

Leon didn't answer. Instead he stared in anger at the man responsible for the Skinner farm's operation—a man who was a doctor, who was supposed to help people, not murder them.

Dr. Sinclair met Leon's stare with a look of smug satisfaction. "Now, if you would be kind enough to hand me that case."

Rene snatched the Neuro-Enhancer out of Leon's hands and raised it above her head. "Never! I'll smash it first!"

"Such dramatics." Dr. Sinclair grinned. "But you won't do that."

"Why not?"

"For one thing, you're a scientist. You don't want to see your life's work destroyed. For another"—he placed the barrel of the submachine gun against Amy's head—"you don't want to see this little girl's brains splattered all over the place."

Rene froze. She lowered the case. "Okay, you win. Let her go." She stepped forward and set the Enhancer on the ground, then stepped back.

"Thank you." Sinclair nodded. "But I'm afraid I can't do that. She knows too much. So do you."

He swung the gun barrel in Rene's direction. "It's a tragedy to shoot a woman like you, Dr. Reynolds. You've got pretty skin, real pretty skin. But I'm sure my men will be able to salvage enough so that your death won't be a total loss.

"As for you," he said, pointing the gun at Leon. "You should feel proud. Even after your death part of your worthless hide will live on. Think of it as a badge of honor on someone else's chest."

Sinclair paused and cocked his head to the side, listening to the gunshots coming from the farm. "I'd love to stay and chat, but there seems to be a party going on. They say when the cat's

away the mice will play. Obviously, I've been away too long."
He aimed again at Rene. "Goodbye, Dr. Reynolds. It's been
fun."

"Aiiyeee . . . yi . . . yi . . . yi . . . yi." Jacob Fire Cloud burst
from the darkness, his face covered with warpaint, eagle feathers hanging from his hair. He came barreling down the narrow
dirt road on his rusty bicycle, heading straight at Randall
Sinclair.

Startled, Sinclair turned and fired, emptying the submachine gun's clip. The bullets tore into the old Indian's chest and
stomach, knocking him off the bicycle.

Leon didn't hesitate. He sprang like a jungle cat, tackling
the doctor from behind, pummeling him with blow after blow.
Although taken by surprise, Sinclair recovered quickly and
fought back with punches and elbow strikes. The doctor was
bigger, stronger; his blows staggered Leon, finally dropping him
to his knees.

Sinclair jumped to his feet and scooped up his machine
gun, pointing it at Leon's head. He squeezed the trigger, but the
clip was empty. He pulled a fresh clip out of his pants pocket
and started to reload.

"Mr. Cane!" Leon turned and saw Amy standing over Jacob
Fire Cloud. She threw something shiny toward him. Jacob's .357
revolver.

Leon lunged for the pistol, catching it in his left hand as he
hit the ground. Rolling over, he aimed quickly and fired twice.
The big Magnum sounded like a cannon going off, a brilliant
flash of fire leaping from the end of its six-inch barrel.

The bullets struck Randall Sinclair in the center of his chest,
tearing through flesh and shattering bone. The doctor staggered
back, his machine gun chattering. A spray of bullets danced all
around Leon, but none hit him.

Leon fired again, and again, emptying the revolver, hitting
the doctor in the chest and stomach. Randall Sinclair fell backward, toppling like an oak tree.

Leon got to his feet. He stood over Dr. Sinclair's body and continued to pull the revolver's trigger, the hammer falling on empty shell casings. Click . . . click . . . click.

"He's dead."

He squeezed the trigger again. Click . . . click.

"He's dead, Leon."

Leon looked up. Rene stood a few feet away from him. "He's dead," she said again. "You killed the bastard." He looked down, saw that Dr. Randall Sinclair was truly dead, and let the gun slip from his fingers and fall to the ground. He turned and saw Jacob Fire Cloud lying on the ground, bleeding.

Oh, God.

Leon started toward the old Indian, stopped and started again, not wanting to see how badly Jacob was hurt but knowing he had to look. He prayed the old man's injuries were not serious, just minor flesh wounds. But they were bad, real bad. Jacob Fire Cloud was dying.

Amy knelt next to Jacob, holding one of his bloody hands in hers. She looked to Leon for help, her eyes wet with tears. But there was nothing he could do for him, nothing at all. Danny was also by the Indian's side, talking to him, comforting him, trying to stop the bleeding. There was a lot of blood.

Leon kneeled beside Jacob, took the old man's other hand and held it tight. Jacob looked up at him and smiled. "I told my son it was a good gun."

Leon nodded, blinking back tears. "A very good gun."

Jacob coughed and turned his head to look at Rene. "I knew you would come. I had a vision."

The old Indian whispered something to Amy. She let go of his hand and ran over to the bicycle, untying the wooden staff from the handlebars. Jacob coughed again and continued, "My people have been waiting a long time for your return, White Buffalo Woman. A very long time. Some said you would not be back, but I knew you would come in time to stop the Great Shaking."

"But I'm not—"

Leon shook his head; Rene stopped. Amy returned and handed her the wooden staff adorned with eagle feathers.

"That is the flag of my people," Jacob said proudly. "It is your flag now; they are your people. Go, White Buffalo Woman. Go teach your children. They are waiting . . ." With those words Jacob Fire Cloud gave a final sigh, and died.

Leon continued to hold Jacob's lifeless hand, not wanting to let it go, feeling the warmth of the old Indian's spirit slowly ebb away. Somewhere in the distance an owl cried out, calling Jacob's name. Calling him home.

EPILOGUE

L eon Cane brought the pickup to a gradual stop, staring out the windshield at the bullet-riddled sign, which marked the boundary of the Pine Ridge Indian Reservation. Beyond the sign, the narrow blacktop road was lined with hundreds, maybe even thousands, of tents and makeshift shelters. In the middle of the vast South Dakota prairie a city had been born, a city whose residents had come from all parts of the country looking for a cure to what ailed them, looking for guidance. It was a metropolis built on a foundation of desperation and hope.

Less than a week had passed since Leon helped Dr. Rene Reynolds escape from the Skinner farm, but it felt like a lifetime. Shortly after their escape, they had notified the authorities about the farm. The State Police moved in quickly, freeing prisoners and arresting the men involved in the farm's operation—those that were still alive.

Rene sat beside him in the pickup, gazing in awe at the village that had sprung up along the reservation's border. Leon turned and looked at her, studying her profile, wondering what thoughts and feelings danced through her head. The mental voice that had been a part of him for so long was now silent; Rene no longer called him. He had heard the voice for the last time when she used the Neuro-Enhancer to direct her anger at the Skinner guards, causing them to turn against one another.

Neither of them felt any sorrow for the guards who died that night, or for the death of Dr. Randall Sinclair, for they had been responsible for the imprisonment, suffering and murder of hundreds of innocent people. But Rene did regret using the Neuro-Enhancer to hurt rather than heal, changing it from a device of mercy into a weapon.

Leon glanced down. The padded case containing the Neuro-Enhancer was cradled between Rene's feet on the floorboard of the truck. Was it a weapon? He didn't think so. Rene had told him that the peculiar side effects caused by the Enhancer were rare; so far, she had been the only one to project a thought with enough force to control a person's actions. No, the device was no more a weapon than Rene was a murderer. Used properly, it could be the greatest breakthrough ever in medical science, a solution to pain and suffering for millions.

But there is some pain even the Neuro-Enhancer cannot cure—the pain of loneliness that comes from deep within the heart.

Leon thought of his wife and daughter. The hurt he felt was still there, but it wasn't nearly as painful as before. Perhaps by helping Rene he had partially redeemed himself for his past failure. Or maybe the pain had diminished because he had finally bared his soul to another human being, sharing the hurt he had keep bottled up inside for so many years.

Two nights ago, he had told Rene everything about himself: his job at NASA, his report linking shuttle launches to severe weather patterns, the firebombing of his home and the loss of his family. His revelation had touched her heart, leaving her speechless. She too knew what it was like to lose a family member, to be haunted by the memory of someone you love.

Rene had held him as he cried, his spirit finally releasing the sorrow he had clung to for so long. They made love later that night, their bodies and souls joining together, sharing a passion and tenderness each of them desperately needed. Afterward, Rene hooked the Neuro-Enhancer to his head, allowing him to experience the wonders she had discovered.

He had a lot to be thankful to Rene for. She had given him his life back, given him a reason to go on living. When he thought of his family now his mind wasn't filled with flames and screams. Instead the memories that floated to the surface from his subconscious were of happier times: visions of moonlit walks along the beach with Vanessa, quiet moments in front of the television, and the joy of giving horsey-back rides to his little girl.

The laughter of a child suddenly filled the air. He turned and looked out the rear window. Danny Santos sat in the back of the pickup, rolling a small rubber ball back and forth to Amy. The young man was lucky; the bullet from Sinclair's gun had passed through the meaty part of his shoulder without striking any bone. With a little rest and recuperation, he should have full use of his left arm again in no time.

Danny was lucky in other ways too, as was Amy; they had found each other. He had invited the little girl to live with him and his family in Billings and she had said yes, the thought of belonging to a real family and having brothers to play with too much to resist. But they agreed to put off their return trip to Montana for a few days so Rene could start them on the teachings.

Leon smiled. Because of Jacob Fire Cloud, Dr. Rene Reynolds no longer considered her work with the Neuro-Enhancer to be strictly scientific. She was no longer experimenting on people, she was teaching them to unlock the full potential of their brains.

Go teach your children. They are waiting . . .

Jacob's final words floated through his mind. The old Indian had died while trying to save the life of the woman he believed to be the third coming of the White Buffalo Woman.

Rene doubted she was that woman, but she felt something was owed to the man who took a bullet meant for her. Because of that debt, she and the others had come to the South Dakota reservation. If the world was going to be healed, if people were going to learn to live together as brothers and sisters, then it had to start somewhere. Why not here?

Both Leon and Rene looked forward to a time when mankind might live together in harmony, free from sickness and disease. A nation built not on war and hatred, but on love and understanding. They knew their dream would not happen overnight, even with the Neuro-Enhancer. There were still those with hearts darkened by hatred and prejudice. Such people were like a tumorous growth; until they were completely removed from society there could be no healing.

Leon had heard rumors of other doctors performing illegal skin grafts, and of Skinner farms in several different states. That was why he could not stay with Rene for very long, no matter how much he would have liked to.

He had found a calling, a battle worth fighting for, a chance to redeem himself even more. He wanted to locate the remaining Skinner farms and turn them in to the authorities. He would leave no stone unturned, driving the snakes out into the light of day where they would be destroyed once and for all. Along the way he would look for those of a good heart and mind, people worthy of sharing in Rene's teaching. He would travel the country, sowing the seeds from which a new America would grow.

But first he was going back to Pennsylvania to visit his family—something he had not done in many years. He knew from experience how painful it was for a father to lose a daughter, but it was equally painful for a mother to lose a son. He was going back to Millvat to see his mother. Leon Cane was going home.

"It is possible to believe that all the past is but the beginning of a beginning, and that all that is and has been is but the twilight of the dawn. It is possible to believe that all the human mind has ever accomplished is but the dream before the awakening."

—H.G. Wells